Praise for
ECHOES OF OLYMPUS MONS

"A fantastic sci-fi horror novel from a rising star of the genre. Gave me chills."

        – CT Phipps, author of *Cthulhu Armageddon*

"This is a science fiction/horror novel that will appeal to fans of both genres. The horror fan in me was pleased with the gore and the body count, but I also started to appreciate the elements of the story that were more science fiction too.

…would recommend it to anyone who likes mysteries and/or science fiction that's a bit on the gorier side."

        – Mindy Snyder, Horror Reviews

"Compelling and engaging sci-fi/horror."

        – Stuart Aken, author of the Generation Mars series

ECHOES OF OLYMPUS MONS
BOOK 1 OF THE ECHOES SERIES

ERIC MALIKYTE

FOREWORD

BY C.T. PHIPPS

Echoes of Olympus Mons is a science fiction and horror novel that I didn't expect to like as much as I did. Science fiction and horror are like peanut butter and jelly but there's always a hesitation to make use of it in literature. A lot of people struggle to be able to find the right mixture of futurism with scares. Basically, a lot of people aim to do the next *Alien* and end up doing *Jason X* (and I like *Jason X*).

Eric Malikyte is the kind of guy who understands that there's really just one simple rule to make science fiction horror work: you have to actually care about the people being slaughtered. Too many individuals mistake the monsters as the stars of horror science fiction. The monsters aren't the stars, whether the xenomorphs of *Alien* or the Predators of the franchise that bears their name. Part of the reason why the sequels to these movies struggle is the fact that they fall into the tropes of slasher movies. In those films, we don't care about the victims and are actively rooting for the monster.

But who do you remember from *Alien*? Ripley, I'd imagine. Who do you remember from *Aliens*? Probably Ripley, Newt, Hicks, Hudson, Vasquez, and Bishop. I bet you remember Arnold from *Predator*. This is the same logic that allows *Resident Evil* to keep on trucking after a dozen sequels. The zombies aren't the stars. The zombies are the *plot*. The monsters are a thing that happens to the characters, and we have to have an investment in their struggle to want to see anything other than a bloody spectacle.

Some people argue that modern audiences don't have the patience for a slow burn. They want to see the monster in its entirety and in the first ten minutes. This is a failure of imagination and why so many movies simply don't have the same staying power as the ones from our youth. Horror is anticipation, creeping dread, and the fear of the unknown. The implication of what a monster might mean is far stronger than having any questions you might have actually answered.

One of the funniest arguments I ever had (something like Indiana Jones wasn't needed in *Raiders of the Lost Ark*) was that the Space Jockey from *Alien* was probably a trucker himself. The implications of the derelict spaceship and the cargo hold full of eggs might be that the xenomorphs are going to some fancy alien restaurant versus being something meant to be the perfect killing organism. Maybe it was designed as a bio-weapon. It is doubtful it was the product of an android from Earth as part of his daddy issues.

But the mystery makes for compelling drama.

Echoes of Olympus Mons reminds me very much of *Dead Space*, *Event Horizon*, and, of course, *Alien*. It postulates a future where we've managed to make it to Mars but the result is just a cramped bunch of habitats where workers are exploited while students struggle to pay off debt. Humanity isn't changed by technology, and it is that just hint of cyberpunk influence that makes it grounded long before the monsters show up. I may not always like the characters, but I know them. They're people. I've met them.

So I feel something when they die.

Sunrises on Mars are always strange to behold. I watched a small white globe cut through a cobalt-blue haze over Olympus Mons, cascading its light dimly across the red planet's dusty surface. I'd been living here almost three years, and the sight never ceased to captivate me. The most morbid part of me imagined what it would be like if I tore off my protective suit and felt the Martian elements for myself. If I didn't die from being flash-frozen first, I'd lose consciousness within little more than fifteen seconds. Hardly enough time to feel the dusty breeze on my icy skin, no? People on Earth don't know how lucky they are, how much they take for granted.

So, until humanity could find the means to terraform Mars, I'd have to enjoy my Martian sunrises from within the confines of the EVA suit.

Within minutes, the sky transitioned into its usual butterscotch tone, and the experience was over. A new Sol had begun.

A familiar jingle rang through my helmet. Akio was calling.

"Answer," I said.

"Yo, Hal," Akio said. "Just wanted you to know Wolfrik knows about your unscheduled walkabout. He's pissed!"

"I'll bet he is." I frowned and turned for the airlock. My heads-up-display was telling me I only had three minutes of oxygen left anyway. "Thanks for the warning."

"Uh-huh, see you at home."

I was always very thorough when hacking the airlock logs and removing myself from the security footage. Someone must have overheard me talking to Akio about my morning walkabouts in the corridor. Whoever it was had snitched on me — most likely fearing that

I was going to end up another lost human popsicle—otherwise there'd be no way Wolfrik could have known about it.

I had to wait a few seconds for the airlock to compress, and for decontamination procedures to finish up. A red light on the far wall turned green, telling me that it was safe to remove my suit. I popped the latches one by one and strolled into the EVA staging area. Most of us found the official term boring. Walkabout always seemed far more fitting, especially after some Australian student named Connor Wilson had gotten cabin fever, suited up, and walked off into the Martian sunset. The last thing he'd said was: "Goin' on walkabout, be back maybe, tell my mum I said hi." At first everyone thought it was a joke, until he'd been gone long past the time that his air supply would support him for. They're still trying to find his body with the satellites. The sandstorms probably buried him long ago; Olympus Mons is a massive area to search for something so small. Since then, no student at Olympus One has been authorized to go out on an EVA without the supervision of a trained Milkyway Unlimited employee. Mars is a desolate, angry world. Never know when, or if, you'll come back.

I removed several layers of insulation and cloth that could almost be considered armor, before I heard the hiss of the door opening and footfalls at my back.

I turned to face Wolfrik; his face was contorted, his eyebrows furrowed, his beady blue eyes stabbing at me. I smiled.

"Why do you smile?" he asked. *Vhy do you shmile?* His German accent always cut through when he was angry.

"I had a nice walkabout."

He folded his arms, probably in an attempt to keep himself from choking me. "Tell me, Geraldo. Why is it that you do not seem to believe in procedure, or safety?" *Tell me, Eralto. Vhy is it that you do not sheem to believe in prosheture, or shafety.*

This was serious. He'd used my legal first name.

I sighed. "It's not that I don't believe in it."

"Then what?" *Then vhat?*

I shrugged. Maybe honesty was my best bet? "Look, I just needed to get out for a little while. See the sunrise without three fucking feet of transparent polymer in the way. There's a world out there and I'm going stir-crazy in here."

As long as he didn't know I hacked the door logs and the security cams, I should be able to get off without much more than a stern warning and a slap on the wrist.

He sighed; the hard look in his eyes did not soften. "Yes, it would seem that your family is no stranger to madness."

"Excuse me?" My fists tightened; my teeth clenched, sending pressure through my skull.

He jerked back, flinching as if he feared I'd knock his fucking teeth out. I was real tempted. When I didn't, he paused and considered me. His eyes softened momentarily. Then, he shook his head, sighing.

"Fine," he said. "If you go out again, and something goes wrong"—he jammed his wrinkled finger into my chest—"it is your own fault. I will hold no responsibility for your actions. Is that understood?"

I gritted my teeth and nodded. Wolfrik turned for the door. I could have let it end there.

But something snapped inside of me.

"So, just like it was with Connor Wilson?" I said.

He turned around, his face contorted. "What did you say?"

"Your solution to my walkabout fascination?"

"This was different."

"I don't think so. You acted in your best interests to keep the investigation team off your back so you could keep your job. It's nice to know that you'll extend me the same courtesy should the same happen to me."

His eyes narrowed; his pale German skin turned a ripe, apple red. "Get out of my sight and get to class!"

I could feel Wolfrik's eyes stabbing holes through me as I made my way to the door. The doors hissed, and I passed through them. I should have kissed his ass and begged for forgiveness, considering he has the power to end my career in academia with a few careful words to the right people.

I stopped in the hall. Echoing footfalls from passing students filled my ears as I remembered her lying in that hospital bed the night she overdosed. My mother had an IV coming out of her good arm. Doctors had no trouble finding the vein.

I remembered the lifeless look in her eyes, and the piercing glare from my father as he held her limp hand by the bedside.

I remembered what his eyes said: *"Your sin did this."*

2

Planetary Physics was lasting about three hours too long. Professor Brown droned on about Martian terraforming theories… you know, if we actually had the ability to kick start Mars's core. Not much point to mowing the grass if your atmosphere gets blown away by the solar wind.

The problem, of course, is that there is no known technology that can force Mars' core to generate a powerful magnetic field again. And even then, there's the possibility that Mars just doesn't have enough mass to sustain an atmosphere. Whatever transformed the planet into a desolate hellhole billions of years ago did a damn good job of it.

I caught myself drawing angry stick people shaking their fists at the solar wind.

The ADHD is strong with me.

I slid my personal tablet out of my pack and began to work on the blueprints to my and Akio's magnum opus, what we called the dark matter camera. I tapped my stylus on the metallic edge of my tablet, staring at the design I'd made. Akio's suggestions from the night before hung over my work like sticky notes. She wanted to redesign the case, fearing overheating, and as much as it pained me to admit it, she was right.

I felt someone kick my left foot. It was Gila, an Israeli botany major. The whites of her eyes were like polished marble against her eye-shadow, to merely call her cute would be an insult to her beauty. She and I had spoken only a handful of times in the past. Most people knew who she was by the Armada tattoo she had on her neck. Apparently, she was a huge gamer.

She leaned in, her pale brown eyes focused on my blueprints. "What's that?"

"Oh, just a little something I've been cooking up," I said.

"Yeah? Looks complicated."

I grinned. "You might say someone who majors in botany might find it a little complicated."

"Come on." She frowned, kicked me again. "What is it?"

"All right, fine. Theoretically, it can detect concentrations of dark matter and three-dimensionally map them."

"Mars has dark matter?"

My eyes drifted from Gila to where Professor Brown was standing, droning on about nanobots or some other bullshit. She was sufficiently distracted with the details of manipulating her lecture program through the tablet interface. I leaned in to Gila and kept my voice nice and low.

"Uh, yeah, dark matter's everywhere," I said. "Well, sort of. It's more that what we *call* dark matter is everywhere."

"What do you mean by that?"

"Well, back in the early twenty-first, it was thought that dark matter and dark energy made up ninety-nine percent of the visible universe. Dark matter was thought to be made up of something other than baryonic matter, and dark energy was this mysterious energy that permeated the entire universe. We went decades believing in a thing we only knew existed through numbers and equations."

"So...it doesn't exist?"

"Not in the way we once thought. The two are in fact aspects of the same force, existing outside our perceptive reality, but occupying the same space. Richard Roth discovered that shortly after the third world war. His gravity well experiments proved that not only were dark matter and energy the same, but that they permeated the whole universe, and the effects could be felt through every dimension. When the discovery was made public, it was Roth who eliminated the term 'dark energy' all together."

"So...it *does* exist?"

"Yeah, but we can't really do much with it. We can tell it's there, and some researchers are developing ways to harness it as fuel for faster-than-light engines, but progress is quite slow."

"If no one can use it, why make a camera that can see it?" She grinned.

"Do you know what causes evolution?"

"Natural selection."

"No, that's the *process* of evolution, not the *cause*. I mean what causes complex life and consciousness to evolve in the first place. What makes a thing decide to become a thing."

"Decide?" She shook her head. "Sounds like you're looking for God."

"Negative." I grinned. "I'm looking for the origin of consciousness, a mechanism through which information is transferred through quantum entanglement."

"Well, I don't know what that is."

"Right, well, no one else does either. I—well, Akio and I—think that dark matter has something to do with how life started on Earth—"

"Is Akio your girlfriend?" I could almost feel her heart beat from where I sat.

"What? No. We're just roommates."

She smiled. "Go on."

"Anyway, we think dark matter is what drives evolution. If we can prove that—" I sighed, strangling my stylus. "—then…"

"Then what?"

"Then I can—"

"Oh…" She froze. The whites of her eyes became widened ovals.

"What is it?"

I looked forward, and the professor was staring right at us.

"Harold," the professor said. She always fucked up my name. "That is a fascinating anecdote on dark matter. Would you care to tell me what it has to do with the study of planetary magnetic fields?"

She'd tapped right into the audio controls in my desk to listen in. Sneaky bitch.

"My name is Hal, Professor, and *gladly*." I stood up and gestured with my hands as if to ask to take her place at the front of the classroom; Gila gave me a worried look and shook her head, as if she knew what I'd do next. "It's a stretch, but, based on the fact that we have equations that utilize dark matter as an energy source for FTL engines, and if dark matter is everywhere—as Richard Roth proposed—then we should be able to use the same technology that would allow for FTL speeds in space craft to reignite Mars' core and get it spinning again. This is, of course, something that could be achieved much easier through magnetic induction, but you asked how dark matter relates to our class's subject matter."

"And why do you think that harnessing dark matter would produce enough energy to reactivate the core?"

"Given the fact that an object that is moved up to or beyond the speed of light has infinite mass, this isn't too much of a stretch from my point of—"

"We don't have the technology to harness dark matter, *Harold*," Brown said. "This class is about applying current technologies and proposing real-world solutions to the problem, not *science fictions* like the one you propose."

"Yes, and we see just how well real-world solutions work out. As I recall, the attempts to create a planet-wide magnetic field generator on the surface resulted in making the Schiaparelli crater three times larger—and three times as charred—instantly vaporizing its inventor, no less."

"Accidents happen sometimes. Just because people die testing a prototype technology does not mean it isn't viable. By your logic, we should have ignored every important scientific discovery made by Marie Curie before she died of radiation exposure."

"It sure would have made the cold war more pleasant."

The class erupted in laughter. The professor fumed at the collar, and poor Gila buried her head in her arms trying to hide her embarrassment.

"It is mankind's folly and arrogance to assume that we can do things better than nature itself," I said. "It would be better to use technology to revive the core than to try to supplement a working one on the surface with technology that's proved to be unreliable. Surely, even you see that?"

"Even me? What the hell is *that* supposed to mean?"

I shook my head. "Nothing, I'm only saying that, while it's a noble pursuit to try to solve Mars' magnetosphere problem solely with our technology, we've already seen that it's far more difficult than we initially thought. It was once thought that living on Mars was a 'science fiction' that would never be realized, and yet here we are."

"I think you've derailed this lecture enough already, Mr. Leon."

"And here I thought I was contributing a worthy debate topic."

"And now you can leave."

Perhaps I should have listened to Gila?

I'm an idiot. Professor Brown had been looking for a reason to throw me out of class again. That made three times that I'd been thrown out of a lecture in two different classes, and the disciplinary committee—headed by Wolfrik—would be breathing down my neck about it. Although, with the most extreme consequence they could throw at me, the expense to send me back to Earth would be more than my degree multiplied by many thousands, and I'd argue exactly that.

The rumor mill would be spinning again after this. I'd got a bit of a reputation around the colony for being a pretentious asshole, and it's not entirely unfounded. My father would be so *proud* of me. The fact of the matter is, I imagined that living on Mars would mean far less human interaction.

It hadn't exactly worked out like I imagined. Most colonies on Mars are forced to conserve space, and Olympus One was no exception. Even though I was an undergraduate at university level, the school component of the colony comprised most degree programs beyond high school. There were only one hundred people on-site, and even so, the colony could feel surprisingly cramped. I could feel it, walking the corridors. How at any moment, one disaster, one mistake, could send us all to our deaths.

Technology had advanced quite a bit since the first settlers came to Mars, with their weak canvas HABs and their rovers, but the danger here was still quite real. They had to rotate the use of each airlock into the colony after one of them imploded from overuse. There was a microscopic hole in the material that sealed the hatch from the Martian elements beyond. Three students and one professor died in that one.

Then there was the smallpox scare that caused a whole sector to get quarantined—some idiot had thought it'd be interesting to see how smallpox would grow in Mars' low gravity.

Hell, you had to sign about thirty legal wavers before they'd even let you on the space elevator, let alone the ship.

It was only 10:30 in the morning; I had the entire Sol to myself. I decided to rush back to my apartment and get some more work done on the dark matter camera. Akio had class till 14:30, so she wouldn't be home for quite some time—I'd have a head start on the prototype.

I waved my palm in front of the keypad and the door to my dorm room; the lights blinked green and the door hissed open. My kitchen was a mess: plastic reusable plates, a half empty bottle of "gin," and what remained of last night's feast were scattered all across the bar where I'd passed out. I grabbed the gin and took a long swig; my eyes locked on the lab and the prototype.

It was scattered in several components on the workstation (which comprised what any ordinary student would call their living room). Wires ran everywhere, leading into a small hydrogen power cell Akio had "liberated" from a rover that was under maintenance. You might call it overkill for a glorified interferometer, but this way the camera would never run out of power if we had to leave it on the surface for an extended period of time. Most automated tech sent out to roam the surface was solar powered; all it would take was one sandstorm and the solar cells would be useless. Akio had originally proposed using a hydrogen cell as a joke, but when we considered long-term surveys of the surface where we might not have easy access to the device, it became clear that no other battery would do.

I shuffled past the other prototype cameras, each in various stages of development. One was to function as a helmet. We'd built it using a headset for one of those augmented-reality games that so many students get distracted by. There were a few that bore some resemblance to the final prototype design we'd come up with; some had bulkier cases, botched wiring jobs (which, despite what Akio says, were not my fault), inferior interfaces, and corrupted operating systems.

Stretching some gloves over my hands, I dropped my goggles over my eyes and got to work.

Once the screen was attached to the casing, I reached to power it on...but hesitated. The obvious, minute danger of testing an experimental hydrogen-powered device aside, I knew that Akio would want to see it. I wouldn't have been able to get this far without her.

My hand dropped back to my side, and I looked around my—our—messy living space.

She had been irate about the state of the kitchen in the morning before my walkabout. If she saw it like this when she came home, I'd end up with a soldering iron burning through my abdomen for sure. I attempted to kill some time by cleaning house, washing the dishes, and throwing dirty coveralls into the laundry vat...but those activities only managed to kill an hour. I grabbed my tablet and sent Akio a coded message.

Hal: *I have a surprise for you when you return.*

She was likely in class, so she probably couldn't respond immediately. I toyed with the idea of hunting down Gila's profile on the shared drive and harassing her about what Brown had done after I was booted out of class, but before I could go through with my plan, I heard a message notification ring on my tablet.

Akio: **GASP* You're going to propose. And after all this time!*

Hal: *Ha. Ha. Can you get out of class early?*

Akio: *Unlike you, some of us value our education and opportunities at Olympus One.*

Hal: *I guess I'll just activate the prototype alone, then.*

Akio: *You finished it?!*

Hal: *Can you get out of class?*

Akio: *And tell Prof. Thornhill what exactly?*

Hal: *Stick your finger down your throat and yak on the floor or something.*

Akio: *Oh, talk dirty to me, baby.*

Hal: *Just figure something out. You have thirty minutes.*

Akio: *Fine, fine, jeez.*

I waited impatiently for thirty-five minutes, putting some old Rush recordings on to keep me company.

Akio shook her head upon entering our dorm room.

"You know, if I didn't know better, I'd swear you were actually a bear," she said. "Think of it, first bear on Mars."

"I did clean, you know," I said.

"Yeah—" she took a careful look at the slight improvement I'd made on the kitchen—"you managed to clean *half* your mess up."

"You came to see the results of our experiment, didn't you?" I picked up the device, careful not to disturb its connection to the hydrogen fuel cell.

"Yes. What the hell have you done to my baby?"

She rushed up and grabbed at it. Her body was small, almost boyish, and her personality matched. She eyed the machine closely, rolling it around in her field of vision, the way a mother might examine her young for lice.

"Looks like you took my suggestion to heart about the casing," she said.

"Yeah, well, seemed like an exploding hydrogen cell would be bad for my health."

"Oh, please, the new cells only have a one-percent chance of exploding." She stuck her tongue out at me, then returned her focus to examining the prototype. "And it seems like you didn't completely botch my wiring, despite your enormous fingers."

"Fuck off."

She smiled and set the prototype back in my hands. "So, should we do it here?"

I shook my head. She wasn't going to like what I was about to suggest. "We're going outside."

She stared at me for a second, her face twisted like a cat freshly doused. It was almost cute.

"You know," she said, "I always defended you when others called you a reckless sociopath, and a pretentious asshole… but now—"

"We don't know if it'll work, Akio. And even if there's only a one-percent chance, if anything were to go wrong, and the fuel cell ruptured, the entire colony would be at risk. Remember the douchebag who released smallpox into the colony?"

"Shit, we don't want to be that guy."

"Yeah, we don't want to be that guy." I grinned.

11

"Did I mention how much I hate you right now? Because I hate you."

"Let's suit up."

4

Daylight was dying in the west behind us; Olympus One's bulbous, round buildings and interconnected tubes and junctures were silhouetted against the dim blue haze of the sunset. Our own silhouettes bobbed and mixed unevenly with the dusty surface as we carefully made our way to the spot where we'd test the camera.

"Turn it on," Akio said.

I turned my whole body to face her, now garbed in her own EVA suit; Phobos was completing its last orbit of the day behind her.

"Here goes," I said.

I opened the camera shutter, pressed the power button.

The machine, cupped in my hands, sent vibrations up my arms. It was almost soothing. The serrated vents on the side gave off a slight glow, giving hints at the internal structure of the interferometer. The lens extended, and the digital display in front of me showed the mirrors and magnifiers shifting into position inside the camera. The hydrogen fuel cell stayed cool on my belt, thanks in part to Mars' sub-zero temperatures. The data started to pour in.

"Anything yet?" Akio asked.

"Not sure," I said. "The data could take some time to compile if the concentration isn't dense enough…"

"But, if we did it right, it shouldn't matter where we are, or how much dark matter there is, right?"

"I see what you did there."

"I know, clever, right?"

I nodded. The data finally seemed to finish compiling, and the three-dimensional image began to render.

It was like looking at the known universe at a distance. The image known as the "universal web" came immediately to my mind. We were but tiny specs at the center of a massive, glowing web of violet energy, with filamentary networks that stretched into and out of everything.

Individual strands of dark matter connected each and every glowing cluster of energy, like strands in a widow's web. There were thousands of those clusters, stretching up into the night sky, a lattice-work of chaos that blotted out even the brightest stars in the panorama. It was a network that stretched through and permeated every dimension, every world, every nook and cranny of the universe. Created from detecting the slight—microscopic—variations in atoms and molecules in our physical reality caused by matter intersecting with dark matter. And we were the first ones to ever see it.

I looked up and smiled.

What was displayed on the screen seemed to jive with some of the reports from the data taken from satellites that had been retrofitted to detect dark matter in space, but those couldn't actually image the dark matter, and they certainly couldn't do the image before my eyes justice.

For the first time since coming to Olympus One, I felt a fire burning inside of me.

"It worked," I said.

"Wow, really?" Akio said. "It's like I haven't been standing here watching you this whole time."

Akio quickly grabbed the machine, spinning me around awkwardly in the process. Her eyes went wide and took on the glow from the monitor inside her helmet. I stifled a chuckle.

"Wow," she said. "I imagined it'd look different."

"We're the first to see it," I said.

"Wicked." She grinned. "We're gonna be stupid rich from this."

"Oh, and just what do you expect to do with money on Mars?"

She stuck her tongue out at me, and I took the machine back.

"We should head back just in case Wolfrik changes his mind about my extra-colonial activities," I said. "I don't want to chance him seeing the machine before we have a chance to patent it…"

"Has anyone ever filed a patent from Mars?"

"Not that I know of…"

I wrapped the cable up and powered the machine down, making sure to save the data gathered. I couldn't wait to get it back inside and take a deeper look at the holographic snapshot. Akio started walking ahead of me.

It's funny how genderless we all look inside a space suit. Most of Akio's features were obscured, but her dainty walk gave her away. The way she always remained dignified with each step…like a cat always seems regal after recovering from a falling on its face.

I remembered my mother getting dressed up for date night. Father was late coming home from work. The makeup she'd used to cover the black eye was convincing, but my mind painted it back into place. Even in her shame, she wanted to feel dignified.

"Hal," Akio said, bringing me back to reality. "Are you going to show it to your dad when you get back?"

"Yeah," I said. "If it leads where I hope it leads."

"If we can use the data to prove our hypothesis."

"I have a feeling it will."

"Darwin would fucking love us."

"Maybe."

"No maybe about it." She turned around, her face lit up under the harsh crimson light inside the airlock. "It's not every day that you discover the mechanism behind evolution. I imagine he'd extend his hand, bow, and say something like, 'righteous job, dudes.'"

"Dudes?"

The chamber pressurized, the light on the door flickered from red to green.

"I watched a lot of cartoons as a kid," she said.

"Obviously."

"Like you didn't?"

"Cartoons were of the devil."

"No way!" She covered her mouth like it was a surprise that my childhood had been sheltered.

"I'm already thinking about how the panorama fits our theory."

"Me too, I can't get the striations that connect each of the clusters out of my head."

"You think that's how information passes between celestial objects?"

She nodded. "It could be, yeah. Like electrical impulses passing from the brain to various parts of the body?"

"We need to be careful not to get too far ahead of ourselves, though. We need to collect as much data as possible."

"Duh."

We were halfway through undressing when she looked up at me, her eyes softened.

I avoided her gaze.

"What?" I asked.

"Don't you think it's cruel?" she asked, trying to hop one leg into her coveralls.

"Don't I think what's cruel?"

"Trying to destroy someone's faith?"

I shrugged. It was more complicated than that. Something I couldn't put into words. "Not like he'll believe it anyway. He'll think it's some devilish trick. Hell, I bet he doesn't even believe we're all really here on Mars, like it's some stage in Hollywood or something."

She nodded. Akio came from a loving family, a sane family most likely. I doubted that she could relate.

We finished getting dressed, stashed the suits where we found them, and hacked the logs on the doors and lockers to make it look like we were never there. I'd erase the footage from the cameras later to complete the job.

When we got home, Akio broke the silence by saying goodnight and retreating to her room. I was too restless to sleep, so I loaded the three-dimensional snapshot onto my tablet and began inspecting it.

The image was, essentially, a panorama of the Martian surface surrounding myself and Akio, with the holographic dark matter network overlaid on top. The sky was a haunting deep purple; the silhouette of a dust storm raged off in the distance, clawing at the frigid air, fighting for life on a world where there was none. The land was almost black beneath our feet, save for the lights on the camera and our suits that illuminated the red Martian soil.

The web was composed of violet striations, which seemed to have thicker concentrations out in the distance of the image. I zoomed into each striation, each cluster, which had striations and branching filaments of their own, curving, bridging, flowing through the planet as if they were the strings on which it dangled.

There seemed to be larger concentrations around (and through) Akio, as well as through my own body. The dark matter around Akio seemed to be spinning, reaching into the air, while the concentration around me was dull, faded. I dragged it around a full 360 degrees.

Something, however, caught my eye. I zoomed in several times. I shook my head, rubbed my eyes.

It had to be a misread of the data...

There was a violet humanoid shape several feet away from where Akio and I were standing in the image.

Maybe the shape was nothing more than a data fragment, or a repetition of the same violet dark matter formations seen around my and Akio's bodies? That would be the most likely explanation; but, something, maybe intuition, told me that wasn't the case, that it was something else entirely.

For one, the violet silhouette's arms and legs were in a completely different position than mine or Akio's. That wouldn't be the case if it was just a ghost image caused by the camera stitching the photographs together to make the panorama.

It was almost as if that violet silhouette was taunting me, daring me to take a trip down the rabbit hole.

And down the hole I went.

The dark matter concentrations around Akio and me reminded me of a research project I'd done last semester on non-local consciousness. There are some quantum physicists who theorize that human consciousness is not merely an effect of the brain. That the human mind exists in the same place as the body, but in a different dimension. My research project was about the idea, and the theory, that consciousness is made of dark matter.

I still remember the argument vividly.

"I just can't accept this, Geraldo," Professor Jameson said. "Your argument for this is heavily biased and it shows."

"And yours isn't?" I asked.

"I'll admit, I don't like the theory one bit, but I would have been willing to give you a higher mark if you'd at least tried to remain unbiased when discussing other theories that contradict your own. You have an almost religious fanaticism when it comes to this."

That set me off. "Seriously? Religious? I was unbiased when I mentioned the other theories. You're using your opinion of me as an excuse to tank my grade on this paper."

"That's a pretty heavy accusation, Geraldo."

"Hal."

"'Hal,' you need to realize that not everyone shares your view on this, and you're going to get laughed out of every class you bring it up in, especially if you use 'remote-viewing' and 'near-death-experiences' as evidence. Hell, I would have been slightly more accepting if you came out and said ghosts were real, and you were the reincarnation of Albert Einstein!"

"I didn't use those as evidence." I crossed my arms. "If you actually read the fucking thing, I used them as an example of good areas that might benefit from further study, considering it's not a huge stretch to imagine that dark matter and quantum entanglement probably have some relationship. If a particle can describe another particle's spin from any distance, who's to say that humans don't have some latent ability to do the same? There are cases of mothers feeling the exact moment when their child dies, and the same is true of twins that experience traumatic events."

"And this somehow means that consciousness is non-local?"

"I'm not the only one who believes in this, you know?"

"Really? Where are these mythical creatures?" He looked around me at the class behind me. "Are there any in here? No? Okay. Looks like you're alone after all."

"I'll prove it someday."

"You won't, not if you continue to try to force-fit the data to your viewpoint. You're just as bad as a twentieth-century creationist who thinks the dinosaurs lived with men."

I slammed my hands on the table. "And you're as blind as someone who thinks the Earth is *flat!*"

I heard chuckles coming from behind me and felt the piercing stare of other students looking up from their terminals to see what all the drama was about.

Professor Jameson glared at me. "Get out of my class."

I smiled. "Gladly."

Professor Jameson and I barely spoke after that. And no other student tried using non-local consciousness as the subject of their paper in one of his courses again.

But, if the dark matter camera were to continuously photograph concentrations around the human body, then perhaps the theory held more water than my professor thought? If the silhouette was reproduced in subsequent tests, things would get even more interesting.

Perhaps it would be *me* who got the last laugh in that particular argument?

I decided to bring these things up to Akio in the morning.

My eyes drifted, lazily, to the clock, and I saw that it was getting late. I moved some papers and boxes off of the couch, and plopped down for a quick nap.

I jerked awake as Akio dumped a bucket of water over my unconscious body.

"Wake up, damn it!" Akio said.

I sat up. "What the hell was that for?"

She sat the bucket down next to the couch and pointed to the clock on her tablet's screen.

"It's almost noon, Hal," Akio said. "You slept through your morning class."

I wiped my face with my palms and watched the water drip off the plastic couch. It pooled onto the hard-plastic floor and slipped down a drain close by. Can't have anything wasted on Mars. Everything must be recycled.

I looked back into Akio's dull brown eyes.

"I'm sure they'll live without me for a day," I said. "You could have just nudged me awake, you know?"

"No," she said. "I tried that. You kept tossing and turning, muttering in your sleep about something. I was almost worried."

I rubbed my eyes. "I must have been more exhausted than I thought…"

"Yeah, maybe. I grabbed your assignments for you, and you can have a copy of my notes to study from. You can thank me later."

That wasn't it. My head felt heavy, as if I hadn't rested at all. I felt the pang of a memory just out of reach. Perhaps from some kind of nightmare?

I got up, strolled over to the kitchen; grabbed the coffee pot, dumped it, refilled it, snatched a coffee packet, turned the brewer on.

"You should get in touch with your professors," Akio said.

"Can't." The coffee pot started to drip, pooling precious black gold into the bottom of the pot.

"Why not?"

"Because we're going on walkabout today."

Her eyes blinked several times while she processed the idea. "Wolfrik will lose his mind if we do that again. If they knew what we did last night—"

"Apparently Wolfrik doesn't care what I do anymore."

"I guess that makes me guilty by association?"

"You're welcome."

"Why do we even need to go outside? The hydrogen cell is stable. Why not just test it in here?"

"I want to see how dark matter interacts with the planet. That's not something we're going to see if we limit our focus to inside the cramped corridors here. Panoramic shots don't work too well inside."

"We should still do some tests inside."

"And we'll do that, but the big picture is out there."

The coffee-pot was almost a quarter of the way full; I pulled it out prematurely and poured myself a cup, then sat at the counter, watching the steam swirl into the air. Akio walked around and grabbed a cup from the sink, rinsed and washed it with her hands. She waited for there to be enough coffee for another cup, poured herself a generous amount, then took the seat opposite me.

"You need to see the panorama in high definition," I said.

"From last night?"

I took a long sip. "Yes. There's a curious aspect of it I want your opinion about before we go out."

"Now you're assuming I'll go." She leaned back, a slight grin wrinkling the skin of her left cheek.

"You will once you see what we got from the test."

"That good?"

"See for yourself." I fetched my tablet from across the living room, brought up the panorama and handed it off to her.

20

She took it in her dainty hands. Her eyes went wide as she manipulated the image, twisting it and moving it in any direction she could. I moved behind her to see what she was looking at.

"What is the glow around us?" she said.

"Getting to that," I said, parrying her finger away and focusing on the part of the image I'd seen last night. "Look at this sector here. See that shape there?"

She nodded. "What is that?"

"Not sure."

"Could be an artifact…or maybe it's just repeating the glow around us farther in the image?"

"If that was the case, why are its limbs in completely different positions than ours? In any case, we won't know for sure until we get up to the summit of Olympus Mons and run another test."

She set the tablet down and rubbed her eyes. "Forget it. You know how long it would take us to walk up to the summit?"

"That's why we're not going to walk."

She pushed me back and walked off to the coffee-pot to pour herself another cup. "You better not be suggesting we steal a rover."

She looked me in the eye; I grinned.

"That's exactly what you're thinking!" she said.

"It'll be easy," I said. "You know the security codes for the hangar anyway, they'll never know that one's even missing."

"And what if something goes wrong? What if the hydrogen cells give out halfway up?"

"Then we use the solar cells."

"What if we crash and the air tanks rupture?"

"Then we die."

She glared at me. "Yeah, I'm out, sorry."

"All great discoveries come with a certain amount of risk. Mars is a dangerous world, yes, but so is living here. Do you realize that any number of things going wrong here could spell doom for us all?"

"What's your point?"

"What's the difference if it happens out there or in here? Death is death."

She tried to avoid my gaze.

"I'll tell you what the difference is, Akio, out there you'll be helping to break ground on something no one's ever seen. A new technology that could open the door to the universe for us."

"A new technology?" She shook her head. "Aren't you making it sound a bit too grandiose? We invented a camera that images dark matter, not a machine that manipulates it."

"And yet, this may grant us the data we need to prove our hypothesis. Look at the glow around us and the silhouette again, there's something you're missing."

She stared at it for a time, squinting and shifting the perspective. "I don't get it."

"The glowing dark matter concentrations around us could be positive evidence for non-local consciousness."

She rolled her eyes. "Not this crap again. I thought you gave up that outdated theory?"

"Just because a theory is unpopular does not mean it isn't true."

"One might suggest the same thing of God, and you're adamantly against the notion that one exists."

"There's a big difference between some bearded idiot sitting in a chair, governing all life in the known universe with a set of arbitrary rules, and the existence of non-local consciousness."

"Not from where I'm sitting. I think it's been widely proven that human consciousness is a product of the brain and nothing more."

"It might be more accepted, but the evidence doesn't necessarily suggest that. There are a lot of things that your theory doesn't explain, like out-of-body-near-death-experiences where the subject is able to perceive their own body and surroundings and even travel to other places before being revived—"

"Clearly just a fabrication of events created by the brain to explain the lack of activity—there's nothing to suggest that the subject's consciousness magically got up and walked off."

"Then how do you explain instances where the subject is able to perceive events and areas that they never could have known of prior to having the experience?"

"Lucky guesses, or maybe the subject overheard bits of conversation that led their subconscious mind to piece together the information later."

"That's a bit of a stretch."

"Not as big as yours."

"Okay, then what about the observer effect?"

"What's that got to do with non-local consciousness?"

"Everything. How do you think the state and spin of an entangled particle is instantly described, if not through a transference of information that transcends the physical relationship of matter? We see this in other forms of matter, where they behave as a wave when observed, and as a particle when they're not being observed by a conscious subject. It's as though the sentient, conscious observer acts as a probability generator when it comes to how it interacts with reality."

"Probability generator—where do you get this stuff?" She made a face at me. "I don't see how the observer effect is affected one way or another by where consciousness comes from. For all you know, dark matter might act as a conduit for the transference of information that serves to facilitate evolution, perhaps as some kind of means of an exchange of information from different parts of the universe. It doesn't mean our mind exists somewhere else."

"And yet, we have the same hypothesis. We arrive at it from different points of view, but what is more plausible for the generation, evolution and organization of complex life in our universe? Your way of thinking—*boring*—" I paused for dramatic effect. Akio rolled her eyes, but I could tell she was holding her breath, so she wouldn't burst out in laughter at my theatrics. "—or, that there are many levels of consciousness, that dark matter *is* consciousness, or is a means of connecting it to biological forms, and that thereby drives and *wills* life into existence."

"I still like my version better." She smiled, then threw a wadded-up piece of paper at my head. "I think you trivialize the role of the brain. The brain is awesome! Who's to say that panspermia isn't a direct result of information being downloaded into the dark matter web and transported across the known universe, thereby causing life to happen on worlds where it's possible?"

"Dark matter web?" I leaned back.

"You like it?"

I smiled. "Has a nice ring to it."

We sat silent for a few minutes drinking our coffee.

I leaned forward. "Fine, then prove me wrong. We can even make a wager on the outcome."

"Provided I help you hijack a rover and violate about thirty different safety regulations?"

"Yes."

"What's your wager?"

"I'll clean the dorm room for the rest of our academic career here on Olympus Mons if you prove me wrong."

"No thanks, I'll pass, your idea of cleaning still leaves me with a metric ton of work to do."

"Fine, then I'll clean it to your specifications for that period of time."

"With no complaints or bellowing?"

"Sure."

She sighed. "Fine, damn it, I'll do it."

I smiled. "I knew you'd come to your senses."

"However." She raised a finger into the air.

"Damn it." I sighed, planting my head on the counter. "What is it? And don't say that you want me to clean naked, that's not happening."

"You have to try requisitioning the rover first…though that would be a nice touch."

"No, it wouldn't, and they'll deny us. Connor Wilson fucked that up for us."

"And if they do, we'll try it your way." She grinned. She had me. "The look on your face tells me everything I need to know."

"Which is?"

"That you'll do it, even if you despise the idea."

I finished my coffee and used my tablet to set up an appointment to talk with requisitions.

2

Akio went ahead to her next class while I strolled over to requisitions. The student rep there was eating one of those new Salad in a Box things that Milkyway Unlimited sent up with the last shipment of supplies. He chewed the green and yellow food bar with all of the slow, deliberate motion of a cow that's just realized how relaxing it is to chew grass and stare into oblivion.

I knocked on the desk. His thin, tired eyes met mine, and he instantly knew me. "Whatever it is, I'm sure you should be in class, Geraldo."

"Hal," I said.

He rolled his eyes. "What do you want?"

"I'm on a mission," I said. "Class project."

"Which class?" His left eyebrow rose. Where did I know this guy from?

"Planetary Physics? I need to do some surface tests on Olympus Mons for the upcoming mid-term."

"Oh, the class you got kicked out of yesterday?" He chuckled. "Trying to salvage what's left of your grade after insulting Professor Brown?"

"Yes, that, exactly that." I smiled, leaned in. "Look, I know I screwed up, and I've got to do something big to make an impression on her."

"I'd be more than glad to help, as long as it falls within safety regulations. What would you like to requisition?"

"A rover."

His dreadlocks almost slapped me in the face as he reeled back in laughter, holding his stomach and everything.

"Are you finished?" I asked.

"Wolfrik would never allow someone with your reputation for insubordination to take a rover out onto the surface!" He shook his head. "You can put in for the request, but I can't promise anything."

I nodded, and begrudgingly put in my request for the rover on the terminal next to captain jackass. I left, headed for engineering to pick up another bottle of "gin."

Dane avoided my gaze when he saw me coming down the corridor. He was looking left and right at his station, dark circles floated beneath his sunken eyes. This time of day, the rest of the Engineering department was usually at lunch, and Dane liked to eat his right in this corridor, where his customers could find him.

"Man, I just took care of you a couple days ago," Dane said. "You wanna burn my whole supply or something?"

"You make it sound like you're dealing in meth or something."

"Quiet down, will you?" His voice transformed into a hushed whisper as he looked behind me. Paranoia was painted on his sweaty face.

"Relax, I just want a bottle."

"Which flavor? I'm working on some new flavors, might even be able to mimic the taste of whiskey soon."

I shrugged. "Surprise me."

Dane grinned. He spun around on his butt, setting his ration bar on the plastic food tray next to him. He hopped to his feet with all the grace of an emaciated stray dog and walked around the corner. I followed him to the door to a supply room, which hissed open after he put in an access code on the side panel. Once we were inside, the door shut, and Dane dug his fingers into a hidden access panel in the wall. He reached his arm into darkness, the sound of bottles clanking together caressed my ears—music to my soul—and he produced a large bottle of clear liquid the size of my forearm, then shut the compartment and sealed it with a love tap from his elbow.

The bottle was cool to the touch when he placed it in my hands. There was a label: CHERRY. "What do I owe you?"

"A favor when I ask for it," he said.

"What'll it be this time? Hacking the feeds again so you can sneak into the showers, a prank against one of your fellow workers in Engineering, or, perhaps, supplies?"

He smacked my arm. "Shush!" Then he came in closer, whispering. "Supplies. Soon. This batch won't last forever, especially with you around, and I can't be seen sneaking into the greenhouse."

"So, that's where you get your corn?"

He nodded. "They're wise to me, though. Put up cameras and shit from what I hear."

"I have ways around cameras."

26

"Good, let me know when you can get me this list." He palmed a small piece of paper into my bag. "Don't look back when you leave, Anderson is getting suspicious."

"You still have the security cameras looped?"

He nodded. "Thanks to you."

"And don't forget it."

We both left the supply room, and I turned away from Dane and left him to his rations and solitude.

When I stepped back into the main corridor, a message ping rang off my tablet. I grabbed at my bag and eyed the message.

I gritted my teeth, squeezed my free hand into a tight fist until my fingers ached.

REQUISITION ORDER: DENIED

Good, I didn't want their fucking help anyway.

3

After depositing my cherry gin at home, I made my way over to the greenhouse. Eyes were on me. Botany majors filled the corridor and I stood out like a dead fly in my mom's menudo. I needed to blend in, and I'd need an alibi for later.

I found my way into one of the research labs. It was empty, thankfully. The lab smelled of fertilizer, and various species of plants were arranged on each desk. A few ferns, a common weed, and a dead watermelon plant that stank like Akio's feet after using the gym. I saw the answer to my problem on the back of a chair: a hooded lab coat and a pair of goggles.

I donned the garb of the botany expert and hoped to a nonexistent God that no one asked me anything about plants.

There were fewer stares now that my gear was in fashion. I made my way to the greenhouse. The door was open, so I walked right in like I belonged. The blood drained from my face.

The greenhouse was a glass dome. It always scared the shit out of me, even though everyone claimed it was made of a reinforced polymer. It was like standing on the surface of the planet without any protection at all.

Standing on the surface of the red planet can be a calming and surreal experience, and I've often wished that I could experience the sunrise without the need for an EVA suit, but this was almost nightmarish. The old fears of vacuum exposure came creeping out as I attempted to get ahold of myself.

I took a deep breath and focused on the plants. That helped.

I slapped the power switch on the wall, turning on the heat lamp that dangled from a magnetic track following the curve of the dome — hoping it might be a distraction from the Martian horizon. I reached inside my bag and withdrew several large plastic bags. I made my way through the greenhouse, picking corn and sugar cane. The other two items on my list — water and yeast — could be found later.

Once the bags were full, I walked right out into the corridor — keeping my head down. There were only a handful of people in the corridor. I got halfway down it, thinking I'd gotten away with it, when I saw her Armada tattoo.

Gila was talking to a friend of hers in the hall. I tried to scoot past her, but her eyes caught mine. My gut sank.

"Hal?" she said, sounding both excited and accusatory.

Her friend crossed her arms and glared at me.

"Gila!" I grabbed both bags with my left hand and waved at her, approaching them. If I was lucky, they wouldn't notice the bags.

"What are you doing all the way over here?" Her eyes drifted down to the bags, eyebrows scrunching together. "And, why are you wearing one of our lab coats…"

"Are you stealing plants?" Her friend's voice had a slight African accent to it. "That is a major violation."

"Chill, Dalla," Gila said, raising her hand. "I'm sure Hal has a logical explanation for this."

"Right," I said, wracking my brain to come up with some kind of explanation that wouldn't end with Wolfrik coming after me for stealing from the botany domes, and Dane from killing me in my sleep if it all led back to him. "It's…for an experiment?"

"Experiment?" Gila's African friend did not look the least bit convinced. I was officially in panic mode.

Gila nodded slowly. There was a tense silence between the three of us. I was sure that I was dead.

"Right!" Gila said. "I did say that I'd help you with that project!"

I nodded. "Gila gave me access to one of the botany domes so I could get a head start."

"Uh-huh." Her friend did not look convinced. She shrugged and turned, patting Gila on the shoulder. "Whatever, plants are dumb anyway. I'll see you later, Gila."

"Later," Gila said.

Once her friend was out of earshot, Gila pinched my arm.

"Ouch, what the hell?"

"Stealing! Really, Hal?"

I grinned, tossing the bag over my shoulder. "If you're so mad, why'd you cover for me?"

Gila shrugged. "I figure you're getting it for Dane. I've been known to partake."

"Really now?" I laughed. "Now that *is* a surprise."

"Anyway, I need to get to my next class, and you need to get those out of here before someone starts asking questions."

"Right."

Gila turned and headed down the hall. I proceeded to get the hell out of that sector before someone else recognized me. I'd send Dane a message later about picking his stuff up. For now, it was time to figure out how to steal a rover without getting expelled.

Returning to the dorm, I set the bags of ill-gotten corn and sugarcane in my room, then opened up my tablet and sent Akio a message.

Hal: *Guess what?*

I sat on the couch and stared at the dark matter camera. If we were going to do this, it had to be done right. There had to be no chance of us getting caught.

Akio: *You've finally realized your life long goal is to open up a taco truck on Mars.*

Hal: *Racist. I don't even like tacos.*

Hal: *No, our request got denied.*

Akio: *Shit.*

Hal: *Yeah…*

Akio: *So…that means…*

Hal: *Yeah, we'll talk about it when you get home. I wanted to get the data today, but I don't think we can do it till the weekend anyway, the trip would probably take two Sols, and someone would notice.*

Akio: *Right. Weekend it is then.*

Akio: *Oh, shit, Prof. Morison is looking right at me. TTYL.*

I set the tablet down.

"Can I do this?" If we got caught, it could mean expulsion. For a moment, I thought about what might happen if I was forced to return to Earth… I was certain my father would just love it if I came home a failure, my head hung in shame and my name forever tarnished within academia. I wrung my hands together until they became numb.

The dark matter camera meant more than even Olympus One did to me. In a sense, it was the entire reason I'd come here to begin with. But, if we could prove our hypothesis…maybe it wouldn't matter how many rules we broke to do it?

I shook my head, stood up, and made myself a cup of coffee.

"No," I said to no one but the walls and the mess of wires in our lab.

I told myself there was no way in hell we could get caught. Sipping a hot cup of coffee seemed to reinforce this idea. We could hack one of the rovers to look as if it'd been put on the maintenance schedule. No one would know it was missing.

If Akio and I were considered one being, we'd probably be the best hacker on Mars. There weren't many people on Mars to begin with, but still.

I sighed.

It was going to be a long wait till the weekend.

■■■

Lightning struck the surface sporadically; the dust rolled itself together like a thousand gargantuan fingers squeezing into a mighty fist. The rover's cage rattled over crimson rocks and spat sand that hadn't been disturbed in millions of years, splashing it backward like a boat cutting through the ocean—if the ocean had gravity of 0.4 Gs. I kept my hands tight around the controls. Akio had kept her helmet and gloves on the whole time since we'd left Olympus One.

I looked at her and grinned sheepishly.

"Fuck you," she said. "I don't wanna take any chances."

"Hey, I didn't say anything."

"Yeah, your stupid face said it all."

I chuckled, and she flipped me off.

Olympus Mons was about the size of France, but Olympus One was situated just a few kilometers up the gradual incline of the volcano, so the journey would take a little over one Sol at thirty-five kph, not taking into account the fact that the rover's speed typically varied due to terrain and incline severity.

I kept the comms down, and the jamming frequency up so the Admins couldn't call the rover back. We could always turn those back on if we got ourselves into any trouble.

"Is the storm going to hit us?" Akio asked.

"The HUD's telling me it's going to miss us by a few kilometers," I said.

"Oh, comforting. Why did I let you talk me into this again?"

"Because you're a real scientist, and not one of those neck-bearded pansies who never leave Olympus One. Also, fame. Also, money."

She rolled her eyes. "Right. How could I forget?"

I watched the dust storm rake its claws across the horizon to my left, red-orange dust licking up from the surface in waves, lightning dancing in the darkness. I tried to imagine what it might be like to be consumed by the storm. Martian winds typically never get any more intense than sixty miles per hour, but that wasn't the chief concern being inside one. Microscopic rocks and debris have a slight electric charge to them, and those lightning bolts could be a big problem if one hit the rover. The biggest challenge would be navigation. Sure, there'd be GPS, but that only told you where you were and where you were going, not what was in front of you and if you were heading for anything that might kill you.

Hours passed, light faded into night, and the controls became stiff in my hands. It was a safety measure baked into the rover to ensure that the stupid human driving it didn't run a four-billion-dollar piece of equipment straight into a giant rock or a crater. I relaxed my grip and let the AI do its thing, allowing me a break to look at the stars.

The constellation Draco drifted across the horizon. The stars glistened like tiny white fires in the night. It reminded me of the surreal feeling of driving through the countryside with nothing but a tank full of gas and a pollution-free sky for company years ago.

Akio had fallen asleep, using some leftover HAB canvas from some old class experiment as a makeshift pillow.

She had the right idea, at least. I set the computer housed in the gauntlet of my EVA suit to wake me before sunrise. I set my seat to recline and laid my head back against the chair's headrest.

I watched the stars for a while as sleep crept up on me.

2

This time, when I dreamed, I remembered it vividly.

I stood on the surface of the red planet. The constellation Draco was bright above me. Each star was a concentration of dark matter within the violet web. Striations stretched from the stars, scattered across the dark matter web, through my own body. Raised me up off of my feet, dangling me like a puppet.

There was something on the horizon, a jagged spire of a silhouette blacker than even the night sky.

A sense of panic tore through me when I saw it. I couldn't move anymore.

"Hal," Akio's voice called to me. Her voice seemed strangely detached.

I felt something move my head to the right.

Akio was still in her EVA suit, but the screen on her gauntlet was dead. She was dangling from threads composed of dark matter, just like me. Her eyes were white, her lips cold.

I woke up wondering where her voice had come from. My heart was racing. I almost reached out and shook Akio awake, but seeing her shallow breathing from inside her suit stopped me.

I looked at my gauntlet. It was still three hours till my alarm would sound.

I couldn't sleep.

3

Before I knew it, the sun was rising through that familiar blue haze against the highest reaches of Olympus Mons's caldera. The coming light gave me back control of the rover, and I guided it down a hill, inside the caldera, and kept driving until I found a large flat area that would suffice for our experiment. By the time I came to a stop, the sky had already transitioned from blue to butterscotch.

I nudged Akio's shoulder. "Wake up. We're here."

She fumbled in her seat. "We're alive?"

"Yes. The storm missed us, like I said." I grinned. "You ready to go outside?"

"You're going to be the death of me, aren't you?"

"Probably. Do you want to stay inside the rover where it's safe while I do all the work?"

"Fuck no!" She flipped me off while I slipped my helmet on, fastening the clamps in place. I pressurized my suit when she was ready and gripped the latch.

"Ready?" I asked.

Akio nodded with stiff, wild eyes and tight lips.

I popped the seal and stepped onto the hard, dusty surface of the caldera. The Martian dirt had the consistency of powdered sugar beneath my boots. Dragging a mounting pole and our invention with me, I checked my HUD. The temperature was minus 45 degrees Celsius, with no other weather anomalies this morning. Picnic weather.

"Are you sure it'll keep working through the night?" Akio asked as I walked the pole out toward a spot that looked soft enough to spike through.

"It should be fine as long as it doesn't dip below minus 70. Even then, the cold won't stop the machine from turning back on when it warms back up."

"You're not typically so optimistic. It's possible extreme cold could do significant damage to the wiring."

"I doubt it." I let out a grunt, arched my arm back, and spiked the pole into the dirt; crimson dust clung to my boots.

I opened up the claw at the end of the pole and fastened the dark matter camera into it, closed it back up and tightened the fasteners until I was sure it wouldn't drop.

"Okay, what about sandstorms?" Akio paced around me, her hands twitching together.

"Winds don't get any stronger than sixty miles per hour, not strong enough to knock over the pole."

"And dust?"

"The dust'll get on the casing, sure, but I doubt it'll be out here long enough for any real damage to be done."

"You're going to come back for it?"

"We."

"Sure, just as soon as pigs roam the surface of this gloriously bleak world in massive packs, creating ozone from the massive piles of crap they leave behind in their wake. That is to say, *no!*"

"So you say." I booted up the machine, let it run through its diagnostic phase and checked to make sure everything was working fine with the screen on my gauntlet. "The systems check out."

"Can we go now?"

"How about breakfast first?"

"Fine, but as soon as we're done, you drive us the hell out of here."

"Deal."

We marched back to the rover, climbed inside the cab, and waited for the pressure to re-equalize. I removed my helmet and set it on the floor to my right, Akio following my lead as soon as she saw that I was not in fact suffocating in a vacuum. I opened a plastic package containing a dried beefsteak and placed another package containing a shortbread cookie on my knee. I stared at the beefsteak for a moment too long, catching a whiff of the smell.

"Well, are you going to stare at it, or eat it?" Akio asked.

I nodded and shoved the beefsteak into my mouth. When eating rations on Mars, the only way to avoid gagging from the taste is to consume what passes for food as quickly as possible.

I made a show of how much I hated that beefsteak by making every grossed-out sound I could manage as it slithered down my throat and splashed safely into the confines of my stomach. This seemed to amuse Akio.

She giggled. "That's why there's no obesity on Mars."

"Makes sense." I rolled my eyes, gagging and looking for something to erase that horrible aftertaste. "Or, they don't choose anyone who isn't in perfect health because they're afraid they'll die from a heart attack or implode."

"That too, but I imagine if you gave a reasonably healthy—and fat—man this shit to live off of for four years, they'd probably end up lean as fuck by the end of their stay."

"Or they'd walk off into the Martian sunset without a spacesuit, because you just took away the man's only hypothetical reason to live."

"Cruel, aren't I?"

"Extremely, but at least now you're not wearing the helmet like a coward."

She smacked my arm, knocking my cookie to the floor.

"Ouch! What was that for?"

"You have to ask? Why'd you have to remind me, jerk?"

I shrugged. She wasn't scared anymore, at the very least.

Akio and I scarfed the rest of our meal down as quickly as possible and consumed enough water to keep us hydrated for the drive back.

She put the helmet back on and I tried not to chuckle.

The return trip went faster than expected. I guess due to the fact that we'd already made the trip once. The Sun kept pace with us for most of the journey and was only beginning to edge behind Olympus One by the time we returned.

Once we entered the range of the campus network, our controls immediately seized, and the rover began to drive off toward the eastern wing of the colony.

Something had gotten through my jamming frequency.

"Well, that's not good," I said.

"What?" Akio's eyes went wide, and her breath was hoarse. Her hand ready and waiting to pressurize her suit.

"Looks like the Admins got through my jamming frequency. There's an auto-recall on the rover, as soon as we passed into network range our controls were seized."

"Shit!"

"Relax." I kicked my feet back and tossed her a mischievous smile. "What's the worst they can do to us?"

"Expel us! Send us back to Earth!"

"Bah! They don't have the balls to spend the millions it would cost to send both of us back to Earth."

"You don't know that, Hal!"

"Relax, I'll just tell them the whole thing was my idea and I coerced you into it—which is mostly true. Most you'll get is a slap on the wrist."

"And you?" Her lip started to quiver.

"I'll be fine. Watch."

The rover twisted and turned around one of the domes, circled the greenhouse, and passed under a bridge, until we entered a large pressurized hangar. The Martian sky vanished behind us, and we were greeted by the angry faces of Wolfrik and the rest of the Admins.

I waved at them, gave them my best smile.

4

"You put me in a strange position here, Geraldo." Wolfrik leaned forward, clasping his clammy hands together beneath the all-encompassing white light of what we affectionately referred to as *The Box*. "What you did was reckless, and even if you care nothing of yourself, you could have killed Akio."

The Box was like solitary confinement. A formless white room that played tricks on the eyes and made one feel as though they were going mad if left there alone for too long.

Despite my reputation, this was my first time in The Box. It had originally been intended to help deal with cases of cabin fever and claustrophobia. There were built-in holographic projectors that could allow you to see any kind of environment: the sprawling, clean flowing waters of the Grand Canyon, the great heights of the Himalayas, the greatest cities in the world...

Wolfrik, however, liked to use it to teach problem students what a big fish he was. I'm not even sure the holographic projectors had ever been used.

"Do you have nothing to say for yourself?" Wolfrik asked.

I leaned back, propped my feet up on the table. "Let's be honest if this is an expulsion hearing, Wolfrik. You don't give a damn about either of us, you're only concerned about what could have happened to the rover."

"This is not true." His accent was coming through, I was getting to him.

"But I think it is." I leaned forward, the humor melting from my face. "You want to label this as a joyride and a woeful disregard for authority. The second part is definitely true, in part, but the first is not. It was not a joyride. It was an experiment."

"An experiment?"

"I can't get into specifics yet, the patents for the device haven't been made. You understand, right?"

His thick eyebrow rose. "I'll believe it when I see it. Even so, if that were the case, I am not understanding why you didn't put in an official request to borrow the equipment, we could have worked with you and ensured that the proper safety—"

"I did put in an official request, and it was denied, you shyster."

He paused for a moment, looking at his tablet to confirm that I was telling the truth.

"Still, you did not have to resort to stealing—"

"Oh, please, spare me with that shit. We both know that you wouldn't have let me take the rover, and why the hell would you? You made that clear yesterday when you brought up my mother."

"Your upbringing has little to do with what you did here."

"Doesn't it, though? I've heard the way you all talk about me. Don't think that I haven't. I've found ways of reversing the mechanism you use in our desks when you want to hear and see everything we're doing, and the things you say are quite revealing. *'That degenerate will never graduate, I'll make sure of that!'* and *'He doesn't belong here, he's not one of us!'* And, my favorite: *'He belongs in the asylum with his mother.'* was what you said. Why, Wolfrik?"

"I never—"

"You did, you son-of-a-bitch!"

His eyes narrowed; he removed his glasses and rubbed them. "Yes. I said that, because you are a problem, Geraldo. You do not follow the rules, you argue with your professors and drive good students to mischief."

"I want a lawyer."

"A lawyer?" He looked genuinely confused. "You don't get a lawyer."

"Then, I want a trial by combat. If I kill you in battle, you have to set me free."

Wolfrik rubbed his eyes. "Is that how you want this to go, Geraldo? Keep playing these games, I can't tell you how well it will go for you at your disciplinary hearing."

"No, Wolfrik, I really want a trial by combat."

"Stop that."

"Stop what, Wolfrik?"

"Calling me that."

"That's your name."

"I have a doctorate, you should address me—"

"It's irritating, isn't it? To be called something other than your desired name."

"It is. So, stop it."

We both grew quiet. I glanced around The Box. I couldn't even tell where the door had been. But I was sure that the other Admins were watching this.

I looked back into Wolfrik's angry eyes. "Do you want to spend four billion dollars to put me on a ship back to Earth?"

"If it comes to that."

"Guess you've all made up your minds."

"That's up to you."

"Is it?"

"I want to hear about this experiment."

"No."

"No?"

I nodded. "No."

"That's unfortunate, Mr. Leon. I had hoped that you would be cooperative, but, as usual, you choose to be difficult. Your expulsion hearing will be held in five days. Until then you are suspended from all academic privileges and are confined to your quarters."

"Oh, joy."

"I trust you're fine with the consequences of your actions?"

"Always."

"You'll be escorted by campus police, now get out of my sight."

"It's been delightful, as usual."

Wolfrik gave me one last piercing glare as a hulking mass of a man seized my arm and shoved me into the hallway outside The Box. The officer wasn't much for conversation, and that was fine by me.

On the way back to my dorm, passerby students gave me downcast looks; whether those were pity or revulsion, I couldn't tell for sure. News travels fast.

The campus officer pushed me through the door to my room.

The door clanked and clacked behind me; the light turned from green to red. Effectively, I was a prisoner in my own home.

My place was just the way I'd left it earlier, so there was that, though I wouldn't have any network access with my privileges suspended. There were ways around that, though, and I'd need access to check on the progress of the experiment.

That was my one saving grace, even if they did ship me back to Earth. I'd have the discovery that Akio and I made.

I paused. Here I was, about to be expelled for breaking the rules, and all I could think about was my work, my obsession. I sank into the couch, staring at the wall. I imagined myself returning home, my head hung low, my father smiling ear to ear.

"¿Ves lo que te lleva tu ciencia preciosa?" *Do you see now where your precious science gets you?* he'd probably say.

"Fuck you, Father."

How had we gotten caught? I'd been certain that my plan was fool-proof. I wanted to feel angry at Wolfrik, at the Admins, for catching us, for locking me up and throwing the keys to my future away. Instead, I only felt empty inside. I told myself that I didn't care. That I'd make it as a scientist one way or another. I almost believed it.

My eyes drifted to the bottle of moonshine on the counter. I poured myself a glass, felt it burn the emptiness away.

I set the glass down. Left in isolation for mere moments and I'd already resorted to drinking. I needed to do something, occupy myself so I didn't polish the whole bottle off…

It had already been an entire Sol since we left Olympus Mons's caldera. The dark matter camera would have plenty of data to review. I grabbed for my tablet and, as expected, saw that there was no access to the school's network. The trick now would be to copy the permissions of another user and trick the system into thinking my machine was still granted access. I only knew of a few off the top of my head, Akio being one, and she was most likely being punished as well. Though, her punishment would no doubt be less severe, she would still be blocked from network access. They only deactivated a user's profile for three reasons: one, if the user is expelled and sent back to Earth; two, if the user graduates and leaves the facility, and three; if the user dies.

Who did I know that I could switch profiles with easily? If I hacked Wolfrik or any of my professors, they'd probably be on to me faster than a Catholic priest on an altar boy. I could probably find Gila's profile pretty easily. She probably wouldn't know it was me, either. The thing about being blocked from the network was that, although you couldn't access anything directly, you were still technically connected to it, and could see other users who were connected to it at the same time as long as you had the appropriate software.

As expected, Akio's profile was blocked, but Gila's profile was open. I made the necessary switch with the permissions and found myself able to navigate the school's web and academic forums, but I wouldn't need it for anything quite so boring. I quickly launched my machine's operation program, the HUD that would allow me to see what it saw out there from the great crater of Olympus Mons.

There was over a Sol's worth of data recorded on the hard drive, and I could see that there had been no hardware or software failures in that time. I copied the files I needed, which took the better part of an hour due to the size, volume, and resolution of the images. Once the data was secure on my hard drive, I restored Gila's permissions and resumed my "punishment."

Now for the real work. I opened the image folder, setting the preferences to display each one in chronological order. The first image was expected, the violet web of dark matter overlaid atop a butterscotch Martian sky; the second image a slight variation of that, and so on and so forth. That was until I got to the fiftieth image, when a shape appeared in the bottom left-hand corner of the vibrant violet web.

I zoomed in on the shape. It was strange, almost animal-like, with round and bulbous shapes, like a squash, or an ant's thorax, where the torso would probably be. It had two thick legs, and four thin, wiry appendages. In the images that followed, the strange violet silhouette was joined by other identical forms. They appeared to be standing on an incline in the distance, despite the backdrop of the massive flat line of the caldera that stretched on for miles and miles.

Then, for some reason, the silhouettes turned around, and began to move, or run, or climb, the incline. This running, or stampede, if you will, continued for almost a hundred images, until they all seemed to be swept away into the normal shape of the dark matter web, like the tide rolling in on a dry beach to wash waiting crabs to sea.

After that, the images seemed to repeat from the beginning, that same shape standing on the incline, perhaps watching the sky for something? Cowering? Then others appeared around it, something happened, and they all stampeded up the incline again. This time, I noticed several forms left behind in the wake of the stampede, crouched, huddled with smaller silhouettes.

I looked at the image number and gasped. The files hadn't looped; they were all in sequence. The sky had gotten darker in the images too, changing to that familiar pink, and then a brief cobalt-blue before final darkness. The sequence just repeated over and over again, always the same, like a video stuck on replay for all eternity.

By the third repetition, I noticed that when the dark matter web returned to normal, it almost looked like a shock wave from an asteroid impact. Like the millions of documentary re-creations that depicted the extinction of the dinosaurs. When I examined each individual "body," or "form," they all seemed to move with an individual purpose, and that purpose was repeated exactly in the next repetition.

I rubbed my eyes. It had been a very long day, and I was starting to get tired. As fascinating as the questions this raised were, some of them could wait for the morning. I'd have plenty of time to write and speculate, considering my confinement.

I cleared a spot on my plastic couch—which would soon not be mine anymore—and quickly let sleep take me.

The New Mexico sun beats down on my back. My skin isn't used to Earth's sun anymore. I swing my duffel bag over my shoulder. My father's house is as I left it three years ago; the lawn of rich grass where I once played as a child is now nothing more than dirt and weeds; the windows are dirtier, and the once-vibrant white paint has flaked and become decrepit.

My father is waiting in his favorite chair.

I say nothing to him.

He turns his head; his smile is ruthless.
"Do you see now where your precious science gets you?"

G

I woke to rustling sounds in the kitchen.

Wrappers crinkling, footsteps tapping.

At first, I thought that it could be Akio, free from her punishment, or whatever they had done with her, but the lock on the front door was still red and, glancing at my tablet, I could tell that no new entries in the door log had been made. My eyes started to close again—

The rustling turned to a deep scratching noise. My eyes opened again; the hair on the back of my neck stood on end. I could feel someone watching me.

I held my breath deep.

With wary eyes, I tracked the noises from the kitchen, to the other end of the living room, and into the bedroom, where the sounds stopped.

Maybe one of the guards was messing with me?

"Hey, who's there?" I asked.

No answer. Maybe it was all in my head?

I exhaled, sighing loudly.

And then, it was like one of those old trains had hit its brakes behind me. An ear-piercing screech erupted through the room; I covered my ears and felt something slam into the back of the couch. The couch rolled, and I went with it, tumbling across the room…

IV

My eyes opened to a white light at the end of a lopsided tunnel. Momentary shock and disorientation subsided when I realized that the couch had been capsized on top of me; I pushed its weight off of me with a certain amount of carelessness. The lights in my dorm room had automatically turned on after sunrise. Whatever had attacked me last night was nowhere to be seen.

Had it all been a nightmare?

Part of me wanted to believe that it was, but the memory of flipping through the air with the couch was all too vivid. And, for once, I hadn't been drinking.

I shook my head and took a deep breath, trying to quiet my own internal rage before I did something stupid.

My tablet was lying face-down several feet from where I was sitting. I picked it up and powered it on. The password and biometric interface came up as usual with no unauthorized attempts to access my files. That was a relief, but still, my rage came to a slow boil as I made a pot of coffee and ran the events over in my head.

Maybe it was some kind of failed attempt to steal the experiment? Or, it wasn't an attack, but some kind of prank by the campus police?

I looked around the dorm room. The place was a mess, but no more than usual. The scattered parts of the prototype dark matter cameras were still where Akio and I had left them, untouched, save for one that was on the floor (which the couch had probably collided with).

Still, that didn't rule anything out. It was possible that they hadn't known what they were looking for. And if I had been attacked, why —

and by whom? The only person I could think of was Wolfrik or one of the other Admins. Maybe he'd paid the campus officer outside to knock me unconscious and search my room for anything resembling an important project? There were rumors, conspiracy theories that Milkyway Unlimited stole promising projects right out from under their inventors. My eyes drifted to the plain gray walls, to the ceiling light fixtures and the air vents. What if they were watching us all?

I sat down with a cup of coffee. I tried to think of what I'd say to Akio when I saw her. She would need to see the data collected from the dark matter camera…but my paranoia and my anger had woven tight binds of stress around my heart. They could have stolen my blueprints, copied the internal bits of one of our prototype cameras without ever having to touch a thing if they knew what they were doing.

I gulped the rest of my coffee down and found myself at the front door, banging on it to get my keeper's attention.

After five whole minutes of banging, the door hissed open. The man towered over me, scowling. He had black hair that was accented with a hint of gray, and dim, blue eyes. "What the hell do you—"

"Yes, what the hell indeed," I said. "I assume you've been here all night?"

"That's my job." He checked his wrist for the time. "Which ends in exactly thirty minutes, so make this quick."

I felt as though someone had doused me in gasoline and lit a match at my feet. "Before you go, you can tell me why the fuck you decided to assault me last night."

"I don't know what you're talking about." His eyes darted away, looking down the hall.

"Who put you up to it?" I shoved my finger into his left pectoral with little effect, catching his attention again. "Was it Wolfrik? Is he so determined to uncover the secrets of my experiment that he'd resort to petty theft?"

The man thrust his palm through my spleen—I found myself on the floor, trying desperately to find the wind he'd knocked clean out of me.

"They're right about you, you know," the man said. "You are crazy."

The door shut, locked, and the light on the console turned from green to red.

Once I could finally breathe again—and I'd sufficiently licked my wounds enough to pick myself up off the floor—I decided not to press the issue again until I saw Wolfrik in person. Attacking campus police probably wasn't going to help my situation anyway.

I switched Gila's permissions with mine again and proceeded to download the most recent images from the dark matter camera. The download took about an hour, so I decided to have breakfast and reexamine the photos that I downloaded the night before while I waited.

Once the new images were downloaded, I immediately began poring over them. I put my tablet into projector mode and set it down on the counter, leaning it on its kickstand. The images came through as a steady slideshow on the far wall.

The strange shapes returned, and repeated just as they had before. Seeing them again, they looked far more lifelike in their movements to me, almost like animals. Maybe I was projecting, but I could make out several figures tossing their "heads" to the sky—perhaps frightened by something descending from the heavens? What could it have been? An asteroid, or a comet? It was no secret that something traumatic had happened to Mars billions of years in the past: the red planet was covered in scars, and its core no longer produced a magnetic field, but there were pockets of magnetism around the planet. They were the remnants of what had been, some said, and a clue to how the catastrophe that forever reshaped the planet had happened.

Professor Jameson's words echoed through my mind. "Hell, I would have been slightly more accepting if you came out and said ghosts were real."

I started to reminisce about a story a childhood friend of mine once told me. He'd claimed that his house was haunted, and said that every night he'd hear footsteps outside his bedroom door, and every night he'd open his door to see the apparition of an old woman in a nightgown walking down the hall with a lantern. The old woman would check on each room, peeking her head in and shining her lantern. I'd called him a big fat liar and punched him in the arm for trying to scare me—I was so good at making friends.

I'd almost forgotten about the story he'd told me till now.

The thing that stuck out most about it was that he described the event like a recording, a video that just plays over and over again.

What if his story hadn't been a fabrication at all? And what if this was the proof that every ghost story in the world was nothing more than an elaborate interaction between non-local consciousness and concentrations of dark matter? What if these were the last moments of an indigenous species that had once lived on Mars? And what if their final moments were so traumatic that they were forever recorded in the dark matter that permeated Mars?

Akio would surely scoff at the idea.

If these were truly the final moments of some ancient species that had lived on Mars, just how old were they? Was there any evidence of their lives left on the surface, or had this catastrophic event completely erased even their heaviest of footprints?

A wave of nothingness wiped the strange wiry animal silhouettes away until the dark matter web returned to normal, but, then, something strange happened.

It was so slow to develop that I almost didn't catch it the first time through the slideshow. Its shape was different from the other silhouettes. Where the ones I'd observed so far had been bulbous and animal-like, this one was sharper, curious, perhaps even predatory. It moved across the camera's field of scope multiple times. Its movements reminded me vaguely of a praying mantis as it got closer.

It appeared in front of the camera's lens. It seemed to pace around the machine several times.

What did that mean? Was it just another layer of the recording? For a second, it almost looked as though it was curious about the camera...

The same wave of nothingness came and washed all of the silhouettes away again, and the mantis shape disappeared as well.

I rubbed my eyes and replayed the sequence again, focusing on the new development this time.

Then the door opened; I restored Gila's permissions, cut the projection off, and wedged the tablet under the couch cushion. When I turned around, I was surprised to see Gila herself standing in the doorway with a pile of books in her arms and a container of what I assumed was some sort of food.

"Why are you sitting in the dark?" Gila asked.

"Thinking about my fate?" I said.

Gila frowned. "Yeah, I heard about your expulsion hearing."

"Word gets around fast." I stood up to greet her. "What's all that?"

"I brought you your assignments from Planetary Physics, just in case you end up not being expelled, and…something I cooked up."

"You…cooked?" No one cooked on Olympus One, at least, not unless it was a special occasion. Everything had to be carefully rationed, so there could be enough food for every resident. There were botany programs in effect, but those were still largely experimental, and only a few people—like Dane—really used the vegetables grown in those experiments for anything. The colony relied heavily on supply drops for rations and basic essentials to make life seem livable.

"Not technically—it's a salad, we had a lot of extra veggies left over from the harvest test. I hope that's okay."

I accepted the books and the salad. "I never liked salad as a kid."

"Oh…"

"Funny how you end up taking simple things for granted out here."

Her lips curled into a smile. "I have to go, they won't let you have any long-term visitors, I guess."

"They're serious about this punishment."

"Well, you did steal a rover."

"I promise it was for a good cause." I turned around and set the salad and books down on the counter.

"Is it the experiment you told me about in class?"

My eyebrows came together. "Did Wolfrik put you up to this?"

"No, why would you say that?" She shook her head and backed away, one hand raised to her chest.

"Don't lie to me. He was adamant about learning the details and I told him no, then someone attacks me last night. That isn't a coincidence. You didn't tell him anything, did you?"

"I'm not lying, Wolfrik didn't say anything to me, I swear."

"Time's up." A different campus guard, with blond hair, loomed in the doorway like a roadblock, arms crossed.

Gila walked to the doorway and gave me one last look. I couldn't tell whether it was guilt or sadness that filled her eyes. "If you don't get expelled, message me. I'll make you another salad."

"I—"

My words caught in my throat. The door shut behind her and the light turned from green to red again, once again making me a prisoner.

I couldn't even apologize.

2

I was napping on the couch when Akio stepped through the door, clutching her tablet close to her.

"Ma'am, he's not to have visit—"

"Yeah, well I live here, buddy, so shove it where the sand won't go," she said.

"Well, that happened quicker than I thought it would," I said, sitting up. "What did you end up getting?"

The door closed behind her, locked. She walked over to the counter and set her things down next to the books Gila had given me; her eyes drifted up to the coffee table where I'd eaten the salad.

"Wolfrik gave me twenty-four hours of isolation therapy in The Box, a ton of questions about the experiment, and a demerit on my permanent record. Where'd you get a salad from?"

"Gila stopped by." My eyes narrowed. "What did you tell him about the experiment?"

"Oh, everything."

My teeth clenched. She laughed.

"I'm kidding!" she said. "It's my project too. Do you honestly think I'd spill the beans to someone like Wolfrik?"

I sighed. "Don't do that to me, damn it!"

"I couldn't resist, the look on your face!" Her eyes drifted off, her lips curled into a sneer. "So…that chick with the Armada tattoo in your Planetary Physics class, huh?"

"You know her?"

"Hard to miss anyone on this colony."

"You haven't tried hard enough."

"We can't all be social pariahs like you." She walked to the other edge of the room with her coffee, resting her weight on the table where we'd assembled the dark matter camera. "I hear she has a really bad temper, takes those strategy games she plays way too seriously. You think she's cute?"

"Who, Gila?"

"Duh." She rolled her eyes at me.

"Yeah, I guess." The question made us both uncomfortable, so I kicked my feet onto the coffee table. She hated when I did that. "I have an expulsion hearing in four days."

Her eyes twisted into a glare and rested on my feet. "I heard, what are you doing to prepare?"

"I'm not."

"Why the hell not?" She walked into the kitchen and set a pot of coffee to brew. "You need to get your shit together so you can mount a defense against—"

"Why? Once we patent my dark matter camera, what will I need this place for?"

"Our camera."

"Yeah. That's what I said." I grinned.

"Did not. You're trying to distract me."

I shrugged. She knew me too well.

She took a sip of her coffee. "And what makes you think that you won't need a degree?"

"I'm sure other schools would accept me."

"Not after getting kicked out of a program like this, Hal. You got a full ride on another planet! They'll probably see what everyone else already thinks they see in you."

"And what do they see?" My fingers clenched into fists.

She took a seat on one of the barstools at the counter. Her eyes were like little brown daggers, piercing through me. "That you don't give a damn about anyone but yourself."

"Is that what you think?"

"I don't know…" She avoided my gaze. "Sometimes…"

"Maybe they're right?"

Her eyes drifted back to me, her eyebrows twisted upward. "You don't mean that."

"I don't know. I don't have much of a reason to care. You should know that by now. I came here to escape, to focus on my work, not get swallowed in petty student bullshit."

"You're honestly telling me that you don't care about your opportunities here, or *any* of the people here either?"

"I don't," I said, trying to keep the anxiety from cutting into my words and betraying the truth. It felt less real, less like my world was crashing down around me, when I lied.

"And what about me?"

"What about you?"

Her eyes opened wide, and I could see there were tears welling up in them. "That's how you feel about all this?"

Before I could open my big mouth again, she'd already bolted for the door and run out into the hall. I got to the doorway in time for my jailer to shove me back inside and lock it again.

I wanted to say: *"That's not what I meant!"* that, *"of course you are important to me!"* that, *"You're my best friend!"*

But, once again, the words caught in my throat. Even in her absence, I couldn't say them out loud.

I sat there for almost an hour, staring at the wall. I hadn't even gotten a chance to show her the newest data before I'd managed to piss her off. As tedious as it was trying to relate to another human being, she was my only real companion on Mars. Despite Gila's good intentions, Akio knew me better than anyone, and I couldn't afford to lose her support; the fact was, we were an excellent team, and she was invaluable to my work.

I pored over the images again to distract myself from my own thoughts, but no new revelations came from another observation. I grew restless and decided to take a shower. We were only permitted one shower every three and a half Sols. I'd had one just two Sols ago, but I figured as long as I was in trouble, I might as well go the full nine. The water felt amazing; I watched it run over my shoulders, down my stomach, down my legs, and swirl down the drain. Seemed like a metaphor for my life, even if my present situation was my own doing and choosing.

The water cut off halfway through my shower. I guess the Admins caught on to what I was doing. I dried off, pulled a fresh set of coveralls out of the plastic drawer and looked myself in the mirror. I had a five o' clock shadow growing where I had once been clean-shaven. The water in the sink was cut off too, so I decided to leave it for now.

I found myself on the couch, holding my tablet. I was so bored without any access to the network. I knew I should wait till morning, when there would be another Sol's worth of data on the Dark Matter Camera to look over, to switch permissions with Gila again, but I was losing my mind. I needed to find something to do.

I located Gila's profile and attempted to switch permissions again...but this time nothing happened. Irritated, I threw myself into the network permissions. A keystroke, two—

Fuck.

Her profile was deactivated entirely.

I rushed to the door and pounded on it. I pounded and smashed and kicked at that door until the pain in my hands was too much.

The door opened. My jailer stared at me.

"What the hell do you want, Leon?" he asked.

"I need a favor from you," I said.

"Why would I do you a favor?"

"Because if you don't, I'm going to keep making noise till you go mad."

"So? I'm paid to ignore you."

"Fine, how about you do it because I think a student might be in danger."

He sighed. "Fine, what is it."

"You know the girl that was here earlier?"

"The one who told me to shove it where the sand doesn't go?"

"No, the short Jewish girl with the neck tattoo."

"Okay, what of her?"

"I need you to perform a student wellness check."

"On the girl with the neck tattoo?"

I rolled my eyes. "What do you think?"

"How do I know this isn't just some kind of ploy to get rid of me?"

"Look, just trust me, I think she's in trouble. Her name is Gila Amos."

"All right, fine, just stand back from the door, and don't do anything stupid while I'm gone."

I stepped back and the door closed in my face.

I found myself pacing back and forth in my living room while I anxiously awaited news of Gila. I waited until the lights in my dorm room automatically turned off. What the hell was going on?

That night, I tossed and turned on my couch, restless. I couldn't shake the feeling that something was wrong. Had the officer been standing out there the whole time? Did he even check on Gila?

Somehow, I managed to fall asleep. I couldn't remember the nightmare I had, but, when I woke up the next morning, cold sweat dripping from my brow, I knew that it had been about her.

I was having coffee when the door opened. The blond campus officer stepped inside, a sour look on his aged face and dark circles hanging beneath his eyes like a blight.

"Where is she?" I asked.

"I don't know how to say this…"

"She's dead."

His eyes opened wide, almost guiltily, but he nodded.

"How?" I asked.

He hesitated, stumbling to find the words. "They found her in her quarters shortly before I arrived to perform the wellness check. The details are being kept quiet to protect her privacy."

"They'll launch a full investigation."

My eyes drifted to the plastic salad container, now empty in my sink. The last remnant of someone I hadn't even considered a friend, yet would still miss, if only for the promise of what might have been had I not been so cold.

"How did you know?" he asked.

"I had a terrible feeling," I said. "I've been having a lot of those lately."

He nodded, staring at me in a way that made me uncomfortable. "I know what you mean."

I found myself grabbing for that bottle of moonshine. I poured two glasses, handed one off to the campus officer.

"I'm not supposed to drink while on duty," he said.

I downed my drink in one gulp and poured another. "You look like you need it."

He nodded, took a sip, and sat across from me. "You never think it can happen, even though they never stop telling you how dangerous living on Mars is."

"Try walking on the surface with nothing but a few layers of cloth-armor to protect you," I said.

"I'll pass."

"What's your name?"

"Clarence."

I poured Clarence another glass, and raised my hand to toast. "To Gila, Clarence."

"To Gila."

The glasses clanked together; we finished our drinks, and an uncomfortable silence filled the air.

The morning came with a heaviness to it. I woke on my bed for once, clutching the bottle of gin I had polished off with Clarence the day before. My head was ablaze, fires spread from my neck to my knees, but I managed to claw my way into the kitchen for coffee and rations. The red light on the door was shining brightly, despite the time I'd shared with my keeper.

I couldn't believe that we'd drunk that entire bottle. Most of the day was a blur. I didn't remember him leaving.

I wasn't in much of a working mood. Something felt wrong, like there was a gaping hole in the pit of my stomach. I wasn't used to that feeling. I'd seen death before in my life, uncles, grandparents, all people I knew on the surface. I'd never once felt the loss; it never seemed real. But, Gila was different. It might have been true that I didn't truly know her, and she wasn't family, but there had been an innocence to her. Maybe that was what made it feel so much heavier?

Maybe it was just my fight-or-flight drive kicking into overdrive, maybe the death made Mars' danger seem that much more real? Maybe I was only thinking of myself again?

I couldn't be sure.

My eyes fixated on the tablet that rested on the coffee table across the room, taunting me with the promise of answers to universal riddles and secrets. I sipped my coffee and resisted the urge to dive headlong into work again. But, then, locked up inside that room, what else was there to do? I found myself holding the tablet, looking through profiles that I could switch permissions with.

My gut sank; Gila's profile icon had a red X through it, but Akio's was green. She was still mad at me, and would most likely know that it was me tampering with her profile permissions. I switched permissions with her anyway and proceeded to download a Sol's worth of images from the Dark Matter Camera.

Once the images were downloaded, I loaded them into a dated folder and began to analyze them. The slideshow drama of strange animalistic forms played out the same as before, further affirming my theory that it was indeed a record in the dark matter.

Then, towards the end of the second repetition of the "recording," two mantis-like silhouettes appeared in the dark matter web near the camera. The mantis silhouettes were anything but predictable. I felt the hairs on the back of my neck stand on end. The first one seemed to be pacing around the camera's position, while the other one stayed off in the distance, completely still. It was almost like they were studying it.

But, that was preposterous.

Then, the static mantis shape dashed right toward the camera. The camera seemed to shake back and forth for a moment. The movement was so slight, though, it could have been the start of a dust storm, an increase in wind speed. I paused the slideshow and went back several images in the file directory.

I rubbed my eyes.

No, there had to be another explanation. They were only imprints, recordings. But, as I went through the panoramas again, I found no presence of a dust storm, nothing that could have caused the camera to shake like it had.

That familiar shock wave of nothingness washed the animal shapes away.

The dark matter web returned to normal.

The hair on my arms stood up. The mantis shapes remained. They paced the camera a few more times, and seemed to lose interest and trail off somewhere out of the range the viewfinder could pick up.

I shook my head. They weren't alive. They couldn't be. I was anthropomorphizing them without any more evidence than the fact that they were different than the rest of the images. It was entirely possible that they too were a part of the recording, just something that the camera hadn't picked up in the first Sol.

The door hissed open abruptly.

"What the hell, Hal?" Akio stormed into the room, holding her tablet up for me to see ACCESS DENIED displayed across her tablet screen in big, bold, red letters. "I was in the middle of a research paper when you hacked my profile! Switch it back!"

"I don't know what you're talking about," I said.

"Don't play stupid with me! I know you switched permissions with me so you could access the data from our dark matter camera!"

"And yet, you're not the least bit curious about the results."

"So, it *was* you!" She pointed an accusatory finger at me. "You better switch it back, right now!"

"Aren't you curious?" I smiled.

She stood there, her shoulders raised, her back hunched — probably contemplating whether it would be worth it to kick me in the balls. "I'm curious, but you can't just subvert the rules every time you want something!"

"If the rules are wrong, why not?"

"You're interfering with my studies!"

"You know there was a death on campus last night, right?" My smile faded.

She grew quiet, hugged herself. "Yeah, that girl you mentioned yesterday…"

"They still haven't announced the cause of death."

"How did you find out?"

"I was switching her profile permissions with mine the last two days, saw hers was deactivated, so I had my jailer run and look for her…that's when he gave me the bad news."

"Are you okay?" Her posture softened almost immediately; she sat down next to me. "Jeez, you smell like a distillery!"

"Clarence and I had a few last night."

She plugged her nose and blinked her eyes. "A few?"

"I'm pretty hungover."

"I can see that…"

I reset the image viewer to the first day's images and handed it to her. "Here's the data. Watch it."

I watched her eyes transform from passive and disinterested slits to wide and attentive globes. Her mouth slowly opened and hung there while the animation progressed through each Sol.

"This is…" She shook her head.

"Unprecedented," I said. "I think they're recordings in the dark matter from an extinction-level event long ago in Mars' history."

She shook her head. "You're jumping to conclusions, Hal. For all you know these images could just be ordinary patterns and energy movements of the dark matter web."

"I don't think so. I've been over it over and over again, and the more I see it, the more I zoom in on each form, the more I'm convinced that they look like some kind of animal."

"I don't know…" Her mouth twisted to one side. "I mean, yeah, they do look like animals, in a way. But, we'd need so much more data to prove that they were. If they were animals, where are the remains?"

"Blown away by whatever cataclysm destroyed Mars' magnetosphere?"

"That would make sense, but every one of our professors would say that's awfully convenient. There has to be some evidence somewhere—maybe underground…" She sat quiet for a minute. "I suppose, if dark matter acts as a conduit for information to pass through like we theorize, it could allow for their last moments to be recorded like that… but if that were true, wouldn't we see recordings on Earth too?"

She was still dancing around non-local consciousness as a possibility, but progress is progress.

"We don't have dark matter imaging devices on Earth, but I think we already have some subtle proof there anyway."

"Oh really?" She raised one eyebrow at me.

"How many ghost stories have you heard where the storyteller makes mention of apparitions that do the same thing, at the same hour, on the same day, over and over again? What if some humans are capable of perceiving subtle changes in the dark matter around the planet? I say it's a possibility."

"You're grasping at straws, Hal. You're way too smart to be using fucking ghost stories as evidence."

"Am I? You said it yourself, if dark matter acts as a medium that facilitates the transference of information, then nothing is stopping human trauma and experiences from being recorded."

She grew quiet again. "Damn it."

"You see it too, don't you?"

"I do, and I feel like I'm going crazy." She ran her hands through her hair. "Everyone is going to think we're crazy. I mean, ghosts?"

"That's why we're going to need a lot of data to back up our theories on this. Think about the test panorama we took. Both of us had concentrations of dark matter around us, so that's a start. The first images of Sol 1 look the same, the camera took snapshots of us climbing into the rover and driving away, and the whole time there was a halo of violet light around the both of us."

She let out a heavy sigh. "I already know what you're going to say. That doesn't necessarily prove that consciousness is non-local. The concentrations of dark matter around us could just be the dark matter interacting with our bodies."

"I might be biased, but I don't think that's the case. Maybe consciousness is composed of dark matter, or at least closely tied to it. That would explain why a traumatic event like this would be recorded into the thickest concentrations of dark matter around the planet. Then there was the other silhouette from the test panorama."

"What about it?"

"Remember Connor Wilson?"

Her eyes opened wide; she shivered. "You don't think…"

"I do. What's more traumatic than suffocating to death on the surface of an alien planet?"

"Just, do me a favor, when we present this data, keep that non-local consciousness shit to yourself."

"Why?"

"It'll make us less credible."

"That's why I have you." I winked at her.

"You're seriously not going to give this up?" She laughed.

"You're just as stubborn."

"Does that mean I win our bet?"

"I was hoping you'd forget."

"Seriously?" She scratched her chin and considered the images on the tablet. "What are these forms that appear after Sol 2?"

"I'm not sure, they look different from the others, possibly another aspect of the recording that the system took longer to render?"

"But, they don't seem to follow the same motion when they reappear the second time…"

"No idea why."

"Next you're going to tell me you think they're all sentient."

"Preposterous."

"No more preposterous than conscious beings recording their last moments in the dark matter across the planet, Hal. Oh, god, do I sound crazy when I say it out loud?"

"A little." I leaned forward, considering what she'd just said. "Well, I suppose if non-local consciousness can be attached to organic lifeforms in our three dimensions, there's nothing really stopping it from existing on its own, perhaps even being composed of dark matter itself."

"Hal…" Akio facepalmed.

The door hissed open again and drew both of our attentions to Clarence. "You both need to come with me."

"Why?" Akio asked.

"There's an emergency assembly being gathered and everyone, even Hal, has been summoned."

"It's about Gila, isn't it?" I said.

Clarence nodded somberly. "Can't say for sure, but it seems like that's the most likely reason."

I stood up and cracked my back. "Well, I guess a bit of a walk will do me some good after three Sols of being a prisoner."

"You might want to shower the smell of alcohol off first," Akio said. "If the Admins catch a whiff it won't look good for you at your expulsion hearing."

"I couldn't shower even if I wanted, the water's been turned off," I said.

"You tried to shower prematurely, didn't you?" Clarence crossed his bulging arms.

"Well, I was going stir-crazy! What else was I supposed to do?" I asked.

"Not waste precious water, maybe?" Akio said.

Clarence gestured to us to leave the apartment. "We need to go now, the assembly will commence in ten minutes."

I snatched my tablet from Akio's hands and followed Clarence out into the corridor. Akio followed shortly behind. Plastic tubes and sterile white walls stretched on and on, interrupted by the occasional black door that led to someone's residence or dorm room. It was eerie: the halls were usually filled with people in the morning, but today they were void. My stomach felt queasy, and I hoped it was just my hangover, and not some impending sense of dread.

"We're here to honor the memory of one of our students," Wolfrik said. "Gila Amos was a treasure among our student body; she maintained an excellent GPA and managed to make good friends with all of her instructors, and she always found ways to help out around the colony with what little spare time she had. She will be sorely missed."

Wolfrik's voice was amplified through the speakers in the dome-shaped auditorium. I stood toward the back with Akio and Clarence; the gathered students created a sea of gray coveralls from one end of the seating area to the next. The rear of the dome was transparent, giving way to a bland view of a butterscotch sky and a crimson horizon littered with rocks and craters.

"I wish I could say that this assembly would be spent honoring her memory." Wolfrik's eyebrows came together, his face becoming long and grave. "But, we have another purpose here as well. This assembly will also tackle the very real subject of suicide and cabin fever. It's an unfortunate way to announce Gila's cause of death, but we hope that bringing awareness to this very real phenomenon will allow others to seek help before causing harm to themselves."

Suicide? That didn't seem right at all. Gila had always been so cheerful. And while I wasn't so naïve as to believe that that alone could rule out any deeper kind of depression, I'd just seen her, and she hadn't seemed troubled at all.

"We want all of our students, staff, and permanent residents at Olympus One to know that all of our doors are wide open if you need help."

I found myself on the network with my tablet. What I was about to do was sure to guarantee my expulsion, but I had to do it. I found Wolfrik's profile on the network and switched permissions. Then I found the security footage from several cameras outside our dorm rooms. Milkyway Unlimited was barred from keeping cameras or listening devices in our dorms, so if she'd died in her room, there'd be little for me to find, but I had to try.

I played the footage at ten times normal speed from the time she'd left my dorm onward. There was no sound, but the image was crisp. She appeared at the other end of the corridor, entered her dorm, and then left minutes later with a towel draped over her shoulder.

The gym was a necessary tool for all of us at Olympus One to maintain our muscle mass and bone density in 0.4 Gs. Sure enough, there was footage of her working out at the gym. Once her workout was finished, she walked toward the shower chamber. They didn't get used much, due to the strict rules regarding frequent showering, but the gym was equipped with a shower unit just in case a student's workout coincided with their scheduled shower day.

There weren't any cameras in the showers, obviously, but there were some near the entrance. I switched to footage closer to where she'd entered the shower room.

"What are you doing?" Akio asked.

"Getting to the bottom of this," I said. "I find it very hard to believe that Gila killed herself."

"Hal." Akio lowered her voice to a whisper. "If they catch you using his profile—"

"This is important, damn it!"

Moments later, Gila came walking out of the shower room, wrapped in a towel and covered in soap. She looked around the empty gym quizzically. She turned around and walked back toward the shower room, but rapidly snapped around with a worried look on her face. Perhaps she heard something, a voice, noises, footsteps?

I rubbed my neck and felt the blood drain from my face.

She walked out into the center of the gym. I switched footage to a camera with a better vantage point on her location. The lights cut out, causing the night-vision filter to kick in. Her face twisted into a grimace again, her mouth opened wide, and she sprinted back toward the shower room for refuge—she tripped over a set of dumbbells, banging her head against a weight rack. Gila backed up along the floor, cradling her head, her chest heaving like she was hyperventilating.

Was something in front of her?

She got up slowly, cautiously, and began carefully walking toward the gym's entrance. Then, her body went rigid, her hands covered her throat, her towel fell to the floor and blood coated her bare chest.

She fell face-first on an exercise mat. The lights came back on, and there was nothing in the gym with her. A pool of blood spread out from where her corpse lay.

Akio's mouth hung wide open. "Oh my god, Hal."

"She didn't kill herself," I said. "She was murdered."

Clarence turned to me. "How do you know? Wolfrik just said—"

"And he's fucking lying!"

My shouting left the dome in a raucous discourse; Wolfrik silenced them again with the raising of a hand. "Surely, Mr. Leon simply shouts in grief. I assure you this is the truth. Gila committed—"

"No, she didn't." I stepped forward, holding up the tablet featuring the still image of Gila's body flat, blood soaking into the exercise mat. "Because I just saw her die on the security feed from the gym last night. She was murdered by something she couldn't see. Her god-damn throat was sliced open and she was helpless!"

Something she couldn't see. I ran the words over in my head. There had been nothing inside that room with her. Nothing that could be picked up by an *ordinary* camera.

"Will campus police please remove Mr. Leon to his dorm room," Wolfrik said. "He's clearly delusional!"

"No, he's not!" Akio said. "I saw it too! Hal is right, what are the Admins trying to hide by defaming this girl's memory and lying to our faces? We've got a murderer loose on Olympus One!"

Next you'll be telling me they're sentient. Akio's words echoed through my mind.

If non-local consciousness can be attached to organic lifeforms in our three dimensions, there's nothing really stopping it from existing on its own, perhaps even being composed of dark matter itself.

The dark matter camera had moved. I tried to explain it away. *I'm such a fool.*

"Akio," I said, my hand grasping her shoulder, "They're alive."

That queasy feeling returned to my gut, and I knew that it wasn't just my hangover. Suddenly I was on my couch again, listening to its footsteps, hearing its screeching, and tumbling with my couch. What if it hadn't been the campus officer like I'd originally thought? What if my observation of the recordings in the dark matter web had inadvertently awakened something and attracted it to Olympus One?

"The recordings?" Akio asked.

I lurched forward and vomited all the filth I'd ingested onto the floor of the auditorium, causing students to scatter and curse. I crouched down and began to hyperventilate.

"Hal, are you okay?" Akio asked, resting her hands on my back.

"No," I said. "I'm not."

"What the hell are you doing, Clarence?" Wolfrik asked. "Get him out of here!"

"It's my fault." My voice was not my own; it boomed through the silent dome. "I killed her."

Something smashed into the back of my skull. I collapsed in my own vomit, and the last thing I remembered was rolling over to see Akio attempting to punch Clarence's perfect, square jaw with her tiny angry fists.

VI

There was a time when I was an optimistic, naive fool, studying for the entrance exams for eight different colleges and one unlikely long-shot program that very few ever managed to get accepted to. My mother had just made dinner and called me downstairs to eat. My father was sitting in his favorite recliner, the one with the patch sewn in the side. Mother always told him to get rid of it, but he always refused. "No hay nada malo con mi silla. Acostumbra tus ojos, mujer." *No. There's nothing wrong with my chair. Adjust your eyes, woman.* To which she would wave her hands frantically, complaining, and return to whatever hobby or task she'd absorbed herself in for the day.

My mother had a sad countenance most of the time. Something I regret never questioning. I couldn't remember how many times I saw my mother come out of the bathroom—nose red, face flushed, pupils dilated. My father was real old-fashioned, believed my mother shouldn't work, that he should be the one to provide for us. He couldn't see that she was trapped.

I came to sit at the table. My father joined us moments later as my mother set the tray of tamales down before us, completing the feast.

My father said grace and I tried not to roll my eyes. Hopefully he wouldn't bring up what happened at work.

"¿Ves? Esto es bonito." *See? This is nice*, my mother said.

"Hubo un accidente en el trabajo." *There was an accident at work*, my father said, glaring at me. "Este idiota estrelló el montacargas contra una pila de paletas y casi mata a una mujer." This *idiot backed the forklift into a stack of pallets and almost killed a woman.*

My mother crossed herself as he jabbed the fork at me.

"I hear the boss is going to fire him on Monday." My father stabbed at the peas. *"I warned him, this is clearly punishment for his sinful lifestyle—"*

"I'm studying for college, father."

My father's eyes narrowed. *"No, you are not. You're going to stay here and help me with the bills."*

"No. I'm going to college." I felt the blood rushing to my face. No longer would I stand by and let this rotten son-of-a-bitch control my life. *"I'm going to be a scientist."*

My mother touched my father's arm. His face was turning a ripe shade of red. He yanked his hand away. *"If you do, I will disown you, do you hear me? Science is not of Christ. It is the work of the devil!"*

I smiled. *"I am the devil, then."*

Veins bulged on his neck, his teeth gnashed together. *"Go to your room."*

I stood up and walked toward the kitchen, leaving my unfinished dinner behind. "Your God is dead."

Regret would follow that statement later when I heard the two of them shouting at each other. I lost count of how many times I heard him hit her as I cried myself to sleep.

I couldn't wait to leave my father's home.

Two weeks later, on her way to my graduation, my mother's car was T-boned on the driver's side after she ran a red light. Doctors said she had a lot of damage to her spinal cord. She was a quadriplegic, and they weren't sure if she'd ever regain consciousness.

They found traces of cocaine in her system, of course. Said she'd overdosed. The police were involved, but nothing really came of the charges they tried to file against her. It's hard to prosecute a vegetable.

A few months later, her condition hadn't improved. I was accepted to Olympus One and my father stopped talking to me altogether. He blamed my academic ambitions for mother's condition, claiming it was God's way of punishing us for my sins.

My mother died in hospice care while I was on the ship that carried us all here. I remember the day that I got the news, how I felt sitting in my bunk in the ship, trying to avoid Akio as she persisted in trying to become my friend, despite my protests against human interaction.

66

It was a simple text message that came through my tablet. A bunch of professional, emotionless text.

I remember listening to the hull, the sound of the atmospheric systems, and feeling completely empty inside.

Akio was the only one who'd realized that something was wrong, and that's when we became friends.

I'd gotten to Olympus One, and within the first few months, I'd already made a few enemies. I never found out who started the rumor—how fucking lucky for them—but it didn't take long for it to spread.

In the mind of the student body, my mother was a mental patient, and many of them thought I should join her—imaginary straitjacket and all.

The story crafted by the twisted tongues of clever liars is often so much more powerful than the truth of things.

I've long since renounced my faith, but sitting in a holding cell on campus for murder awakened an existential dread in me. The fear of fire and brimstone is always strong with those who are raised Catholic.

One of the campus officers came in and escorted me to The Box. He closed the door behind him, leaving me in a whiteout, that familiar abyss with no end. Wolfrik came through a door on the other side of the room that melted back into the formless white behind him. He sat at the white table across from me.

He sighed and opened up his tablet, which probably contained notes pertaining to the incident.

"This does seem to be your week for getting into trouble, Mr. Leon," Wolfrik said. "There's no question about that. To go from an active student, an undergraduate so close to earning your first degree, to pending expulsion, and then to confess to murder just shortly after that. Well. I don't think I have to tell you what kind of position that puts me in, do I?"

"I didn't actually kill her," I said.

"You confessed in front of everyone." He smiled. "I have at least thirty witnesses that will testify to that. Everyone is already jumping to blame you and Akio for the murder."

"What does Akio have to do with this?"

"I'm getting to that."

"You must really enjoy this," I said. "Me in all this trouble and at your mercy. But you're making a grave error here. It wasn't murder."

"Then what was it?" He clasped his hands together, the way he had done after we were detained for stealing the rover. "We know you were locked away in your quarters, but according to one of the campus officers assigned to guard your dorm, you and Akio had a heated exchange shortly after Gila came to see you. Then, you had Clarence perform a wellness check on her, as if you knew something had happened. So, what was it? A lovers' triangle? Did she get jealous of your relationship with Gila and decide to end her life? Even if you don't comply here, we've got Akio in another box, and I'm sure she'll be much more willing to tell us the truth."

"What the hell are you talking about?" I shook my head. "Have you even watched the footage, man? Nothing is going on between Akio and I."

"Once again, you confessed. Every student, as well as at least ten Milkyway Unlimited employees, bore witness to this. Clarence has testified as such."

"Did you not hear me? You're ignoring the footage I found while you prattled on about suicide, making an ass out of yourself."

"It makes little difference what footage you found." He gestured to his own tablet. "You're quite capable with creating forgeries, are you not?"

I swallowed a lump in my throat. I had to tell him, even if it placed our invention into the greedy hands of Milkyway Unlimited.

"That footage was only accessible from your profile," I said, leaning back in my chair. "If I'd made any type of change to the files it'd be pretty damn obvious. I'm not *that* good. But, I'll tell you what I *am*."

"And what's that?"

"I'm completely capable of exposing a cover-up and ruining your fucking career, Wolfrik. The fact of the matter is, you would have had to move Gila's body back to her quarters for Clarence to buy that load of horseshit. He doesn't strike me as the type to go along blindly, or to cover up a student's death. I may be hopeless when navigating social situations, but I know how to read people. I can easily prove this. So,

68

this means that you not only tampered with evidence, but you also know that Akio and I couldn't have perpetrated that murder."

"Sure, we found her in the gym—" He was starting to sweat. "— But that hardly proves that you didn't have something to do with—"

"You're full of shit. You're already sweating, which means that I'm right and you haven't got shit for evidence." I grinned. "You don't want to see me when I've got nothing left to lose, Wolfrik. Unless, of course, you think you might be willing to hear my side of the story out."

Wolfrik glared forward at me. I had him. "I'll...listen."

"What I'm going to tell you now is going to be hard to swallow, given your background. It involves the experiment that Akio and I are conducting up at the Olympus Mons caldera."

I hesitated.

"We invented a device," I continued, "a camera, that's capable of imaging dark matter, seeing how it interacts with Mars." A strange air, like static, passed between us when I brought up the dark matter camera. The hairs on the back of my neck stood on end, and I felt myself grow colder. "The camera is still there, taking panoramas of the caldera and the dark matter web. When the web is in its normal state, it looks like a computerized simulation of the known universe, of every galaxy and cosmic structure in existence."

"That was the reason you and Akio stole the rover the other day?" His tired eyes were wide open, but there was a subversive quality to his voice. "Why are you all of a sudden so talkative about the experiment, when you wouldn't give me a single hint before?"

"It's complicated."

"We know that you switched the network permissions with her. Akio gave you up."

"I needed to get at our research data. That's how I was able to download the panoramas."

"You expect me to believe that?"

I slammed my hand on the table. "It's the truth! Give me access to my tablet and I'll show you what we've discovered."

"You say that this camera is able to image dark matter." He scratched at his beard. "How could that possibly lead to the death of someone here? As I understand it, dark matter doesn't really interact with our three dimensions except for gravitationally."

"Have you ever heard of the theory of non-local consciousness?"

"Yes, and I've also heard complaints from one of your professors, that you threatened to have him fired after giving you a poor grade on a paper of the same topic. What does that have to do with dark matter?"

"The camera images what we call the 'dark matter web,' as I said, but there's something else being recorded." I took a deep breath. "Images began appearing in the dark matter web, thousands of them. At first, I didn't know what to think of them, but then I zoomed in. They appear to be animals of some sort, or silhouettes of animals that lived here millions of years ago. The images repeat three or four times a day; they cower, they look to the sky, and run for the hills, and they always end the same way, by some kind of shock wave that resets the web back to its normal state."

Wofrik scoffed, rolled his eyes. "And, what, you believe these *recordings* killed Gila?"

"No, of course not." I sighed. I was losing him. Should have led with the other shapes. "I believe that these recordings in the dark matter were made at the time of an extinction-level event. That through quantum entanglement, they burned an image of these events into this world. But it doesn't stop with recordings. I began noticing other silhouettes appearing before the dark matter camera. These were different from the others; they looked vaguely similar to a mantis. They follow no particular pattern, and have even been able to interact with the camera physically by pushing it. I believe that these things are not only a form of non-local consciousness, but that their *'bodies'* are composed of dark matter.

"The first night that I was confined to my dorm room, I downloaded Sol 1's data from the camera. That night I heard footsteps and strange sounds around my living room that culminated in an ear-piercing shriek and something smashing into the back of my couch. I think that by observing these creatures, I've inadvertently become entangled with them, summoning them here.

"They're the ones that killed Gila."

He was silent for a time, his eyes studying me. I could tell he was having a hard time with my story. "You've really outdone yourself this time, Mr. Leon. I'm almost impressed by the complexity of this tale, but that's all that it is, a tale. It's no secret that your mother died in hospice several years ago, and clearly you're beginning to exhibit whatever mental disorder she had. I can only recommend that you—"

"My mother was hospitalized after overdosing on cocaine and getting into a near-fatal car accident, you imbecile—" I stood up and jabbed my finger at him. "She became a quadriplegic and had to be hospitalized, where she died of complications due to spinal cord damage!"

A campus officer came in from the same door Wolfrik had used earlier. He approached me, grabbed my arms and forced me back down into my seat, holding me there.

"My mistake," Wolfrik said. "Still, it makes little difference. There's no way in hell that I'd believe a story like yours."

"Let go of me, meat-stick!" I wrenched free of the brute behind me. "Then, bring me my tablet, let me show you the data from the camera so you can see for yourself!"

"And how do I know that you didn't fabricate the images with some 3D imaging program?" He sighed and shook his head. "I don't think there's really anything more to discuss, other than the charges for Gila's murder."

"I didn't kill her!"

"Prove it." He chuckled. "You say that you can ruin me, my career, but what you don't realize, Mr. Leon, is that Milkyway Unlimited is what decides your fate. If they think you're guilty, you're guilty."

My heart sank.

"How about this," I said. "Akio and I will show you the data we've gathered, and then take you out to the Olympus Mons caldera to show you the prototype itself."

"And why would I do that, risking a billion-dollar piece of equipment in the process?"

"Because, if you don't, and I'm right, a lot of people are going to die. Those deaths won't be on my hands. They'll be on yours."

"I think I've heard quite enough." Wolfrik stood up. "Adams, escort Mr. Leon back to his cell."

Adams manhandled my thin arms and dragged me back to my cell.

The corridor was devoid of people. We were in the part of the colony known by students as The Brig. It was usually empty, which isn't surprising. When you live in a colony as cramped as Olympus One, everyone tends to at least try to get along—or stay out of the way—but there are occasional students or employees of Milkyway Unlimited who lose it and commit crimes or contractual violations.

Now I was one of them.

"How much of that did you hear?" I asked the walking wall that Wolfrik had called Adams.

"Enough to know you're crazy," Adams said.

"You really believe that?"

Akio was in one of the cells that lined the dimly lit corridor. I wasn't sure if I'd ever see her again, if this went Wolfrik's way.

We stopped in front of my cell. Adams opened the door and shoved me in.

"You have to pass a lot of tests to get a job here," Adams said. "Physical and mental stuff. I know that there are no such things as invisible monsters."

"But, don't you find the footage strange?" I asked.

Adams let the door close in my face.

"The old man said it, didn't he?" Adam's words echoed over the intercom, reverberating in my ears. "You're good at making forgeries. Could be, you're better than you let on."

The comm went dead, and I was left alone. At least I wasn't stuck in The Box for the night. I wasn't sure my sanity could take that.

I lay awake for hours, replaying Gila's last moments over and over again in my mind. Trying to make some kind of sense of what had happened. But there was no sense to be found, not without further investigation, and Wolfrik had already made his mind up about the situation. I spent a good while blaming myself, regretting my own caustic attitude toward the man…if I'd spent just a little bit of time placating his ego, maybe things would have been different?

My dreams were feverish things that night.

It is as though I never left my father's den. My father sits before the fire, reading the Bible. I sit in the chair opposite of him. He reads aloud, but I'm not listening. Finally, he says something other than recited scripture: "You were always a troublesome child."

I look him in the eyes; his face is wrinkled and tired. "And you were always so strict."

"You gave your mother so much pain when you were born," he says. "Almost killed her, your head was too big. They had to give her a C-section. C-sections are not of God."

"Of course they're not."

"Your head was always so big. Filled with ungodly ideas, masquerading as theories. Just another word for sacrilege!"

I sigh, and let myself sink deep into the chair. "Why couldn't it have been you, instead of mother?"

The dream shattered.

Someone stood over me, silhouetted by the dim light flooding into my cell from the corridor. It was Clarence. For a moment, I thought maybe he was going to kill me.

"Get up," Clarence said.

"Why?" I asked.

He grabbed me and dragged me into the corridor. Wolfrik and Akio were standing there, wearing EVA suits. Now I was really confused.

"What's going on?" I asked, rubbing my eyes.

They avoided my gaze.

A conflicted torrent of emotion reared through me. A hot flash of guilt and the simultaneous rush or relief. "Someone died…"

Akio nodded. "The footage was pretty gruesome, and it followed the same pattern as Gila's death."

"You're off the hook, Mr. Leon," Wolfrik said.

"So, you believe me now?" I said.

"No, not yet. But Akio somewhat corroborated your story," Wolfrik said.

"You made this decision pretty fast." I crossed my arms. The interrogation Wolfrik had given me the day before was still fresh. It was hard for me to believe that he'd let me off without a fight.

What was he hiding?

"Yes, well, the other Admins felt that, in light of the security cam footage, we needed to explore all avenues of possibility." His teeth gritted together. He wasn't happy about this. The other Admins had forced him into this. Perhaps I had a faceless ally somewhere within Olympus One? "I've decided that, after reviewing the evidence that Akio's shown me on your tablet—"

"You hacked my tablet?"

Akio shrugged. "It's only fair, you hacked my profile."

Wolfrik cleared his throat. "Yes, she hacked your profile, I think that's hardly the biggest problem now. Anyway, I believe that there's a reasonable doubt that something is going on here that requires an explanation, and I'm willing to see if your hypothesis holds water."

I shook my head. "So, you believe her and not me?"

"To be fair, Mr. Leon, her track record is far more reliable than yours."

Akio cleared her throat. "I believe you."

"What?" I gasped obnoxiously. "Can you say that again? My heart nearly stopped."

Akio rolled her eyes.

"I believe that these things are extra-dimensional creatures." She took a deep breath. "But I'm still not convinced that non-local consciousness is a thing."

"You're still sticking to that, eh?"

"I still say there's not enough evidence to support that part of your hypothesis."

"This banter can wait until we're in the rover," Wolfrik said as he started down the corridor.

"Where's my tablet?" I asked.

"I've got it here with me." Akio withdrew it from her bag and handed it to me.

Akio had already bypassed my security and the screen was still resting on the files from the dark matter camera.

"Wolfrik, do I have access to the network again?" I asked.

"You've been given provisional access until I can decide what to do with you," Wolfrik said.

"Comforting," I said.

I opened up my connection to the satellite that I'd used as a link to the camera and saw that the connection between the camera and the satellite had been severed.

"That's odd," I said.

"What?" Akio asked, snatching the tablet from my hands.

"The camera isn't linking to the satellite anymore," I said.

"You linked to one of our satellites?" Wolfrik's voice became hoarse. "Add that to the long list of violations you've committed in the last couple of days."

"Without that link, there'd be no way to get the images from the camera; it's not as if Olympus One's network stretches up past the caldera."

"And if your hypothesis is correct, none of this would be happening if you had simply kept your ideas to yourself."

I turned off the tablet and tucked it under my arm. We walked in silence the rest of the way.

3

The ground stretched on and on, a sea of red and black, accented by the sand-colored, dull, dusty Martian horizon. Clarence drove the rover, while Wolfrik silently pawed through the images on my tablet. The ride was bumpy, and I could hardly stomach the idea of being stuck in a confined space with the man for over two Sols.

Clarence drove like my grandmother.

Wolfrik was sweating bullets behind me, always staring down, never looking at the Martian landscape.

Akio kept her helmet on, just like last time. Still, she seemed less anxious.

"There's something I need to know," I said.

He didn't look up. "And what is that?"

"Who died?"

Wolfrik hesitated for a moment, his words stuttering in his mouth and catching in his throat. "It was Adams."

"He was campus police, wasn't he?"

"He was."

"How did he die?"

He looked away. "Akio already said that the manner of death was similar to Gila's."

"That doesn't tell me how he died, only that it was similar to how Gila passed. Answer the question."

"He died after leaving one of the public bathrooms in Sector 1b. His throat was opened up."

"Just like Gila's?" My stomach tightened.

"Similar, yes. A nearby student reported hearing a loud shrieking sound, ran toward the bathroom, only to find Adams clawing his way into the hallway, leaving a trail of blood behind him on the floor. He didn't last long after that."

I shook my head. "Adams had direct contact with me too."

"Lots of people have had contact with you since we turned the camera on," Akio said. "That doesn't necessarily prove your hypothesis."

"Then what about the similarity in their wounds?" I said.

"Like I said, it could be some other phenomenon tied to dark matter, or..."

"Or?"

"A murderer."

"Yes, a murderer who can turn themselves completely invisible."

"It isn't unheard of—as I recall, we've got some new stealth technologies on Earth that can function as a cloak to what the human eye can see."

"Not to mention what the security cameras can see," Wolfrik said. "Who's to say we're not dealing with someone who's hacking the security footage to throw us off? Both of you are quite capable of that."

The cabin was quiet. The rumbling from the rover rolling over rocks sent vibrations through our seats.

"Why target Gila and Adams, though?" Akio asked.

Wolfrik shook his head. "I don't know. Maybe it's someone that Hal angered? Let's face it, you're his only friend. Perhaps they altered your camera's data to make you think there are invisible monsters out to get you?"

I crossed my arms. I did not like this idea…but it would make some sense. For a moment, I wondered if I could trust my own judgment. Maybe Akio had been right? Maybe I was letting my personal viewpoint color the data before me?

I felt like I was losing my mind.

"I sometimes feel like I'm being watched when I'm guarding Hal's dorm," Clarence said, causing the cabin to fall into an uncomfortable silence.

Finally, Akio broke the silence: "Technically, we're all being watched. Could be the security cameras."

"Or they're studying us," I said.

We stayed quiet for the rest of the journey. I ran over the images again to keep my mind from wandering, and to keep the vision of Gila bleeding out on the gymnasium floor from flooding into my mind. Part of me wished I could be one of those ancient Martians, doomed by the onset of an asteroid, or a comet, or, hell, nuclear war, just so I wouldn't have to deal with the thoughts in my head any longer.

The Sun had fallen and risen by the time we arrived at the place where I'd planted the camera. Clarence drove the rover down into the caldera and I located the pole. My eyes opened wide as I focused on it. It had been knocked over on its side.

"That's not how we left it," Akio said.

I nodded. "That's probably why it got disconnected from the satellite. Gear up, I need to link up with it directly."

We donned our helmets and pressurized our suits. The horizon was brilliant and cobalt once more. My feet sank into the dust. I plodded over to the capsized dark matter camera and scooped it up in my hands, like a father cradling a son who'd fallen off his bike. I could feel the vibrations in the soil from the others running to catch up.

"It's not damaged, is it?" Akio asked.

I examined the casing and hooked my tablet up to the camera directly. The link showed that most of the systems were still functioning properly, save for the link to the satellite. I downloaded everything leading up to us arriving in the caldera and linking up with the camera, then dismounted the camera from the pole and shut it down.

"It's not damaged," I said. "I just downloaded the images from the last two Sols, hopefully they shed some light on these things."

"You shut it down?" Wolfrik asked.

"Yeah," I said.

"How will we know if your hypothesis is correct?"

"I don't know," I said. "I guess we'll just have to wait."

"Wait for someone else to die, you mean," Akio said. "No offense, but that's a terrible plan."

"I agree with Akio," Wolfrik said. "But I guess we'll know soon enough. I'll have to confer with the other Admins."

Clarence looked to the horizon suspiciously, his fingers twitching anxiously with the oxygen tubes of his suit. "We should leave now. Something's not right."

"Don't be superstitious," Akio said, her voice quivering.

"I got what I came for." I stood up and walked back to the rover.

The others piled into the cabin with me. Once it was pressurized, we all removed our helmets. Clarence started the rover back up and we began the long journey back to Olympus One. I opened up the files that I had retrieved from the camera. The diorama of alien shapes played as it had before. The strange mantis-raptor-like forms didn't return until the fourth repetition, and this time there were four of them. They paced the camera, and even nudged it again, causing it to move back and forth.

I continued to watch the slideshow play out until darkness fell in the images; that was when it happened. One of the mantis shapes appeared to take a swing at the camera with one of its appendages. The camera fell, kicking up dust into the viewfinder. The camera continued to record, but it only managed to capture faint glimpses of them pacing it, as well as the weaker concentrations of the dark matter web in the sky.

Just then, I had a terrible feeling. What if these things, whatever they were, were beyond our comprehension?

I remembered the nightmare I'd had in the rover. Akio and I dangled on strings of dark matter, her lips cold and dead.

I looked at her.

"What is it?" Akio asked. "You look like someone just killed your dog."

"I have confirmation," I said, trying to mask the shakiness in my voice. "They knocked over the camera…which means they can affect things in our dimension."

Akio nodded solemnly. "And it would be a stretch for someone to come all the way out here to tamper with the data on the camera. So there's a good chance the data is raw."

"A good scientist tests and retests his findings," Wolfrik said. "Perhaps you've forgotten this, Mr. Leon?"

"Yes, but for once I'm agreeing with Hal," Akio said.

"Wow, thanks," I said. "Nice to know you have so much confidence in my judgment."

I watched Phobos complete its first orbit of the day, its surface illuminated unevenly against the putrid orange sky. My thoughts drifted to the Greek god of the same name. He was the personification of fear brought by war, and he was known to accompany Ares, or Mars in the Roman pantheon, into battle. It felt like an omen, considering everything that had happened.

The Sun had set when we finally returned to Olympus One. No new deaths had been reported, so I was hopeful that my theory was right after all. Once we had removed our gear, Wolfrik stopped Akio and me in the hall.

"I've talked it over with the other Admins," Wolfrik said. "We're giving you a provisional reinstatement."

"Why?" I asked.

Akio elbowed me in the ribs. "Be nice!"

"In light of the tragedy," Wolfrik said. "We're willing to forgive the trespass so long as you do not cause any more trouble for the remainder of the semester."

"Which means no arguing with your professors, Hal," Akio said.

"Thanks," I said.

"Don't thank me yet." Wolfrik began to walk down the sterile hallway. "Just get some rest and try to catch up on the work you've missed in the morning."

I nodded, clutching the camera in my hands tightly.

4

Sleep was far more elusive than I'd thought it would be. With my status as a student in good standing, I purchased another bottle of gin from Dane after delivering his shopping list.

Dane looked at me strangely as he passed me the bottle. The label read: LIME.

"What?" I said.

"They say you murdered those people," Dane said.

"And you believe that shit?"

He shrugged. "That's what I was trying to figure out."

His face was three kinds of screwed up. His eyes were bloodshot, pupils dilated, slurred speech.

"You ought to stop drinking the merchandise, Dane."

"Is it true?"

My fists clenched tight for a moment, but then I saw something in Dane's eyes that made me want to retch. There was fear in his eyes. Fear of what I was capable of.

"No," I said quietly. "It's not true."

I placed the "gin" in my bag and left him standing there, wondering if I was some kind of serial killer.

In a way, maybe he was right? After all, I was the one who had come up with the initial concept for the dark matter camera. Akio had been there from day one, but I was the one who convinced her to work on the project. So, maybe, in the same way that the men who'd built the atom bomb were culpable for the deaths at Hiroshima, Nagasaki, New York, Moscow, London, and all the others, maybe, I was just as guilty for the deaths of Gila and Adams?

I returned to my dorm. Akio wasn't home. I sat down on the couch and dragged the bottle out of my pack, stared at it for a time. I walked over to the cupboard and withdrew a glass. I poured until it was full, then tossed it back, neat. Anything to shake this feeling of guilt. A few more glasses, but I still couldn't get Gila off my mind. I watched the life drain out of her eyes over and over, clutching her throat to stop the blood from rushing down her breasts.

I was on my fourth glass when my door hissed open. Akio stepped into our dorm.

"I thought you were going to sleep?" Akio said.

"I tried," I said.

"Are you drinking again?"

"Couldn't get her out of my head." I tossed the drink back.

"Hal, if you need to talk—"

"I'm fine."

She stood there for a moment, silent in her worry.

"What?" I poured myself another glass. "If something's on your mind, just say it."

"I don't want you to screw this chance up," Akio said. "Drinking won't solve your problems—in fact—" She stormed forward and swiped the bottle of moonshine off the table and stuffed it in her pack. "It's against school regulations to drink until you've graduated, so I'm taking this."

"What the hell is your deal?"

"My deal is that I care about you for some stupid reason, my deal is that I don't want to see you self-destruct over some whore who—"

"Some whore?" I polished off the drink in my hand and stood up. "Seriously? Gila was top of her class! Top of her—"

"Yeah, in fucking *Botany*."

"And our invention got her killed!" I shook my head and pushed my finger into Akio's solar plexus. "I killed her, Akio. It's my fault! My *fault*! That's why I see her dying every time I close my eyes…that's why I can't sleep…and that's why I've been drinking!"

"It's more than that, though." Akio pushed me back onto the couch. "You wanted to fuck her, just admit it!"

"And what if I did! What business is it of yours?" I started to laugh. The alcohol had my head swimming, the room spinning. "What is it? You think there's a chance for you and I, or something?" I shook my head. "News flash, Akio, I'd never date you, and I couldn't fuck you no matter how drunk I was…"

Because I'd ruin you, just like he ruined her.

I saw the effect of my words in her eyes: rivulets of tears cut canyons in her mascara.

"I didn't mean…"

"Yes, you did," Akio said, turning for the door. "You meant every word!"

"Akio, wait!"

But she was gone. The hallway was empty, and so was I.

5

I got to class early, despite my splitting headache and the fact that I hadn't slept. I moved through a sea of sullen students and found my seat next to where Gila's had been. I considered moving…but when I tried to move, I felt like I was going to vomit all over the floor.

Professor Brown was not her usual self. She was sitting at her desk, staring forward blankly at the rest of the auditorium. Tears came streaming from her eyes, and before long, she broke down, flailing to get control of her emotions.

Something inside me writhed, and it wasn't my hangover. I had a feeling it wasn't over. We had failed.

Professor Brown stood up and cleared her throat, wiped the tears away best as she could, and attempted to address the class.

"I'm sorry," she said. "Some of you already know, but our Dean, Dr. Alexander Wolfrik, passed away last night in his quarters. Class is canceled today."

And just as I had processed what she had said, the classroom was empty. I sat there for a time, staring at the blank front screen. It wasn't long ago that I would have delighted in news like that, and that alone was cause for me to feel guilty.

It was my fault.

All of it was my fault.

VII

The whole colony was in mourning. Not long after the cause of Wolfrik's death was announced, rumors started to circulate that the Admins were talking about evacuation or quarantine, but so far, they hadn't made a decision.

The video wasn't shown, but I tracked it down myself to confirm my own guilty conscience. The footage had been captured from his main terminal, a log file from a communication feed he'd made to Earth. He'd gone home that night, shortly after pardoning me of my impending expulsion.

He sat down at his chair, opened a direct link to Earth. His son was on the other end of the call. I could see both of them in the recording. His son's face was contained in a small rectangle in the top right-hand corner of the screen.

"Hello, Fredrick," Wolfrik said.

"Father," his son said.

"How's your mother?"

"You know how she is."

"Still won't talk to me?"

His son nodded.

Wolfrik took in a deep, heavy breath and sighed. For the first time, I could tell how old he looked, how old he felt, with the weight of guilt—perhaps from the resentful family that he'd left behind on Earth—that hung heavy beneath his eyes. I knew that look well: I saw it in the reflection of the mirror every day now.

Wolfrik reached under the desk, pulled out and opened a bottle of wine, poured himself a generous amount in one of those fancy wineglasses they pass out to faculty before they leave Earth.

"You know that I love you both, right?" Wolfrik asked.

His son nodded. "She thinks you're going to die up there."

"She'll forgive me when I come home." Wolfrik didn't look convinced.

"Maybe…you've been gone for six years, father."

He didn't even have a chance to raise the glass to his lips before he heard the sounds. Wolfrik turned around, his eyes darting, panning, from his kitchen to the study to the bedroom. Even in the recording, the distinct sound of disembodied footsteps was present, and hauntingly oppressive.

"What is that noise?" his son asked.

"No…"

The lights were on, but there was nothing there, nothing that you could see with your eyes.

Still.

Something cut him in half. I'll never forget the look in his eyes when the top half of his body went one way and the other half went another. Blood circled the drain as he screamed for help, clutching at his own spilled entrails. His cries for help were answered by a slash to the throat.

His son saw all of it from Wolfrik's desktop camera feed. He sat staring in disbelief, tears drifting down his cheeks. He kept calling for his father.

The log file ended with Fredrick sobbing, pawing at his own camera for the father he'd never see again.

It was my fault. I had awakened them.

All my theorizing and plotting. I wished I'd never built that damned camera!

The camera was resting on the counter, inactive. I thought about disassembling it and playing golf with the parts outside. But, against my better judgment, I grabbed it, tucked it into an overnight bag, and gathered up the pieces from the other prototypes in the room.

I stood before the front door, my hand on the access panel.

Turning the camera off hadn't helped. They'd still gotten to Wolfrik. And they would get to others.

I turned around. My eyes traced the contour of the wires that snaked through various components throughout the living space that we'd converted into a lab.

I'd screwed everything up. All my theorizing, my plotting, my goddamned ambition. What good was it if the things that came from my mind, from my intelligence, only got people killed?

I was better off dead.

There was enough wire to make a decent rope if I used the industrial strength tape. I could make a noose. I could end it.

And, if I was lucky, maybe I'd see her again?

I pictured my mother's hospice room, where the machines had pumped her lungs full of air and tracked her unchanging vitals.

My father was standing next to her when I arrived, clasping her hand right around a crucifix. His eyes opened and cast a wave of guilt at me; Catholics are professionals at casting guilt.

"¿Qué estás haciendo aquí?" *What are you doing here?* my father said.

"I'm here to see my mother," I said in English.

"You don't even speak Spanish now to your own father?" He stood up, leaving my mother holding the crucifix in her lifeless hand. "Is this what they teach you in this devil's school?"

"I got accepted to Olympus One." I crossed my arms. "I'm going to Mars to earn my degree."

"Mars?" His liver-spotted face contorted. "You go to space now to do your learning?"

I nodded. "I didn't plan on telling you."

"You're going to—"

"Burn in hell, I know." I smiled. There was freedom in what I was about to say. "Your belief is a crutch, father. You blame my 'sin' for mother's condition, when the truth is, it was your abuse that drove her to using. It was *you*."

He shook his head. "That was her weakness. The driver was God punishing—"

"Keep telling yourself that."

"It is the truth." The fire and brimstone that burned deep in his bloodshot eyes told me that he believed it.

"I guess I'll leave you to commune with your imaginary friend, father." I turned for the door. "I'll come back to see mom later."

"God will get you."

"Sure thing. And maybe he'll ride in on a unicorn, impaling me on its rainbow horn, while he's at it?"

I closed the door behind me. I didn't get a chance to say my goodbyes to my mother before she died. Doctors said that it was a blood clot that did it. Maybe it was there for years, just waiting for the accident to happen and set it free, where it would march into her heart and end her suffering. My father needed to blame me for her drug addiction, for the accident, and for her death. He couldn't face the fact that he'd done things to another human being that had led to her demise. He hid behind his faith, like a corrupt politician hides behind loopholes in the law.

My fists tightened. Tears darted down my face, bringing me back to the present.

Thoughts of suicide faded from my mind and were replaced by a clear resolve to stop what was happening. I would shoulder the responsibility and the guilt for what Akio and I had created. I would push through. I would take responsibility in a way that my father never had.

I opened the door.

The few students that passed me gave me suspicious looks, almost like they knew what I'd done, and maybe they did. I wished they'd just come out and say it.

I was the last person she wanted to see right now, but there were things that I needed to say. I knew where to find her, too. There was one place she always went when she didn't want to be around me, one place where she could clear her mind and focus on her studies, a place where she might be mourning the passing of Alexander Wolfrik, our one-time adversary and reluctant ally.

I followed signs to the Planetarium.

She was sitting alone in one of the stadium-style seats toward the back, staring at a shifting real-time view of Saturn. Titan was eclipsing over the gas giant's surface.

"Go away, Hal," she said.

I froze at the bottom of the stairs; the whites of her eyes were bloodshot in the light from the overhead dome projection. "Akio, I know you're mad at me…"

"Mad?" She shook her head, wiping at the heavy bags beneath her eyes, painted black with her running mascara. "You think that's what this is?"

I shook my head. "I know what this is."

"Then what is it?" She waved her hands about hysterically. "Tell me what's going on inside my head, you narcissistic shit!"

"You're mourning," I said, taking a step forward.

She shook her head. "Oh, yeah, *real* insightful. No, *Hal*, I'm not just mourning Wolfrik's passing. I'm heartbroken."

"Look, what I said—"

"Was fucked-up to say the least."

"To say the least." I shook my head, looking at my feet. "But it's not what I said that you should be mad at me for, it's what I meant by what I said."

She rolled her eyes. "Oh, please, I think you were pretty clear."

"You're my best friend." The words came out in a whisper.

"What?" She cupped a hand to her ear. "I didn't hear you, Hal. Say it a little louder so those of us in the back can hear."

That's when I noticed the bottle in her other hand. She uncapped it, took a long swig of the gin and wiped her mouth with her sleeve.

"You're my best friend," I said.

"Oh?" She stood up and nearly tumbled over into the row of seats in front of her before steadying herself. "You have a funny way of showing it, by constantly insulting me and getting me into trouble. Best friend? Horseshit! You only care about yourself."

"I mean it. I'm not good with people. And I know I can't really make up for what I said back there, but I think we both know why I push people away."

Her head bobbed up and down in an exaggerated, swinging arc. "Yeah, we all know why you're so fucked-up. Cause Daddy and Mommy never loved you. Daddy was an overbearing Catholic and Mommy was always high. Is that it? Is that all, Hal? Is that why you're always such a prick?"

"He used to beat her." I was standing next to her row of seats, inching my way towards her.

Akio fell silent, falling back into her chair.

"I'd lie awake at night waiting for it to stop, sometimes crying myself to sleep in the process."

"You never told me that."

I sat down next to her, setting my bag between my legs. She offered me the bottle; I took it. "It's not something I like to discuss."

"So, that's why you're such an asshole."

"Because I'm afraid of becoming him."

I took a long swig of the gin, felt it burn all the way down into my core.

"You realize how cowardly that is?" Her eyes were bold now, eyebrows creased.

I nodded. "I do."

"And the logic of it. You're an asshole so you can avoid becoming like your father, who was an overbearing asshole?" She pushed me. "What the fuck, Hal?"

She sobbed into her hands. Part of me wanted to comfort her, to wrap my arm around her and ease the troubles from her body and soul, but I couldn't. I knew it was too late for that. There was nothing that could repair this damage between us, and that was my fault.

"Turning the camera off didn't work," I said.

The real-time video changed to a satellite view of Jupiter. It might have been the alcohol starting to take effect, but sitting there, watching the storms churn within the great red spot, it felt almost as if we were about to plunge into the storm clouds—where we would be ripped to nothingness by 618-kilometer-an-hour winds and crushed by the planet's immense gravity.

"Yeah?" She snatched the bottle of gin out of my hand and took another long swig. "What the fuck am I supposed to do about that?"

"We need to stop it."

She shook her head.

"Akio, we're the ones that caused this, and we're the ones that have the best chance of stopping it."

She was quiet for a while, taking occasional sips from the bottle. Was this what I was like when I was drunk?

"I'm moving out, Hal," she said.

"Akio…"

Her eyes rose up to meet mine; there was a darkness in them that hadn't been there before. "You want to know what I think? I think you should take that camera and flush yourself out an airlock. That'll probably solve it."

I reacted so fast, I was barely conscious of what I was doing. I grabbed for the bottle of gin. She held on tight.

"No!" she shouted. Veins popped out of her forehead as she struggled to keep her grip. "You're not the only one who gets to get drunk and tell the world to go to hell!"

I ripped the bottle from her hands and smashed it on the floor. "Maybe none of us should."

Her tears dripped, pooling on the floor. "Screw you, Hal. Just, go fuck yourself! Leave me alone!"

I nodded and descended the stairs.

I spent a long time alone that night, pacing the dorm room that had once been ours. My newfound resolve to solve this mystery seemed to have ebbed. I thought that if I told Akio the truth, if I told her what was really going on with me, that she'd help. I needed her. But I'd screwed up our friendship, even our professional relationship, beyond repair.

I considered getting another bottle of gin to ease the pain I felt, to ease my guilt, to make it easier to give up. I found myself wandering the corridors, semi-aimlessly.

I walked by Gila's old quarters. Someone new was staying there now. I almost knocked on the door, almost said hello and introduced myself.

I kept walking. Found myself in the gym, where she had died. They'd since cleaned the mess up. There were a few students and Milkyway Unlimited employees present. They stopped their workouts to stare at me. Their stares were a mixture of confusion, fear, and, perhaps, anger.

A young man stopped hitting the punching bag, sneering at me, and left.

It would have been so easy to disappear into my own depression, to give in to the desire to drink. That's what my mother would have done, isn't it? My father would have turned to his faith to absolve himself of his own guilt, were he in my shoes.

I found myself in front of the punching bag. The others present in the gym went back to their workouts, taking time for occasional wary glances in my general direction as I watched the punching bag slowly stop swinging from the previous man's assault.

Then, I did something that surprised even myself. I reached back and took a swing at the bag. It hardly budged; my knuckles hurt. I hit it again, and again, and I kept hitting it until my knuckles bled. I screamed, I shouted, louder with each successive punch. At first, I imagined that it was my father that I was hitting. Then, I imagined that it was the mantis shapes that I assaulted.

I collapsed on the exercise mat. I stared at my bloody knuckles as I tried to get control over my breathing and ease the stitches that pierced my sides.

I rolled onto my back, staring at the ceiling. The punching bag drifted into and out of my view as it slowly came to rest.

I wondered what had passed through Gila's mind as she lay in this very room, bleeding out her throat. Was it sorrow that she felt? Confusion? Or, was she satisfied with the life that she had led, even if it ended so anticlimactically?

There were no answers.

How many others would be forced to have their final words or thoughts while bleeding out on the floor of an alien world, a cold and lifeless colony, millions of miles away from the places on Earth that they called home?

How many others would I be forced to watch on the very security cameras that were designed to monitor us, to protect us, sometimes even from ourselves?

My eyes drifted to one of the security cameras in the gym. How many of those were there throughout Olympus One? Those cameras observed a vast portion of the colony.

If each of those cameras were capable of imaging the dark matter web, it would make collecting data much easier.

I sat up.

"That's it," I said, drawing awkward glances from the other people in the gym again.

I stood up and collected my pack and left the gym.

I wasn't sure what I could do alone to stop this, but I couldn't just give up. I couldn't allow myself to excuse my guilt.

I no longer desired that drink.

My resolve returned.

2

Once I was back at my dorm, I cleaned myself up and ate some rations. There was no telling if Akio would change her mind, and I'd proceed with the assumption that she wouldn't. Just as there was no way to tell if it was possible to stop what was happening.

It was my responsibility anyway.

I needed more data, and I needed it fast. I entered the corridor, while I held my overnight bag with a death grip. I'd need help, though, whether the Admins liked it or not.

That's who I had to see first.

Since Wolfrik's death, Emma Williams had taken over as Dean. She'd be the one to convince. Hopefully she knew as much as Wolfrik did about our theories, and about the dark matter camera itself.

Wolfrik's old office was in the eastern wing of Olympus One. I ignored the receptionist and the campus officer standing guard, barging right into her office. She was sitting at Wolfrik's desk.

She'd already replaced his awards and photos of his family with her own. His stuff was tucked away in a box in the corner of the office.

"Can I help you?" she asked.

She was a woman I knew only by her name. Emma Williams' eyes were bold, her lips tight, and a wave of gray salt that she no longer tried to hide painted the left side of her head.

"Actually, yes, you can help," I said, taking the dark matter camera out and placing it on her desk.

The campus police officer I had dashed by came rushing into the room, grabbed me by the arm. "Listen, you little shit! You can't just go barging into the Dean's—"

"Ah. You're Hal Leon." Her eyes narrowed at me. Whatever the officer had been about to say was silenced by the expression on her face. I couldn't tell whether she was disgusted by my presence, or intrigued.

I wrenched my arm free of the campus officer's grip. "I see—my reputation precedes me, as the cliché goes."

"Do you want me to remove him?" The officer asked.

Emma shook her head. "No."

"Then what should I do, ma'am?"

"Get lost. Mr. Leon and I have business to discuss."

The officer nodded and quickly made his exit.

"Sorry about that," Emma said. Her eyes drifted to the dark matter camera resting in front of her. "I'm aware of what this camera of yours does, but—"

"Save your breath." I took a seat in front of her chair. "No offense, but we don't have a lot of time. I need a team of students or employees at Olympus One who have a background in quantum physics or engineering, both would be best."

She reeled back in her chair, eyes opened wide in shock. Guess she didn't expect me to be so blunt? "And what would you want this team to do for you?"

"I want to retrofit all of the security cameras on Olympus One to be able to see the dark matter web, and I want it monitored day and night to collect data on whatever the hell is killing people here."

Her brow furrowed for a moment. She closed her eyes. "Done."

"What?"

"Was that not the answer you expected?"

I nodded. "Not gonna lie, I thought it would be a tougher sell than that."

"Well, you still have to convince the men and women down in Security to help you as well. But I'm well aware of your experiment. Alexander kept a detailed file of your interrogations and your claims. He was planning to send it to Milkyway Unlimited."

"That son-of-a-" I jerked forward, feeling the anger course through me briefly, before I stopped myself. The man was dead. There was no point in cursing him.

"Don't blame him, it's in our contract to report any and all potential new technology developed by students here to the company. If we don't, and they find out, they can sue us for up to forty percent of our cumulative wages."

"I didn't know…"

"They make us sign several documents before sending us out here. Milkyway Unlimited wants a monopoly on any new tech that could lead to exploring the known universe. There's also the fear of us becoming autonomous from the government, so they threaten that they can levy this threat against our families posthumously if necessary."

My eyes narrowed, our eyes locking. "I'm assuming you already contacted the company then?"

She nodded. "I'm sorry. I hope you understand."

My teeth gnashed together. I wasn't sure how to feel about this news. "I suppose that was unavoidable."

"Is there anything else?"

I thought about asking her to get Akio for me, to convince her to work on this…but I'd already caused enough trouble in her life as it was. I needed to do this without her.

I shook my head. "No. That should be it for now."

I picked up the camera and shoved it back in my bag. Somehow, it felt strange now. "I need to get started on those cameras."

"I'll get your team together then."

I nodded, and left. The officer outside tossed me a dirty look, but I ignored him.

3

I followed signs TO SECURITY, against the flow of occasional passing students. All but one didn't notice me. And even so, each person that I saw looked angry or depressed.

There was something in the air, it seemed. A tangible sense of dread so thick you could slice it with a kitchen knife.

I found the room I was looking for. The sign above the black double doors read SECURITY, and also AUTHORIZED MILKYWAY UNLIMITED PERSONNEL ONLY.

I buzzed the intercom. The door opened without so much as a hello. I stepped through.

The walls inside the Security room were an uncomfortable metallic blue, accented with a black variation of Olympus One's plastic, sterile floors that reflected the light from the myriad of screens and consoles in the room in a way that was oppressive on the eyes.

I stood in the open doorway. The men and women there stared at me blankly, as if I was some idiot freshman who'd gotten lost.

"You're not supposed to be here," an older Latina woman said. She had a nametag on her coveralls that read: LIZETH.

"You know who I am?" I asked.

She nodded. "You're the one they say killed Wolfrik."

I nodded, setting my overnight bag down. "Then you saw what happened on the security feed?"

She nodded. "At first I was certain someone doctored the footage…"

"No one did." I dug through my bag and retrieved the dark matter camera. "How much do you know about the experiment Akio and I were conducting?"

She shrugged. The others had a strange mixture of looks painted on their faces, from curious, to horrified, to apprehensive. I tried to recount the events as best as I could without making myself sound like a mental patient. The reactions were mixed at best. Even though Emma Williams had Wolfrik's file on my theories, she and the other Admins hadn't allowed that information to get to the general population of the colony for some reason…maybe this was it?

Lizeth leaned back in her chair. "So, you're saying that there are creatures in this dark matter web?"

I nodded. "But, we're losing time here. I came here because I want to modify the security network to use the dark matter camera design to detect these things. I thought that shutting the camera down would break entanglement with them, but it didn't, and Wolfrik died because of it. So, we need to collect more data, we need to understand them, before we can stop more people from dying. I've already gotten the go-ahead from Emma Williams to do this."

"Then why explain this all to us?" Lizeth asked.

I shrugged. "I don't know how else to start. If I modified the cameras, and you didn't know what to look for in the renders, that'd get us nowhere. And, along with the team that Emma's putting together, I need everyone on board."

"Why haven't these things killed you?" A man with a posh British accent and a balding scalp asked, sipping at a thermos that I imagined was full of tea. "Strikes me bloody odd that they haven't killed you yet, when you're the one who flipped the switch, eh?"

I think you should take that camera and flush yourself out an airlock. That'll probably solve it.

"I don't know why that is," I said. "But, as long as they haven't killed me, I'm going to do everything I can to stop them."

"What if they're sentient?" Lizeth said, toying with her glasses. "What if viewing them with the camera was like some kind of affront to their culture or something?"

The others looked at Lizeth like she'd lost her mind by entertaining the ideas I'd presented to them.

"Not that I believe your story yet," Lizeth said.

"A simple case of misunderstanding between vastly different cultures?" I scratched the stubble on my chin.

Lizeth shrugged.

The man with the posh accent sighed. "There's not much point to us arguing, if Emma's already signed us over to you, is there now? We just do what MU tells us."

"Right," Lizeth said. "We don't actually get a say, do we?"

"I guess not, when you put it like that," I said. "But, I wanted to try to explain anyway."

The door opened, causing me to jump. Clarence walked into the Security room.

"What are you doing here?" I asked.

"Emma sent me over to keep an eye on you," Clarence said.

"And why's that?"

"She fears that someone may make an attempt on your life."

I wasn't sure how to take that.

"I guess we should get going, then," I said.

I said goodbye to our new unwilling comrades in the Security room. Clarence and I went to hunt down a security camera to dissect. Retrofitting the cameras throughout the colony would take most of the week to do, if not longer. I spent that first night tearing one apart and attempting to come up with a new design on the fly. I got odd looks from passerby students, some of them scowls, and who could blame them? That crazy guy who got Wolfrik, Adams, and Gila killed was disassembling a security camera on the corridor floor.

It made the idea of a threat on my life seem more real. Why hadn't that occurred to me before? Even I'd had times when I doubted myself, wondered if I was just going mad. But, the Admins seemed to believe my story now, and maybe that was enough?

It was well into the next morning when I finally finished the first modified security camera. It was quite a bit bulkier than before, but the mount in the ceiling should still be able to hold its weight. If it worked, then I could easily hand out instructions to others to get the rest retrofitted.

I reattached the camera to its mount in the ceiling and reconnected the wires. Clarence had fallen asleep in a chair at some point, arms crossed and a scowl on his face. Seemed to be his default look lately.

I woke him up and returned to the Security room. It was empty at this time of the morning, and that was probably for the best.

I found myself at one of the terminals. My hands worked like they had a mind of their own, tearing into the circuitry where it needed to be modified. I had pieces of the other prototypes jury-rigged into that

96

first camera, but the core system needed a software and memory upgrade before I could use it.

I got myself under the terminal, found the motherboard and soldered some extra ram into it—taken from one of the older prototypes.

I uploaded a version of the OS we used for the original camera and modified the code as needed. Then, I patched my tablet into the system so I'd be able to monitor the camera feeds directly once all the cameras were retrofitted.

I stood up, and gave the system a quick test. The camera feed was devoid of anything strange, no mantis shapes. It would take time for the OS to render a 3D image of the dark matter web, let alone update changes. That could be a problem if I intended to use the cameras to try and predict who the next victim would be. Especially if the victim was me.

I rubbed my eyes.

"You should sleep," Clarence said.

I turned around, trying to rub the slight burning sensation from my tired eyes. He'd gotten a cup of coffee and taken a seat at one of the terminals in the rear of the room. Sometimes he was so quiet, it was like he wasn't even there. "I have no idea when Emma will finish assembling my team—I need to be ready to give them the blueprints and instructions, just in case."

"You can't keep going at the rate that you are. You'll burn yourself out."

"Yeah, but with Akio gone…"

"But nothing, you're only human."

He was right. But, part of me knew that as soon as I closed my eyes I'd see the faces of Gila, Adams and Wolfrik. They would consume my nightmares, and I'd be unable to rest anyway. Naturally, I was working myself so hard to keep my mind off things.

"Tell you what," Clarence said. "Take a nap; I'll wake you when the others show up. I doubt the Sun's even come up, so you might have a few hours."

I didn't bother arguing. As soon as I admitted that sleep was a possibility my whole system started to crash, like an exhausted swimmer being carried out to sea by a powerful tide.

I crawled under one of the terminals and used my bag as a pillow. The slow hum from the computer fans was almost soothing.

Within seconds, I was asleep.

4

The flames rage within the fireplace in my father's living room. He sits reading lines of scripture again. I stand by the fire, staring into the flames as they dance, licking at the air. I can feel the heat from my chair. I can feel the fire's hunger, its need to expand and consume everything.

"You're being punished," my father says.

I ignore him, continuing to watch the flames.

"They won't kill you because you're just like them," he says. "A monster. A devil."

The flames grow, consuming the wood within the fireplace; sparks dance, threatening to ignite the carpet.

"And when you bathe in the blood of your fellow sinners, then they'll cart you off to hell where your mother is."

"Well, at least I'll be far away from you."

Sparks explode from the fireplace, igniting the carpet. The flames spread from the carpet, to the chairs, to the upholstery. I stand there, watching it climb my pants, singeing my hair and melting my skin. It is a welcome feeling.

It's strange, because my skin doesn't hurt when the fire melts it; but, for some reason, my side does.

5

My eyes opened to a kaleidoscope of images and a cacophony of sounds. I felt like I had been skewered over a firepit. The room was spinning. Had one of my kidneys gone?

Damn you, Dane, and your moonshine.

"He's waking up." An unfamiliar voice, female.

The room smelled different than it had when I'd fallen asleep, like stale coffee grounds and dirty laundry. Somehow my overnight bag was a much softer pillow than it had been before.

"Mr. Leon," the female voice said, "you've been stabbed."

Stabbed? I tried to speak, but it hurt to move my lips.

My vision sharpened; I could see I was resting on my couch. Clarence stood at the other end of the room, arms crossed and leaning against the wall. The doctor waved her hands in front of my eyes.

I coughed, and waved her hands away. She gave me a glass of water, which eased my tender throat.

I felt at the bandage on my stomach.

"How bad," I said quietly.

"Missed your vital organs. It was a kitchen knife."

"I opened the door to go to the bathroom and he rushed into the room," Clarence said. "I tried to grab at his shirt, but he was already across the room, sticking you with the knife.

"I managed to pull him off of you before he got to do it a second time. He must have been waiting there all morning for the door to open."

"Who was it?" I asked.

"A colleague of yours from Planetary Physics. His name is Kal Drestner."

"Unusual name."

"Emma's launching an investigation."

I tried to sit up, but the pain in my stomach told me to lay my ass right back down. "Ouch."

"You're not going to want to move until the bandages have a chance to solidify. Even then, you're going to be in a considerable amount of pain if you try to do anything too strenuous."

"I need to get the blueprints to the security staff."

"I'll let Emma know you need to see her."

The doctor left me alone with Clarence. My eyes drifted, struggling to stay open, closed.

When I woke again, it was dark, but I was certain I hadn't been moved. I tried sitting up, succeeded. The pain wasn't as bad as the doctor had suggested. I spent a little while testing my range of movement. Walking to the bathroom, to the sink, twisting this way and that. When I finally felt up to it, I left the room and made my way to security.

It didn't seem real at first. It was a slow realization as I traversed the twisting corridors of Olympus One, the blinking hallway lights and twisting, interconnected tubes and wiring above leading me to my destination.

Someone had made an attempt on my life. It was a strange sensation. Clarence had been there, and I had still almost died.

The thought made me feel naked.

Before, I had felt a sense of apprehension at turning a corner, as if any moment could have been my last. Death by some invisible threat with unknown goals or motives. But, now? I had to face the fact that humans, flesh-and-blood people, wanted to kill me. Death by the seen or the unseen, two unknowns, one physical and one beyond normal means of comprehension.

The airlock was starting to sound real cozy. At least then I'd be the master of my destiny.

The overhead lights in the hallways and corridors were dimmed at this time of night. The lighting system was designed to mimic the phases of the day, attempting to trick the brain into perceiving morning, afternoon, dusk, and night. It was almost surreal being awake at this hour, traversing nearly empty halls, where cast shadows loomed forlornly. What secrets did those shadows hold? Perhaps the eyes of those mantis creatures stared out at me, mocking me in my attempts to understand them, to stop them.

The Security room was empty when I arrived. The modifications I had made to the boards and panels hadn't been changed or messed with. I sat down at one of the terminals and brought up the feed from the modified security camera.

There were about forty-eight hours of footage recorded so far. I played through it at ultra-fast speed.

The dark matter web clusters took shape after hour three. It looked like a splatter of violet ink on a dirty canvas. Its twisting tendrils and branches wound up and down the corridor. Students passed through it without even causing a ripple. Would it take three hours to update and render every time a change occurred?

If that was the case, I'd have to find some way to improve the rendering time.

The next three hours passed, and the cluster moved a few degrees to the north. No mantis shapes. Yet. Another three hours of footage went by, and a figure started to take shape in the web.

My heart seized in my chest for a moment.

But, it was only a human silhouette, possibly a concentration of dark matter clinging to one of the passing students.

I had to fix that rendering time. I broke open my tablet and started messing with the code. Maybe there was something that was slowing it down? Would increasing processing power help?

I glanced back at the sped-up security feeds. Violet humanoid silhouettes crowded the corridor, mixing unevenly with passing students. I paused the recording for a moment. The silhouettes froze, each with a different posture…and, something else: each silhouette was unique, a different level of luminosity and shape for every form on the screen.

The unique confusion and knowing of déjà vu overtook my senses.

I glanced at my tablet, opened the test panorama Akio and I had taken. The concentration of dark matter around her was so much more vibrant, while mine was dull and washed out.

The silhouettes on the security feed were similar. There were bright ones, with twisting tendrils of dark matter that tethered down the corridor to other silhouettes. Then there were ones that were smaller, isolated, and washed-out—like mine.

I shook my head, rubbed my eyes.

"There's just not enough data," I said.

I went back to modifying the code for the security cameras, but the entire time I was doing that, those silhouettes were there at the back of my mind, scratching and clawing for attention.

There had been one like that, but disconnected from us, the first time we tested the dark matter camera too.

The door hissed open, I jumped in my seat.

It was only Lizeth. She was holding a coffee, her hair was up in a bun, and she had heavy bags dragging beneath her eyes. "Good to see you're up and running, but shouldn't you be resting?"

I shook my head. "You know why I can't."

She took a seat next to me. "You did a number on our systems, we could barely figure out how to navigate your OS."

"I meant to leave a note, but getting stabbed kind of halted that plan from coming to fruition."

"So, what are we looking at?" Lizeth sipped on her coffee.

"The dark matter web is taking three hours to render on top of real-time footage." I rubbed my eyes. "To say the least, that's problematic."

"Add more RAM?"

"That's what I thought, but where to get it when supplies are limited here?"

"I'm sure Emma can help procure what you need."

"Yeah, I need to see her anyway." I dug through my bag and retrieved the original dark matter camera. "In the meantime, I'm going to take some photos."

I left Lizeth behind, her face aglow in front of a monitor.

The dark matter camera was much faster at rendering images at just under thirty seconds. On my way to Emma Williams' office, I snapped several images of student—and faculty—filled corridors. Nervous stares and angry scowls came from those who recognized me.

When the images rendered, I gained context to what the security footage had showed me earlier. The students each had a mixture of different dark matter concentrations around their bodies. The brighter the concentration, the more connections it had. A new-agey *nut* might call them "auras."

Tendrils and branches stretched between two women walking together in the hall, their hands clasped together and sly, knowing smiles etched on their faces.

A boy, probably a freshman, huddled at the door to a lecture hall. The dark matter concentration around him was muted, save for a small area near his stomach, where he clutched his tablet.

A woman screamed at a man in the hall, drawing a crowd of onlookers with mixed expressions. The concentration around the woman was bright, jagged, almost like lightning, while the man's was dim and washed out, matching his sulking expression. Perhaps they were lovers?

It made me think of Akio.

"You're Hal, aren't you?" A hand grabbed at my shoulder, twisting my stomach wound in the wrong way.

I turned to face a young Caucasian man with a reverse Mohawk shaved down the middle of his head—a stupid trend all the freshmen were doing lately that was almost as bad as those face-brands that had started in Los Angeles.

"Let go of me," I said, trying not to wince at the burning needles in my side.

"Answer the question, asshole," he said, his grip tightening.

"Look at my face, trench-head." I pushed him back, but his grip remained locked tight. "What do you think?"

"I think you're the one who killed Wolfrik and the others!"

He took a swing at me, and I ducked, cradling the dark matter camera like a boxer might protect his head from incoming injury.

My head was rattled. I remembered slamming into the wall, my face numb and tingling. And then Clarence stepped in like a battering ram and knocked head-trench sliding on the floor.

"Are you okay?" Clarence asked.

"Where the fuck were you?"

"Shower and breakfast, I can't protect your sorry ass at all hours of the day."

Head-trench got up, holding his shoulder. "You watch your back, Leon, because sooner or later your muscle isn't going to be there to protect you."

"Next time bring an angry mob." I held up the dark matter camera and took a snapshot of my attacker as he fled from Clarence. "And pitchforks!"

Clarence was about to dart after him, but I grabbed his arm and shook my head. "Don't."

"He needs to be punished for assaulting—"

"He's just ignorant of what's really going on," I said. "Honestly, if I was him, I'd want to punch my face too."

103

Clarence smiled. "You probably shouldn't have egged him on."

"Eh." I shrugged. "People say I shouldn't do a lot of things."

"What are you doing out here anyway?" Clarence asked. "I thought I left you back at your dorm."

"Yeah, well, I needed to get to work."

"You should have waited for me."

"And miss you swooping in like some nineties pro wrestler all hopped up on smack?"

He slapped me on the back; I winced. "Rick James!"

"I don't think Rick James was a wrestler."

"Then who the fuck is Rick James?"

"A musician, I think."

"Oh, then who was a popular wrestler back then?"

"I don't know, do I look like an expert on dead forms of entertainment?"

"No, but you're an expert on finding new ways to get yourself killed."

"Ha. Ha." The image rendered, but I decided I needed to get the ball rolling and head to Emma's office. I tucked the camera back in my bag. "I need you to get me to Emma Williams' office without any more angry villagers trying to eviscerate me. Think you can handle that?"

Clarence nodded, his moment of levity passed, and a familiar scowl stretched across his face as if he'd momentarily lapsed out of business mode.

We walked down the corridor, and for some reason, I couldn't keep my mouth from running. "Why'd you come to Olympus One, Clarence?"

He was quiet for a little while, like he was processing how best to answer the question.

"My son goes here," Clarence said. "He's a freshman, and I didn't like the idea of me being stuck on Earth while he was all the way out here."

"Were you a cop on Earth?"

He nodded. "I was also fifty pounds heavier. I miss pizza."

"No way."

"I passed the psych evaluation and the first round of physical testing, but they said I had to lose the extra weight to come here, so I did."

"Just like that?"

"No, it was hard. I spent every day with a personal trainer before I hit my beat. Somehow, I made it to my goal before they hired everyone they needed. It's good too, because we don't really spend money when we're up here, so my son will have a nice little nest egg when he gets back, something to pay down those student loans."

"Yikes, I think I'd rather die out here than have to pay those back."

His eyes drifted to my injured side. "Careful what you wish for."

My stab wound ached; I eased it with pressure from my hand. "Yeah…"

I barged into Emma's office. This time the officer standing guard didn't bother acknowledging me. Clarence waited outside, made small talk with the guard. Emma was on a treadmill she'd set up next to her desk—sweat stains soaking her coveralls—when I walked through the door.

"You're up," Emma said.

"I am, nice to see that everyone's surprised by that fact."

She took a hard look at my face, stopped the treadmill and got off. She'd put pictures of her family up on the walls, except for a blank area on the wall to my left; more pictures and awards were in boxes waiting to go up. The box of Wolfrik's things was gone. "Your face looks red."

"That's because someone used it as a punching bag."

"Where was Clarence?"

"Shower and breakfast he said."

"I'll have to talk to him about that."

"It's not a problem, I was the one that left my dorm."

She took a seat at her terminal. "So, what do you need?"

"What I requested before. Anyone who can follow directions and has a background in quantum physics. Before I got stabbed, I modified one of the security cameras with parts from the other prototype dark matter cameras. I think I can do the same for the others, but I can't do it alone."

"You have blueprints, I presume?"

105

"What do you take me for here?"

She rolled her eyes; I was stunned by how beautiful that made her look. "Well, I've been looking, but it's taking longer than I expected. I have to screen each potential team member to make sure none of them want to see you dead."

"Not that I'd blame them."

"Stop that," she threatened with her index finger, I almost ducked. "That morbid attitude you have going isn't helping anyone. You know how many people there are who have invented things that got people killed throughout history? Imagine what it must have been like to be a member of the Manhattan Project after Hiroshima."

"I am become death. The thought has crossed my mind."

"But, you're not the destroyer of worlds."

"No. Not yet."

"And not ever, if you can manage to get a handle on this situation." She shook her head. "Imagine if you were able to make contact with these beings, bridge the gap of communication and culture between the organic and the non-physical. Your name would go down in history as the first person to ever make contact with an alien species."

"Excuse me, but that doesn't fix the fact that people have died, and I'm not going to pretend otherwise. Gila died—she tried to befriend me with a salad and it got her killed. She didn't deserve that. Wolfrik gave my theories the benefit of the doubt, same result. He had a son back on Earth and I have to live with the fact that it's my fault his last memory of his father will be of seeing his body split in half while he held his wineglass with a firm death grip. And Adams wasn't even my friend. He was ordered by campus police and Wolfrik to guard my dorm, to keep me hostage. He was just doing his job. And now he's dead too."

"And yet, any one of them could have died from any manner of freak accident here." She leaned back in her chair and flicked her wrist and palm from her screen to the wall. The wall lit up with a still image of a student in the middle of somersaulting off of a classroom desk into a row of stairs. "Take this *genius*. He decided it would be smart to leap off of the desks to test out how far he could jump in Mars' gravity. He was lucky to only break his arm." She switched to a video of someone moving a supply crate with a forklift, the forklift veered off to the side and ripped a hole in part of the hangar wall. "And this idiot almost tore right through the wall, a centimeter more and most of that hangar would have imploded, which would have been a bloody mess."

"But those people didn't die."

"Yeah, but Connor Wilson did, and he just walked off in a random direction, never to be heard from again. Are you going to shoulder the guilt for his death too?"

"No, because I didn't cause it."

"Did you cut open Gila or Adams' throats?"

"No."

"Did you cut Wolfrik in half?"

"No."

"Then shut up."

"I can see this conversation is going nowhere."

"Then get back to work, and I'll get you your team as soon as possible."

I turned for the door, but hesitated. "What happens if these things know what they're doing to us? How does my name go down in history then?"

"That's the risk we take as scientists. If you can't handle it, maybe you're not cut out for this."

"Thought you'd say that."

The door opened, and Clarence and I walked back to the Security room where Lizeth and the others were waiting.

6

I was asleep on the couch when they buzzed my intercom. A smart person would have asked them questions. I had a death wish, so I opened the door.

The four of them filed into my messy living room. One African girl with dreadlocks and an Armada tattoo like Gila's on the back of her neck. She had augmented yellow eyes, and they were piercing in their contempt for me. A skinny, pale boy with short, spiked hair. A Caucasian man with an afro. There was a crucifix around his neck, and he smiled, avoiding direct eye contact with me. And a four-foot-nothing Asian girl that reminded me too much of Akio for me to feel anything more than guilt when looking at her sneering face. One thing was certain, none of them wanted to be here.

"Wow, what a very big mess." The African girl paced my living room, swiping one of her fingers over my coffee table, blowing the dust off of her fingertip. "How do you live like this?"

"Very carefully," I said. "Are you the team Emma said she'd assemble for me?"

The pale boy nodded. "Rumor is, you're at wits end."

The pale boy's voice was like an angel's, if angels existed. I was thankful that I hadn't called her a him out loud.

The African girl extended her hand. "I'm Abdalla."

I took her hand and shook it.

"I'm Hank," the pale girl said.

"Hank?" I asked.

"Hank." She nodded.

The Caucasian man with the afro saluted me. "Then call me Jenna."

"Is that your name?" The Asian girl asked.

He shook his head. "I just felt like being edgy."

"Just tell me your name before I actually start calling you Jenna," I said.

"Mike," he said. Mike palmed the crucifix, and his smile was beyond uncomfortable.

"Where'd you get Jenna from?" Abdalla said.

Mike shrugged.

My eyes drifted to the short Asian girl.

"Bao Liu," she said.

I nodded.

"I'm going to send you each some blueprints," I said. "The blueprints have a supply list attached. I need you to divide up the security cameras in the colony and modify them to my specifications."

"All of them?" Bao asked.

"As many as possible," I said.

"That won't be easy, considering the rarity of some of these parts." Abdalla thumbed through the specifications.

"Emma's given us full authority to gather what we need," I said. "If anyone gives you any trouble, let me know."

"There are stickies here that say that the renders take three hours to complete? Is that for every frame?" Abdalla looked up from her tablet, confused.

I nodded. "Yeah, but the footage isn't synced right now. The original OS was designed for still images, so having to keep up with the security footage being captured at sixty frames per second is causing it to lag a lot."

"Then, why not adjust the security cameras to function like cameras instead of making them film?" Bao said. "This way, you reduce the number of images captured significantly, but at least it won't take so long to see what happens."

"Man, this project is gonna piss my guild off," Abdalla said, rubbing her neck.

"No offense, but people have died because of these things, and we don't know why," I said. "I think that's slightly more important than some game."

"Yeah, Gila was a rival of mine, a friend." She flipped me off. "So, I think I know what the stakes are, asshole."

"We wouldn't be having this problem if you hadn't made the camera," Hank said. "So, I think Abdalla has every right to be irritated. Technically, you interrupted the flow of our lives, our studies, with this shit. I have to go to lunch today and tell my boyfriend why I'm working with someone he thinks might be a murderer."

"Sorry," I said. "I didn't think—"

"We're not your friends," Hank said. "We didn't want to do this and we didn't want to work with you. Not with your reputation. But, since people are dying, and Emma believes your story, she made it worth it for us to participate."

"How so?" I asked.

"None of your business," Abdalla said, crossing her arms.

"I think we've outlived our welcome," Mike said, turning for the door.

They each filed out into the corridor. The door hissed shut.

I missed Akio. Where was she staying?

It wasn't my business anymore.

7

With my mandatory nap done, I brewed a pot of coffee, poured it into a thermos, and returned to the Security room to continue my work.

Clarence was sitting in his chair, playing on his tablet. He was humming the melody from that new ACOS song. I didn't care much for the song; it was a depressing guitar-driven piece about the life and death of a mentor. Frankly, I was surprised that it was so popular, considering the current climate of the music scene. Guitar-driven, melodic musical pieces were a bit archaic in today's atmosphere of super distortion and instantly gratified mental projection. I sat down at the main computer terminal and set my coffee down next to me. The hummed melody, combined with the bad acoustics of the room, made Clarence seem a lot farther away from me than he really was.

The dark matter camera was still sitting in my bag as I pored over the security feeds. I considered making the modifications to the cameras that Bao had suggested. I couldn't lie, though, it did hurt my ego a little bit that I hadn't thought of the solution first. It was an easy fix in the code and the security camera programming to alter how many images they captured.

And sure enough, that fixed the issue. Now the rendering time was down to the standard thirty seconds. I saw the feeds come in from the camera that I had modified first. The dark matter silhouettes around each student were as I had imaged them with the original camera.

They really did look like auras!

I dug the camera from my overnight bag and looked at the screen. The picture I'd taken earlier of the freshman who had attacked me was still up. Trench-head's "aura" of dark matter was vibrant, if a bit chaotic. My eyes tracked all over the image; my finger hovered over the button to turn to the previous image—

I stopped.

It was there, in the right-hand corner of the screen. A mantis shape. It appeared to be lurching after the freshman.

I shot out of my chair, my mouth hanging open like an idiot's.

"What is it?" Clarence's face contorted.

"Do you remember the freshman that attacked me in the corridor earlier?" I asked.

He nodded. "What of him?"

"We need to find out who he is. Now."

"Is he in danger?" He paused. "Are you in danger?"

"He's in danger. I think he's the next victim."

Clarence tapped a finger to his ear. "Emma. This is Clarence. We need a wellness check performed on a freshmen with a reverse Mohawk shaved into his head."

"Tell her I've got an image of him on the dark matter camera."

He held up his finger. "Is that right?"

"Don't shush me, Clarence, tell me what's going on!"

"When?" The color seemed to drain from his face. "Yeah. I'll tell him."

Clarence's hand fell to his side.

"What happened?" I asked.

"Your *friend* is dead."

My heart raced. Pressure filled my ears like a balloon that was about to pop. "Akio?"

He shook his head; my blood pressure fell. "The kid that attacked you. His roommate found him in his quarters, his head cleaved in two, resting on his bed."

"Jesus fucking Christ." I sat down, held my head. "I was too late."

"Emma said there'll be an assembly tomorrow, and that you can't let this distract you from your job."

In my anger, I was about to say something sarcastic, but I stopped myself. I sat back down.

"I know that, damn it," I said.

"Then prove it and get your ass back to work."

He was right. Moping about the death of someone whose only connection to me was their attempt to pound my face in was pointless, but it didn't change how guilty I felt. It'd be a strange coincidence if the dark matter creature targeted that freshman at random, and so far, it seemed like it was anything but random.

Somehow, it was connected to me. I stared back down at the image. But, what was the connection? Were they protecting me from perceived threats? No. That didn't make any sense. If they were somehow connected to my thoughts on individuals, why would Gila have been targeted?

Then, my eyes traced the outline of the freshman's chaotic aura.

I dug out my tablet and scrolled all the way back to the test panorama. Looking at the picture, specifically at the dark matter concentrations around myself and Akio, there was one clear difference between myself and the freshman who had just been murdered.

The concentration around me was muted, washed out. His was vibrant, bright.

Like Akio's.

VIII

I elected not to show my face at the memorial assembly for Davin Pace, whom I'd referred to as trench-head only days ago in a crowded corridor after he'd attempted to pound my face in. Emma thought that it would be far too risky with one assault and one attempt on my life already. That didn't bother me so much.

I welcomed another attempt.

As for the ceremony, I could look it up later if I wanted to make myself feel more guilty than I already did. I would have already done so if I wasn't so busy. Small comforts.

Like Adams, there was no security video of Davin's death. As far as we knew, it had happened when he was in his dorm room. As much as my nightmares didn't need more ammunition, not being able to see the event didn't help matters. Even Emma had her doubts, with half of the deaths having been unobserved.

It's standard practice for the scene of any death at a Milkyway Unlimited–owned site to be photographed with a forensics camera for later review by the authorities on Earth. I had little doubt that the deaths were caused by the mantis creatures, but I needed to see the crime scene images for myself. Maybe there was some clue in them that would shed light on how they were killing us?

My dorm room would have been lonely if it wasn't for Clarence's constant presence. Clarence was sitting on one of the stools at the kitchen counter, reading his tablet and drinking from a reusable water bottle.

I brought up the crime scene photos for both Davin's and Adams' deaths and projected them on the wall, then turned the lights off. Clarence glanced up at the images once, and went right back to reading on his tablet.

I had the images of Davin's body lined up with the ones of Adams' body. I approached the wall, zooming in on the wounds by sliding my fingers over both images. Davin's head was taken off of his shoulders. The decapitation was clean. He likely didn't even realize what was happening until it was too late. But, Adams' throat had been sliced open, much the same as Gila's. He had likely bled out, clutching at his throat…just like Gila.

"You're gonna lose it if you keep staring at those," Clarence said.

"It can't be helped," I said. "The common fear on campus is that there's a serial killer loose, and a lot of them seem to think I'm as good a suspect as any."

"And you're looking for evidence to show otherwise?" Clarence grunted.

I nodded. "The proof is in the wounds."

Clarence looked at the photos I'd zoomed into on the wall-projection. "I don't get it, they both look like they were made with an industrial cutter."

"Except that there's no cauterization. They're too clean to be made with any kind of bladed instrument so…"

Clarence stood up. His demeanor changed. He held his hands behind his back and approached the images. He must have done that a thousand times when he was a cop. "Are these taken with the standard forensics camera?"

I nodded. "I think so."

"Can you zoom in up to the cellular level?"

I nodded, zooming all the way up so we could see how the skin cells had been divided or damaged. The luminescent forms of each cell reminded me of the dark matter web. That alone set my nerves off, caused tears to threaten to spring loose from my eyelids.

The orange, luminescent skin cells for both wounds were divided completely evenly. Even the cellular walls between skin cells hadn't been disturbed.

114

The room felt colder for some reason.

"That isn't possible," Clarence said.

"And yet it is," I said.

"Don't be an ass."

"You could explain why this is impossible, then, *Mr. Former Cop*."

He inclined his head, his expression seeming to say, *Very well*. "A knife wouldn't create a clean separation in these cells. It shouldn't be like this. The blade cuts some cells, pushes others around."

"Kind of like a bulldozer?"

He nodded. "Sort of. I've seen a lot of these. Detectives left them on their screens and tablets sometimes, watched a few for the fuck of it, morbid curiosity, you know?" I shook my head at him. "Anyway, the knife cuts the skin as much as it pushes into the body. Each layer of skin cells would have been affected, if the murder weapon was something a student would be able to get access to."

"And these divisions are exactly even," I said, nodding. "As if something pulled them apart at the seams, like opening a doorway."

We both looked at each other, as if the same shiver had passed through our bodies.

I cut the projection off. "I need to get to the Security room, get the ball rolling on today's tasks for the others."

He nodded, and followed me out into the empty corridor when I was ready. It was odd seeing the corridors so empty at this hour of the day. There were usually at least three people going to and from classes, or visiting friends or lovers at any hour. Hell, even in the middle of the night. The colony rarely ever slept.

Now, I could almost feel the tension permeating the air, clinging to the twisting tubes above, the constant rattle of atmospheric pressure that carried air from one part of the colony to the next.

I could tell that others felt the same way too. I'd stayed up late last night watching the feeds from cameras, watching passing students and their auras mix with each other. Their body language said everything. Shifting eyes that said, "Is someone watching me?" Hunched backs that said, "Please don't notice me." Hands in pockets that betrayed nervousness. The slight discomfort between acquaintances in conversation. I'd seen at least three sets of images of different students

115

and Milkyway Unlimited employees engaged in conversation, and it seemed like there was a unifying thing in common.

Fear.

And I know what fear looks like. I'd seen it in my mother's eyes every morning and every night before my father walked into the room.

I put out a call to Abdalla, Hank, Mike, and Bao to meet me in Security. They hadn't answered my PM's, but I'd figured they were still in the assembly.

The team and I managed to get fifteen percent of the cameras upgraded to the new design. I spent the next few days watching still images come in from each of the feeds, looking for any hint of who the next victim might be, but so far, all I'd seen was the collective discomfort Olympus One seemed to be in.

I studied the images for clues in the absence of the mantis silhouettes. But, they could show up at any moment.

There were scattered images of those familiar animal shapes, playing out that same diorama. It was strange seeing them overlaying the passing students and angular corridors of Olympus One.

There was a blind spot in our network, and it was starting to worry me. There were only so many feeds I, or anyone else, could track at the same time. The closer we got to one hundred percent conversion of the cameras, the bigger that blind spot got. Even with Lizeth and the other Security staff helping, there was no way to track everything going on. That meant that sooner or later, another Davin Pace, another Gila Amos, another Alexander Wolfrik, and another Breac Adams, was inevitable.

Clarence and I entered the Security room. Its blue metal walls, black plastic floors and glowing myriad of screens were not a welcome change to the comfortable clutter of my dorm room. He took his usual spot, ignoring Lizeth and the others, and I took mine. The security room was always several degrees colder than the rest of Olympus One, as if we were all placed directly beneath an air duct. Lizeth smiled at me as I sat down. If she were a few years younger…no. Eddie and Jaidon kept their distance from me, but did their jobs well enough. Looking at the back of Eddie's balding scalp got me thinking about what he'd asked me.

Why haven't the creatures attacked you yet?

My mouth hung open like I was about to tell him something, but I said nothing. He didn't seem to notice.

I had a theory, but I wasn't ready to show it yet. Maybe soon I could answer his question?

Something caught my eye on the security feed.

I saw Akio walking through the corridor in Engineering. My hand immediately went to change to another camera—but I hesitated. Her walk was different now. Still dainty, like a prissy house cat, but also full of anger, missing some of that familiar grace.

I was the cause of this change in her.

The camera I was using had not been modified yet, so I couldn't see if the concentration of dark matter around her had changed.

Akio stopped in a familiar spot, crossing her arms and tapping her foot as she impatiently looked at her tablet for the time.

She mouthed something.

I shook my head. I didn't want to see what was about to happen. I hadn't touched the stuff since our fight. A vow, spoken only through action.

Sure enough, Dane showed up. He was looking more fucked-up than usual. Dark circles rotted away beneath his bloodshot eyes. It was surprising that the Admins would allow him to continue working in such a state, especially in Engineering.

Dane extended his hand, Akio extended hers. He gave her a crooked grin. They exchanged some words; the traditional pact made between Dane and one of his customers. What favor would he have you do, Akio? Dane caressed the side of Akio's face; her chest rose and fell, and she rolled her eyes. My face flushed with warmth.

I felt like a voyeur. She'd be furious with me if she knew I was watching. This was none of my business.

Dane walked around the corner, disappeared in the utility room, and Akio followed him inside. The door shut behind him. I imagined him reaching into that access panel to his hidden stash, dragging out a bottle and placing it in Akio's shaking hands.

They emerged a moment later. Akio's bag looked slightly bulkier.

She'd just given me a lecture on drinking that shit before graduation. I had to resist the urge to confront her. I had a job to do.

I changed feeds just as the doors hissed open behind me.

Hank walked in first, sporting a glare on her face. Bao and Abdalla filed in with similar expressions. I expected that reaction from the three of them. It was Mike's that unnerved me. He was smiling, always smiling.

"Thanks for coming," I said, turning around in my chair. "I know it can't be easy after what just happened."

"Don't," Hank said. "You don't get to do that."

"Do what?"

"Try to pretend that you care about what happened to Davin."

I wrung my hands together.

"Look, he's getting mad," Abdalla said. "Better watch out, Hank. You might be next."

I stood up. "That's enough!"

Each of them, save for Mike, flinched at my outburst. Silence filled the room. Lizeth and the others were at attention now too.

"You might not believe in what's going on here," I said. "But the evidence is there, and that's all that fucking matters. Say what you want about me behind my back, but when I call you here, I'm the project leader and I'm trying to stop this from causing any more people like Davin to lose their lives.

"I am tortured every god damned night"—Mike's face twisted into a grimace—"by the faces of those that have died because of my research, my invention. I already blame myself for this, and I don't need your shit too."

I shook my head. "But, I suppose you need some kind of tangible proof, right?"

I saw mixed expressions on each of their faces. I took out my tablet and brought up the crime scene images of Davin and Adams, projected them on the wall.

"Turn and face the images," I said.

"What are you trying to prove here?" Mike asked.

"These were taken using a sophisticated forensics camera, capable of zooming in up to the cellular level."

I zoomed in to each of the wounds, as I had earlier. "Clarence could tell you, based on his experience as a police officer, that the damage to these cells isn't normal. The cells have been divided evenly, which is essentially impossible."

Bao approached the wall. She ran her hands along one of the cellular walls. "Why aren't the cells reproducing?"

"Huh?"

"These photos were taken postmortem. The skin cells in question should have had time to reproduce. Whatever made these wounds, it must have completely shut down the surrounding cells from being able to receive electrical impulses from the brain, or other parts of the body." She pointed to a point where the skin cells weren't damaged on the surface of Davin's neck. "See, here, the skin cells are bunched up, replicating, but here they're completely dead. The life's been sucked out of them."

"Well, fuck, *that's* not creepy at all," Abdalla said.

"You never said you had a background in cellular biology," I said.

"You never asked," Bao said.

"Well, in any case, it proves my point," I said. "The fact is, there's nothing I could have used to cause those wounds. There are crime-scene photos of Wolfrik and Gila as well that will likely show the same."

Abdalla's bold golden eyes glared daggers at me; she crossed her arms.

"And with that said"—I pointed to the door—"get your asses out there and convert some fucking cameras before I do it myself. Because I will. And I don't care if someone walks up behind me and slits my throat as I'm doing it."

For a moment, they just glanced at each other. After a second that seemed to last for an eternity, they nodded, and everyone besides Mike left. The doors closed.

Mike's smile returned.

"What's so funny?" I asked.

"You were raised Catholic, weren't you?" Mike said.

My eyes narrowed. "Don't go there."

His eyes opened wide for a moment. "You haven't thought about it at all, have you?"

"About what?" I crossed my arms; my finger nails stabbed into my flesh.

"That all of this might be divine punishment."

"I don't believe in divine punishment."

"But *I do*."

My eyes focused on the silver crucifix hanging from his neck; its very presence seemed like an affront to everything that we had accomplished on Mars. "Give me a break. A quantum physics major who's also a believer? That's ironic."

"Is it?" He chuckled. "As I see it, our discoveries in quantum physics do not disprove the Lord's existence, but reaffirm his truth."

"I don't believe in—"

"And that's your problem, but don't worry, I'm not going to try to reawaken your shattered faith. No. But, consider this for a moment, Hal." He cleared his throat. "What if your invention is peering at something that we shouldn't see? What if it is the hand of God almighty that you have stolen a glimpse at?"

"I'm sure if that fairytale were true, all our water would turn to wine and burning bushes would sprout from every sandy hill on Mars."

"Sarcasm, how cute. Consider what I've said. Maybe we're being punished for your sins?"

"Get the fuck out of my face and get to work."

He nodded, held his hands behind his back, and walked out.

Lizeth glared at me. I rolled my eyes and took a seat at my terminal again.

"What?" I asked.

"Do you really look down on others because of their religion?" she asked.

I sighed. "Can we just get back to work?"

She shook her head, turning around in her chair. "No. I'm really curious."

I shrugged. "It's complicated."

"No, it's not."

I rubbed my eyes. "But, it is. Just drop it, okay?"

"And why should I do that? You realize that bigotry goes both ways, right?"

"Yes, well, history kind of shows who does the most damage, and it's rarely ever scientists who go building concentration camps and committing genocide, is it?"

"So, you haven't thought about it at all?"

"Are you religious or something, is that why you're giving me shit?"

"No. I'm not. I just don't think you should belittle people just because of their beliefs."

"Whatever, let's just get back to work."

She scoffed, turned back toward her screen, and started rambling off curse words in Spanish. I stood up and slung my pack over my shoulder.

"I'm gonna grab some air."

"Whatever."

I headed for the door and didn't look back.

I didn't know why she was defending that jackass.

The corridors were slightly less empty now that the assembly had let out.

Clarence filed in behind me, said nothing.

I saw a man exchanging tense words with his girlfriend. They stopped and looked at me. Hunched backs, shifting eyes. Fear twisting their mouths into downcast frowns.

Was it me they feared? My brain said yes, but my body said it was everything.

We reached my dorm. I set my bag down and took a seat on the couch.

"When you said you needed some air, I figured you didn't mean the same air that shares your empty food containers and unwashed jumpsuits," Clarence said.

"I need to do something without prying eyes." I took my tablet out, started browsing profiles.

"I don't count?"

"You don't count."

He nodded. "What are you looking for anyway?"

"Looking up our friend Mike, gonna try to learn more about him."

"And why would you want to do that?"

"Learn what I'm dealing with."

"Isn't that a little…"

"What?"

"Creepy?"

"You're the cop, you tell me."

He shrugged.

I grabbed Mike's name from the list that Emma forwarded to my inbox before sending them over. Something I'd discovered *after* they'd knocked on my door. Mike Smith. His profile was surprisingly empty. Just a birth date.

No country of origin.

No other schools, high school or otherwise, listed. That got me feeling suspicious. My profile listed my residence on Earth, my birth date, and each of the schools I'd graduated from.

I decided to hack his inbox. Once I was inside, I saw that he had several recent messages from his mother. I opened one.

Message Detail: Re: Be Careful: 6/1/2045

Do you know these other students she's putting you with? Be careful, Mikey. I worry about you so much being so far away.

I wasn't sure what that meant. I opened the next message in the thread.

Message Detail: Re: Be Careful: 6/1/2045

Nothing to worry about, mother. I doubt anyone suspects. We were very careful in the enrollment process, and Milkyway Unlimited doesn't disclose that kind of information.

What wouldn't we suspect?

I kept reading. There seemed to be missing messages, going further back in the thread. He was likely deleting anything that had sensitive information in it. Maybe he'd known I'd hack into his inbox and snoop around?

There didn't seem to be anything else useful in his inbox, so I backed out and opened up one of the camera feeds.

"You look disappointed," Clarence said.

"I am."

"Didn't find what you were looking for?"

"Nothing useful. No country of origin, nothing. Most of his messages were deleted as well. But, it's odd." I stretched out on the couch, staring at the ceiling. "Something's bothering me about the few messages that I did read."

"Think he's hiding something?"

"Yeah. I do. I just wish I knew what."

"Might be nothing."

I looked at Clarence's disheveled blond hair; his eyes were bloodshot with fatigue. "You wouldn't be able find out where he's from, would you?"

Clarence shrugged. "Maybe. We're usually here to keep the peace, glorified hall monitors most of the time. Until all this shit, that is."

"Yeah…"

"I'll see what I can find out." Clarence stood up, headed for the door. "You going to stay here awhile?"

I nodded.

"Don't get yourself in any trouble while I'm gone."

"Sure thing. Think I'll take a nap."

"It's barely even noon."

"Time is irrelevant in space."

"You're not in space, you're on a Mars colony."

"My senses can't tell a difference if I can't see the sky."

"Point taken." The door opened.

"Let me know what you find out."

He nodded, then disappeared. The door closed, and I rolled over on my side to take a brief nap. Only, I couldn't stop thinking about Mike.

I sat up. My stomach growled.

When was the last time I had eaten? I couldn't remember. I walked over to the fridge, opened it, and a quick glance at my rations told me that Akio had taken half the remaining ration packets when she moved out. I grabbed one and sat back down on the couch.

I read the label on the ration packet. My heart sank. I'd grabbed a beefsteak.

I tossed the packet onto the coffee table. I wasn't hungry anymore.

2

Unable to sleep or eat, I retreated to the Security room and grabbed a coffee. I watched the video feeds as I shifted positions in the room, from chair to chair, to the floor, to the cot that Clarence sometimes used when he was watching over me. The coffee only made my restlessness worse.

So far the team and I had managed to get the conversion process up to thirty percent. I had eyes on the dark matter web in every sector of Olympus One now. Yet, I was still blind.

While I switched from feed to feed, I found myself distracted by the animal-like forms in the dark matter web. I found myself wondering about their story once again. They were scattered throughout various parts of Olympus One's corridors, not even close to the display recorded by the original camera at the caldera. The few animal forms I saw bled through the walls, cradling what appeared to be their young as they looked to the sky at their doom while oblivious students walked right through their forms. It made me wonder if the camera would be able to see these things all over the planet.

Were the mantis silhouettes connected in some way to them?

It was fortunate that the two types of silhouettes were so vastly different. As long as I paid attention, I'd be able to tell when a form was recorded, and when it was acting on its own. Hopefully.

The intermixed mess of recorded animals versus human forms with dark matter auras surrounding them was enough to give me a headache.

But, I couldn't look away. Not if I was going to stop the next murder from happening.

Then I saw her. Akio's hair was a mess. She sported dark circles beneath her bloodshot eyes and coveralls that looked like they hadn't been cleaned in days. She was buying another bottle of moonshine from Dane. The once-bright concentration of dark matter around her body had dimmed considerably. Now, it resembled mine in that original test panorama. Dane's aura was brighter, but not as bright as some of the others I'd seen.

I felt flames dance at my shoulders. She was spiraling and it was my fault. She was becoming *me*.

I'd sworn I wouldn't get involved…and yet I found myself power-walking out of the Security room and down the corridor all the same. I had to stop this.

Bands of tensions wrapped tight around my heart when I saw her. She almost didn't see me.

"Akio," I said. "Stop."

Her face twisted into a vicious scowl at the sound of my voice, her shoulders raised up, and she clutched at the bottle in her hands. "What the fuck do you want, Hal?"

"You've been hitting that bottle a lot?"

"So?" She shook her head, I could smell it on her from here. "As I recall, you drank every night."

"You're drunk already? How many of those have you had?"

She shrugged. "Like it's any of your business."

"What I did and what I said were terrible." I tried to close the distance. "I know that. But, I can't just stand by and watch you self-destruct like this."

"Funny, I remember saying the same damn thing to you." She cackled. "Now you're an even bigger contradiction."

"Akio, get help."

"Like you did?" She shook her head, wagging her finger at me. "No way, *Geraldo*. You don't get to tell me what to do."

"Don't call me that."

"What? Geraldo?" A grin twisted across her face, distorting the lines of running mascara that ran down her cheeks. "That is your real name, isn't it?"

Now she was closing the gap. She stood in front of me, poking her finger into my solar plexus.

"So, what is it?" she said. "Why so down on your culture? New America is gone, man. Are you so damn desperate to be a white man that you're willing to bend over and get fucked by the American dream too?"

"You know that's not it. We've had this conversation."

"Oh, yeah. I remember all right. I remember. Your daddy was a piece of shit, right? And so you act like a piece of shit so you don't have to be held accountable for your actions."

"No."

She cupped her mouth and lurched forward, vomiting all over my shirt.

"I think I'm maybe gonna be sick," she said, clutching her stomach and kneeling on the floor.

"I'll get you to the nurse." I picked her up and slung her over my shoulder. The fight had gone out of her, it seemed.

She was still rambling. Passing students gave us odd looks as we made our way to the Sickbay. Each step made the wound in my side throb, but I shouldered on. If I'd been in Earth gravity, I was certain that lifting Akio would have been an impossible task.

"I gave you everything," she said. "But you never noticed. Why? Is it because I'm ugly?"

"No, you know why, Akio."

"Oh, right, cause you're a c—" she held back another wave of vomit—"coward."

"I was." I sighed. "I am. But, what's done is done."

"You missed out, buddy boy!" She was shouting a little too loud now. "I woulda fucked your brains out!"

The color drained out of my face.

"I'm sure you would have," I said quietly.

"I wanna know what it's like to fuck in no gravity."

Thankfully, we arrived at the Sickbay. I crossed through the glass sliding doors. The nurse on duty gave me a strange look. This time of night there was only a skeleton crew on duty, just in case of an emergency. There were plenty of students, as well as staff and workers, who kept odd hours.

"She needs a detox and a stern lecture," I said.

The nurse rolled her eyes and waved me on in. "That fucking twat Dane and his moonshine."

"The very same," I said.

I followed the nurse into a hospital room. She directed me to lay Akio in the bed.

"Honestly, I don't know how they haven't caught him yet," the nurse said.

"His customers are probably very loyal. They keep his secrets."

"Well, they shouldn't." The nurse took Akio's temperature, hooked her up to an IV. "I've got it from here, Mr. Leon, so…"

I nodded. Even she knew who I was. I turned to leave.

"Leon?"

I stopped. "Yeah?"

"What they're saying about you—" Her voice trembled; I watched her eyes drift to Akio. "—is it true?"

"Which rumor? The one where I killed Gila, Wolfrik and Adams, or that I'm insane, just like my mother?"

"The first one."

"It's much worse." I rubbed my temples. "I discovered something terrible in the dark matter web. And now I'm not sure I can stop it."

She was speechless. I knew how strange I sounded, how crazy she must have thought I was. I left before I made things even more awkward.

I was in luck. My shower day was today. I'd been in the Security room, watching the feeds, for so long that I'd completely forgotten about it. I went home and let the hot water scald my skin, burning my fears and my self-loathing away, albeit only temporarily.

I thought about Dane. I'd gotten along with him fine before all of this started. I'd known he was kind of a creep, but that hadn't stopped me from taking his moonshine.

The way she looked.

It was true that it was partly my fault, but…

I felt something overpower my fatigue, my anguish, like a roaring fire lit in the core of my gut. I gritted my teeth.

I was going to have a talk with Dane.

Once I was dressed, I grabbed my overnight bag and filled it with a couple of pillows, then headed over to Engineering. That fire that I'd felt while in the shower burned even hotter. The more I thought about him, the more I wanted to break his face.

Dane wasn't at his post. That meant he was probably in his quarters. I'd only been there a handful of times. Dane didn't like to be disturbed where he made his poison.

I found myself in front of his door and buzzed the intercom.

"Is that you, Leon?" he said. "Fuck, man, you know better than to come here. What if someone sees? If you need a bottle, just come back tomorrow, I'm closed for the night, man."

"Is that so?" I held up my overnight bag to the tiny camera in the comm, gave him my best smile. "Because I brought you a present."

"Damn, you shoulda led with that, man. Give me a second."

Shuffling sounds echoed over the comm. The door opened. Dane's bloodshot eyes were naked in their shock as I tossed my overnight bag into his chest and punched him in the face.

He hit the floor, holding his nose. I shook my stinging knuckles out and stood over him.

"What in the fuck was that for, Hal?" he said.

"Stop selling to Akio Sato," I said.

"The Asian chick with the incredible ass?" He chuckled. "Man, you should have seen what she did for that first bottle. I didn't think she had it in her."

"Had *what* in her?" My head started to swim. The floor was crawling, and the hair rose on the back of my neck.

"I told her to be in my centerfold, man." He laughed again, sitting up. "I got pictures and everything. Gave her my strongest recipe."

My fists clenched; I felt my teeth cracking as I gnashed them together.

"She has a great rack for a petite little—"

I kicked him in the mouth. He spat a tooth out and tackled me. My adrenaline was running so hot, I barely noticed the pain in my side at all. I blocked his first punch, but he nailed me in the face with the second. I'd never been in a real fight in my life, but something had snapped inside me. I caught his third punch and slapped his ear as hard as I could. He screeched, lurching to the side. I rolled him over and locked my arms around his throat in a choke hold.

"You know about the rumors, right?" I whispered in his good ear.

"You didn't kill those people," he said.

"Are you so sure?"

"You?" I tightened my sleeper hold on him; he coughed, tapping my skinny arm to ease up. "Fine, fine, I believe you."

"Even if they aren't true, this is. I will beat you bloody and flush you out the airlock if I ever see you selling to Akio again. She's off-limits, do you understand?"

"You wouldn't, they'd catch you, they'd—"

"I'll hack the logs so it looks like you went on walkabout like Connor Wilson, you stupid fuck. They still haven't found his body, do you honestly think they'll find yours?"

He was quiet for a moment. His eyes darted one way or another.

"Fine, I won't sell to her."

"Good. Then we have an understanding."

I let him go and stood up. My side started hurting again.

I heard footsteps in the kitchen. "Do you have company?"

"What?" He shook his head, pushing himself up off the floor on all fours. "No. Man, you really have lost it."

Something wasn't right.

I felt something like static pass off to my right. Then, there was a pressure in the air.

One of them was here.

"Dane, run!"

His head turned to me, his mouth agape.

At first it was like someone had drafted a straight line all the way down to his crotch; his skin sank inward, his lips curled, tongue splitting in two as he attempted one last scream. Then, blood began to ooze from that perfect dividing line in the center of his body. His eyes rolled back into his head as his body split in two, like a cell undergoing mitosis. Brain and muscle fibers stretched and collapsed as each half of Dane went in opposite directions.

Like opening a doorway.

A pool of blood gushed out in all directions around Dane's collapsed body. I tasted iron on the tip of my tongue. I fell to the floor on all fours. I was in shock, half conscious of what I was about to do.

My grip on reality shattered. I could almost see the silhouette of the mantis form assaulting, cutting at reality as it had in my nightmare.

129

My fingers writhed at my face as I sobbed, muttering nonsense into the aether. I could almost feel Dane's consciousness fade from the room.

I sat back up and thrust my arms up at the ceiling. "Come on, you stupid fuckers! I'm right here. Take me too!"

I felt a wall of static pass by me, and then it was gone.

I tried to walk away, but fell to my knees again. It was like the strength had been sucked right out of my legs. I remembered the footage from earlier. Dane's dark matter aura had been brighter than Akio's, brighter than mine. It killed me that that was all I could think of when he was in pieces, lying in front of me in a bloody dead mess.

"Take me too…" I whispered.

Minutes passed as I stared at the blood oozing from his split halves. I had to do something, I had to do something. My mind clawed its way back to something resembling sanity, if only temporarily. I grabbed at my tablet and called Emma.

This was going to look very bad.

IX

I stared blankly as the cleaning crew scrubbed away at the mess on Dane's dorm room floor. They wore masks; their eyes seemed disinterested with the bloody horror that rested at their feet. They placed the two severed halves of his body into thick black bags as if they were simply cleaning some mess left over from a chemical spill in one of the labs. The smell of bleach and chemicals burned my nostrils. They were sweeping Dane's blood down the drain when someone grabbed me by the arm and dragged me into the corridor. I was too lost in my own head to focus on the face of the person who dragged me out.

Was it my anger toward Dane that had caused this? Maybe my dark matter aura was a beacon for these creatures? A flash of emotion, and it pulsed, luring the creatures to it, like blood at the bottom of the ocean might bring a hungry shark to unsuspecting prey.

"I'm away for half a day, and you go and do something completely stupid." Only when he spoke did I realize that it was Clarence who'd dragged me from the room. "What were you thinking?"

Dane was guilty of making and distributing contraband, there was no doubt about that. The investigation that followed would show that. The cameras outside his room had been compromised, hacked by an invested party to play the same loop over and over again so prying eyes wouldn't guess that he was making contraband for students. Emma would know I wasn't a murderer—at least not in the traditional sense—but the general population of Olympus One would be hard-pressed to believe that, despite evidence to the contrary.

In my mind's eye, I kept seeing Dane's body split down the middle. His mouth agape, a thin line of blood oozing from a cut that was perfectly symmetrical with the rest of his body. And as his eyes separated with his two juxtaposed halves, blood gushed forth, pouring out into a puddle around his feet.

A fountain of death.

Why? the halves of his horrified expression asked. *Why would you do this to me?*

"Don't let this distract you," Clarence said.

But, how could I not? It was hard to ignore the connection each victim had to me. Would it be better to simply shut myself off from the rest of the colony? Would that solve the problem?

I think you should take that camera and flush yourself out an airlock. That'll probably solve it.

I had been piecing a theory together since Wolfrik's death, and now I was almost sure that I was right. The concentration of dark matter around me in the test panorama, and every other image after, was muted, dulled, while Davin's had been bright with youthful rage and a healthy hatred for the corporations that seemed to dominate our society. My theory was that my dark matter aura did indeed pulse like a beacon, but only briefly, possibly during an altercation, at the climax of an emotional high or a fit of rage.

That would lure them.

And what they would find when they arrived was a sea of burning candles. Once my emotional high was over, maybe they couldn't see me at all? Maybe that was why I was still alive?

The next several hours were a blur. I remembered Emma debriefing me about Dane's death. The remainder of his contraband stash had been confiscated and an assembly was set to mourn his passing. When I wasn't in the Security room, monitoring feeds, I lay awake for hours on the couch, staring at the ceiling as I saw him die over and over again in my head.

Flush yourself out an airlock.

I was tempted to. Perhaps that was the true answer to all of this? That my continued existence was what put this colony in danger.

Clarence and I were on our way back from the second or third trip to the Security room. My eyes burned with fatigue. I wasn't even sure what time it was. I was deliberately avoiding looking at my tablet.

I stopped at my dorm room door. Hesitated.

"What is it?" Clarence asked.

"I need some time to process this," I said.

"I won't get in your way—"

"I meant alone."

His eyes hardened as they studied me.

"Don't worry, I'm not going to leave my dorm."

"That's not what I'm concerned about."

"And I won't kill myself, either."

"Emma won't like it, not after what just happened."

"I'll take full responsibility."

He was quiet for a moment. I opened the door and stepped inside.

"Go home, Clarence. Please."

He nodded. "Fine."

I closed the door, and waited for him to leave, watching through the intercom's camera. I made my way out into the corridors and twisting hallways. The dim, blinking lights along the plastic floor guided me. Anyone who might have seen me wandering the halls might have said I was aimless, no destination in mind, but they'd be wrong.

I found myself standing in the same airlock that Akio and I'd used for our first walkabout with the dark matter camera. My hand hovered over the airlock control panel. It'd be so easy. It was what everyone wanted me to do.

I pressed the button. The first door opened to the airlock with a compressed hiss. I stepped inside, and the door hissed shut behind me. The sky was black and blanketed with stars. The floodlights outside lit the crimson dusty surface for several hundred feet until the night sky and a drifting view of Phobos turned the surface a dark navy blue.

All that separated me from a quick death was several inches of solid steel and transparent polymer developed to withstand anything short of a direct asteroid impact.

I caressed the release latch as a lover might caress the hand of their significant other. I gripped it. The metal was so cold, it was like grabbing solid ice.

It would be so easy.

I might even be saving her.

I remembered the first time I met Akio. My feet had ached from standing in line all day for the space elevator. She had been standing in front of me. I was perfectly content to stare into the clear blue sky all day, never sharing a word with another human being.

She wasn't having that.

Akio turned around and smiled at me. "I'm so fucking bored, I could amputate my left pinky and reattach it just to pass the time."

I was silent at first. Part of me was shocked that she'd started talking to me in the first place. Another part of me wondered if she'd stop talking if I didn't respond. She was a small thing, with soft skin the color of wet sand and brown eyes that were almost black against her whites. Her hair was styled like what you'd expect from David Bowie and an anime character's love child.

"Are you going to respond?" she asked, crossing her arms. "That's kind of rude."

"What should I say?" Damn it, now I was in a conversation. "Yes, it's boring standing in line all day. Small price to pay for seeing the Earth from low orbit."

She sighed. "Yeah, but I wish we could just take a rocket or something."

"This is safer."

"But boring."

"It is that."

She turned back around. I thought she was done, but about a minute later, she started shuffling her feet again and turned to face me once more.

"What are you majoring in?" she asked.

"Quantum Mechanics with a minor in Engineering," I said.

"Holy shit"—she slapped her forehead—"I'm majoring in those same things, except in reverse."

"You're mocking me."

"No." She blinked at me and tilted her head to the side. "Why would I be?"

I shrugged.

"We should room together."

"Do they have coed dorms?"

She slapped my arm. "What century are you living in? Of course, they do. Besides, it's not like we'll be fucking…" She grinned. "Unless you want to?"

"I've always been told not to screw your roommate until you're about to move out."

She laughed. "You do strike me as someone who colors inside the lines."

My eyes narrowed. "And what's that supposed to mean?"

"I don't know, guy, you just seem stiff, that's all."

"I'm an introvert who's being forced into talking to a stranger. It's also hotter than the Sun's corona today."

She extended her hand. "My name's Akio Sato."

I shook her hand. "Hal Leon."

"There."

"There what?"

"Now we're not strangers."

Tears broke from my eyes. My hand fell limp at my side. I was too much of a coward to do it. No matter how low I sank, no matter who died, I still couldn't kill myself. Even if it was for the greater good.

I stood there for a few minutes, staring at the horizon, hoping that I'd find the nerve, but I never did.

I sulked back into the corridor and retreated to the discomfort of the Security room's glowing screens and blue walls. It was empty. I sank into a chair and started poring over the security feeds. There were few actual shots of me, and certainly none that showed my dark matter aura doing anything other than looking like a dull, washed-out cloud.

I watched a group of boys, probably freshmen, talking outside one of the corridors. Their appearances were disheveled, backs slouched, eyes wary, their dark matter auras were muted. Dane's death would probably be the topic of conversation. Now there'd be no one to fuel their habits and on-campus frat parties. But, even if that was the conversation on the surface, the real subject would be, *who's next?*

At some point, I fell asleep at my console.

Hank nudged me awake. The remnants of a fading nightmare begged for my attention, but no matter how hard I focused, the memory of it was gone, as if it had evaporated with the sudden rush of consciousness. "You been at this all night?"

I rubbed my eyes and sat back in the chair. "What time is it?"

"Early."

"Where are the others?"

"Not here yet, obviously."

Hank took a seat on the other side of the room. Silence filled the empty space between us.

I flipped through feeds, watching students pass through halls, oblivious to the dangers that surrounded them. Hank stared at the back of my head; I could feel her gaze like a constant pressure.

"What is it?" I asked.

"I heard about Dane," she said.

I said nothing.

"You were there when he died." Her fingers dug deep into the arms of her chair. I could hear the plastic stressing, creaking.

"I was."

"Kind of convenient, don't you think?"

"I don't think it's convenient at all."

"I mean that it's suspicious."

"Are you suggesting that I killed him? I didn't, even if he was a piece of work."

"My boyfriend seems to think you did." She crossed her legs on the chair, her masculine hands meeting on top of her knee. "Thinks you hacked the crime scene photos somehow."

"I take it he's not a big fan."

"Thinks your whole theory is some elaborate attempt at keeping an alibi for your crimes."

"And what do you think?"

She tilted her head at me; her beady brown eyes scanned over me like someone staring at a police lineup. "I don't know. If it is, you've got the Admins eating out of the palm of your hand."

I turned around again to get back to work.

"But," she said. "I do know that if you were lying about this whole thing, if you were actually some kind of brilliant mastermind serial killer, I'd probably put a knife right through your throat myself."

"I'm sure you would."

My heart jumped. The door hissed open, slicing through the tension in the room like a blade through my own flesh. Abdalla came in, holding a cup of coffee in her hand, followed by Mike and Bao.

Abdalla's augmented eyes avoided me; her sneer wrinkled the cocoa-colored skin to the left of her nose ring.

"I'm glad you're all here," I said. Part of me hated this, the business of it all. To speak to these people, who should be my peers, with a semblance of authority, while trying to mask from my voice the anguish that burned deep within me. "I have to tell you all something."

Hank's hands drifted over to her knees. She strangled the life out of the fabric with a grip that was surely meant for my throat.

Abdalla's eyes smoldered with contempt as she sipped her coffee.

"I witnessed Dane's death," I said, staring down at my hands. "He'd been giving my friend moonshine, she was self-destructing."

"You have friends?" Mike said.

"She *was* my friend, anyway, before I fucked everything up. I confronted Dane, told him to stay away from her. When he started prattling on about how he got her to strip for him as payment for his moonshine, I beat the shit out of him."

"Did you kill him?" Mike asked, smiling. "Is this a confession?"

"I heard footsteps first, and asked him if we were alone. He thought I was mad. Then there was a charge, like static electricity." Tears darted down my face. "I saw him split in half. Blood pooled at his feet."

"We've heard this," Bao said, crossing her arms. "You're not going to get sympathy from me."

"I'm not looking for sympathy," I said. "I'm telling you I know why this is happening, or, at least, I *think* I know why."

Abdalla's eyes opened wide, though her mouth was tight. "Tell us."

137

I turned around and gathered a slideshow of images on the screen. "I'm sure you've all noticed the concentrations of dark matter that seem to radiate around people in the images we've been taking."

A unanimous nod waved through the room. I projected the images from my tablet onto the pristine white floor between us. "Well, in the test panorama that Akio and I took—and every other subsequent image after—my dark matter aura was always muted, washed out, while Akio's was always brilliant, flowing and reaching to the sky.

"I think that my aura flares when I hit an emotional high, like with the adrenaline spike I felt when Davin attempted to pound my face in, or when Wolfrik canceled my expulsion hearing—"

"—Or when you beat the stuffing out of Dane," Mike said, his grin fading, a knowing expression falling on his face like moonlight on a shadowed forest.

"Yes," I said. "I think that emotional high fades quickly. I think these things, whatever they are, can see that flare-up. It calls them like a sonar pulse. But, when they reach the source of the pulse, they only see a sea of bright lights, candles in the dark to guide their path. Maybe they're attacking, maybe the light offends them—if they even see it as light—maybe they just kill whatever isn't like them."

"So, what do we do with this?" Hank asked. "If that's true, then how do we know flushing you out an airlock won't solve this problem?"

"Maybe it will," I said quietly. "Maybe it won't. That's my problem right now. I don't know if it's just me that's entangled…or her too."

"Her?" Hank asked.

"Akio, he means," Abdalla said.

"You should have the balls to find out," Hank said.

"Are you seriously suggesting he flush himself out an airlock?" Bao's eyes became wild. "What's wrong with you?"

Abdalla was staring at me. Somehow, I got the idea that she didn't think it was such a bad idea.

"Don't tell me you actually believe this crap about flaring auras?" Hank shot up from her seat. "He's losing his mind, trying to make up any fucking explanation he can think of. There's no evidence that the dark matter concentrations lure them, whatever they are."

"There would be only one way to find out for sure." The words left Mike's mouth and seemed to float in the air. "We'd have to perform an experiment."

I tried to respond, the words caught in my throat.

"Someone would have to attack you," Mike continued. "And wait to be slaughtered on camera."

"That's insane!" I shook my head. "Not to mention incredibly dangerous!"

"I'll do it," Mike said.

Everyone's eyes drifted to Mike. A mix of horror and bewilderment on each of their faces—or maybe I was simply projecting? He was grinning. Silence filled the room as their haunted stares turned back on me.

"No, it's a terrible idea," I said. "We should think of something else."

"In order to take you seriously with this, we must conduct an experiment," Mike said. "We need to bury any doubt that remains and finally prove, or disprove, your hypothesis."

"Mike's right," Hank said.

I didn't know what to say. My eyes fell on Mike's crucifix.

I needed to leave. I could feel the steady beat of my heart drumming in my ears. I wanted to vomit. I wanted to run. I rubbed my sunken eyes.

I needed sleep.

"I have to think about this," I said, stumbling from my chair.

"The answer needs to be yes," Mike said.

I passed through the doors into the corridor beyond without looking him in the eyes. The students I saw were blurry phantoms to my tired eyes as I stumbled toward my dorm.

I barely remembered opening the door or crashing onto the couch.

It was as if something had claimed my soul.

If I had a soul.

2

My father's living room was always an uncomfortable place for me. Even as a child, I would rather spend hours alone in my own bedroom, reading books and studying, than sitting in the living room in front of the TV with my father.

I'm eight again. My wrists are shackled to the carpet, while a cartoon featuring Jesus and his twelve disciples plays on the screen.

"Watch closely, boy," my father says. I try to turn and face him, but the chafing collar around my neck keeps my head facing the TV, staring into Jesus's knowing eyes. "He knows what you've done. Seen it all. And he's going to punish you for peeking behind the curtain."

I'm about to mouth a reply, when I notice that Jesus is staring back at me, grinning. His smile spread from ear to ear. His teeth rotting, black and yellow.

"I hear you've been a bad little lamb," Jesus says. His voice is soft, but not in a soothing way. Not soothing at all. "God's hand is not for mortal men to sneak a peek at. Shame on you, little lamb, shame on you."

"You're not real," I whisper, tugging against the collar that squeezes my neck, making me feel dizzy. "You're not real, you can't be!"

Jesus's face droops into a sorrowful frown. "Maybe you're back in your room, being strangled by some disgruntled heathen? Why did you abandon me, Geraldo?"

"Stop calling me that! It's not my name!"

"Oh, but it is, it's the name that my father gave you."

"No, my father named me. The same man who hurt my mother. Beat her over and over and over."

"Your mother was a sinner." Jesus's smile vanishes. His skin looks faded, pale. "She took the devil's powder. We do not accept those kinds of people into heaven, you know?"

"What about him?" I try to gesture my head at my father. Cracking sounds echo through the room. The pain is too much. My head hits the carpet; tears bleed from my eyes, soaking the carpet fibers red. "Why can't she get in heaven if you'll let him *in?"*

"Your father repented every night of his trespasses. Your mother only made excuses. Like you."

A fire rises up within me. I lift my head, ignoring the pain, the choking feeling, the cracking noises, and look Jesus right in his eyes. "I'm not making excuses! You're not real, you're not—"

"Excuses," my father says. "You stare at the Son of God himself, and yet you do not believe."

"Go fuck yourselves!"

With all my strength, I pull at the shackles around my wrists, breaking the chains to silver shards. I turn to face my father. "You can—"

My father is a violet two-dimensional silhouette, a mantis shape that cuts at reality, offending it without care to my senses. In that violet silhouette there appears to be a starscape, a view of a spiral galaxy at a distance. The chair groans as the mantis silhouette stands up. It has a grin made from the fibers of the abyss, teeth of blackened nothingness and the souls that they've consumed as my punishment. The stars shift when it moves. Madness takes my mind, embracing me.

Two arms rise on each side of the figure, each with a talon shaped like a bladed scythe that drips with blood.

"Geraldo, my son," Jesus says. His eyes pulse with hellish crimson light. "Behold my angel."

The creature swipes down at my midsection—

I woke up to the unique sensation of my eyes bugging out of my skull while the blood rushed to my head. The still-healing wound in my side ached. Locks of hair draped down the silhouette's shoulders. I could see the glint of a nose ring in the light from my charging tablet.

Abdalla was strangling me.

I struggled to speak. Something writhed inside of me; tears broke from my eyes. I thought of my mother's lifeless husk of a body, machines beeping to keep her breathing. Pinpricks of pressure danced on my nose and cheeks. I thought of Gila and Wolfrik and Adams and everyone else my invention had destroyed.

I thought of my responsibility.

I thought of Akio, her disheveled appearance as she'd entered the storage room with Dane.

The lack of oxygen made me want to kick my legs out.

I resisted.

I stared into her eyes.

"Do it," I whispered.

She stopped. Her hands trembled.

She sat back against the arm of my couch, her breath steaming in the air. I could smell cherry moonshine on her breath. Another gift from Dane.

"I can't do it," she said, sobbing into her palms.

I could still feel her grip around my neck. My throat felt like sandpaper. I felt a wave of nothingness spread out from my core.

The sobbing echoed through my dorm room. I sat up, gritting my teeth through the stitches that stabbed in my wound, crinkling the plastic material of the couch. I watched her as the blood pressure rushed back to my head.

She looked up at me, her lips trembling in the glow from my charger. I wasn't sure what she expected me to do. The look in her eyes. Something like panic, or rage, or both?

She was about to say something.

I reached out, put my arm around her. She fought me at first, but soon collapsed into my chest, sobbing.

"I'm sorry," I said. And it was the second time that I'd actually meant it.

"She was everything to me." The whites of her eyes stabbed up at me from my chest, tears sparkling like opal stones in a cave long lost to the world. "And you were the only thing she could ever talk about. You were all she wanted. And you got her killed."

She pushed me off of her and ran for the door.

I sat there, staring into the darkness. My body was a lifeless husk.

I wished she hadn't stopped.

I sat there for a while, staring off into the abyss of my ceiling, watching the light blink on my tablet. It was probably night. It was hard to be angry at Abdalla for what she'd done. I couldn't stop thinking about what she'd said.

I got off the couch and slipped on a fresh set of coveralls, grabbed my overnight bag, and headed out. At this time of night there'd be very few people in the greenhouse. I slipped in easily enough, just as I'd done for Dane when picking ingredients for his moonshine.

I grabbed what I needed and slipped out. I didn't need much. I returned to my room and cleaned off the kitchen counter. Akio would have seen me as a new man, standing there wearing gloves as I soaked the counter in three coats of bleach before it was safe to prepare anything meant for human consumption.

I removed the gloves and washed my hands. Grabbed a draining bowl, soaked the greens, chopped the carrots, onions, and tomatoes—picturing the way Gila's salad had been. I blended it all together in a large bowl and filled two containers, sealing them.

Then I used the camera network to find Abdalla. She was sitting alone in the gym, her head in her hands.

I darted out the door.

4

Abdalla hadn't moved an inch. I entered through the front, and at first she didn't notice me. Then, her eyes followed my movements like a wounded doe in a forest might keep watch on an approaching predator.

She was crouched on a workout bench. Maybe one that she and Gila used to use?

I set the two containers down. Abdalla crossed her arms.

"What's this?" she asked.

"A peace offering," I said.

Her eyes widened. Her eyebrows tightened, coming together. "Salads."

"Gila gave me a salad just before she…"

Abdalla wiped tears from her eyes. "Why are you doing this?"

"I thought we could each share something about her. Honor her memory with a salad."

She was quiet, her eyes locked on the tossed greens, carrots and tomatoes within the container. "The same ingredients she used."

I nodded. She gave me a long, careful look. I opened mine first, squeezed a packet of ranch onto it and started eating. She followed my lead after that, taking little nibbles here and there. Perhaps she thought I'd poisoned them?

I stopped eating for a moment. "She kicked my foot in Planetary Physics the day before all of this started.

"I was looking over Akio's notes on top of the blueprints for what would become the dark matter camera. She was curious, or maybe she just wanted to talk. I was surprised that she'd grabbed my attention the way she did.

"We whispered back and forth about dark matter. Professor Brown was listening." I stabbed the salad with my fork, mixing the veggies around again. "I remember the look on her face as I stood up and lectured the professor about dark matter. She was horrified, her cheeks had turned a bright red. She shook her head, trying to dissuade me from doing what got me thrown out of class.

"I remember thinking how beautiful she looked that day."

"Gila wasn't as shy as everyone thought," Abdalla said, still taking careful, dainty bites from her salad.

"Akio said she had a temper."

Abdalla nodded. "She did."

"I never got to see that side of her."

"She and I used to be rivals. She was so good at Armada and I was jealous. I really sucked, but I thought I was better than half the people in my guild. I remember going to one of her matches against one of my friends to scope her out. She lit up when she was playing, taunted him and kept baiting him into traps, ambush after ambush. It was like she had a psychic link into his mind, because she perfectly predicted every one of his moves.

"I remember how he stood up and accused her of cheating. She leaned back in her chair, brushed her hair off to one side and smiled.

"Then he called her a stupid Jewish cunt, and she responded by standing up and kicking him in the balls so hard that he fell over cradling his manhood."

She laughed, tears broke from her eyes, but she kept eating her salad.

"She told everyone that she helped him grow a vagina," she said. "That's when I fell in love with her."

I was quiet. Despite the fact that I'd finished my salad, I felt empty inside. My eyes felt like they were sinking into my flesh. "I'm sorry I took her from you."

Abdalla shook her head, wiping the tears away with her sleeve. "You didn't."

"You said—"

"I know what I said!"

Silence.

"Anyone could have done what you did," she said.

I clasped my hands together, squeezed and wrung them. "That doesn't fix it."

"It doesn't, but you haven't killed yourself yet."

"Yet."

"Now, do you have any idea why these things are killing us?"

"I have a theory, but not enough data yet."

"Then, what should you be doing?"

I nodded, stood up and headed for the door.

"And, Hal?"

I stopped, turned to her.

"Thanks."

"Let's make a pact."

One of her eyebrows rose. "A pact?"

"That every day, we'll take a break to have a salad to remember her."

She gave a jerky nod, as if she was fighting off another fit of tears. "Yeah, we can do that."

"Good night, Abdalla."

"Just Dalla, that's what my friends call me."

"I'm not a friend, though, am I?"

"You are now, so…"

I stuck my hands in my pockets and slipped out before the tension got any heavier.

5

I'd gone maybe ten paces from the entrance of the gym when Clarence found me.

"There you are," he said. "I saw that someone tampered with the codes on your door—"

"It's fine," I said.

"Are you—"

"I'm sure."

He was wary, but dropped the subject.

"Did you find anything out about our friend?" I asked.

He nodded. "He's from New America."

My mouth hung open for a moment. It explained so much. "I should have guessed…"

"You look like shit, by the way."

"Thanks." I walked, he followed.

"Have you slept?"

"Barely. I was just going to try to get a few more hours before I have to make a very difficult decision."

"Mike's already petitioned Emma for some kind of experiment."

"He did what?" I stopped.

"She seemed pretty upset about it."

"She didn't tell you what the experiment would entail?"

He shook his head.

"You don't want to know," I said, and kept walking.

I lay down on the couch. I couldn't stop thinking about Mike's experiment. The logistics of it. The insanity that would likely result.

The fact that he was from New America didn't help matters. What was left of the country was incredibly isolationist. They didn't like outsiders, either. That didn't mean that their students didn't get accepted to other universities in the world, but it was rare.

Eventually, these thoughts turned to ashes in my mind, silent whispers, and I fell asleep.

G

I dream that I'm in my father's den again, sitting in a dried puddle of blood. The collar has been tightened around my neck, and all four of my limbs are shackled to the floor. I'm in a permanent kneeling position. There's a slash in my shirt around my belly, and beneath the hole in my shirt, I can see a scar.

"I put you back together, boy," my father says. I don't want to look at him, fearful of the thing that he's become. "Even though you don't deserve it, I did. That's the kind of father I am."

Jesus's face was decomposing on the TV. Stringy bits of rotting flesh and exposed muscle fibers dangle from his face, revealing the skeleton beneath. "I couldn't agree more. Truly, one of my children."

"Why do you not repent, boy?" I struggle with my shackles; they cut deep into my wrists. "You know you're going to hell, right?"

"I thought I already was in hell," I say.

That's when I hear my father's old chair groan, and I know that his weight is no longer a burden to its aged frame. Violet feet, the shape of talons, claw into the floor. Staring into its body is like peering into another universe: in its mantis silhouette I see the death of worlds and stars alike, and I hear the screams of men and women going mad from the sight of things not meant for mortal minds to know.

"You will learn to be more respectful." My father tilts his mantis-shaped head. There are no eyes staring back at me, yet I feel his piercing gaze all the same.

"The way mother did?"

He raises a claw above his head. Jesus's face is nothing more than a skeleton.

"Kill me, so I can be done with this farce!" I grab at my shackles and feel my father's blade tear through my neck.

7

I was coated in sweat when I woke. The morning overhead lights irritated my eyes. I sat breathing, getting control over my pulse as I stared at the ceiling.

The nightmares were getting worse.

I felt like I was going mad.

I looked at the clock on my tablet. It was 7:45 in the morning.

There was a new message in my inbox. It was from Mike.

All it said was, *You need to make a decision.*

For once, I agreed with him.

I sent out messages, calling everyone to the Security room as I had my coffee and ate rations. Clarence met me at the door and followed me to the Security room.

I rubbed my eyes.

"Did you sleep?" he asked.

"Not well," I said.

My joints ached. The stab wound that I'd suffered just days ago throbbed.

I saw a couple pass us in the corridor. Their conversation quickly turned to hushed, awkward silence when they saw me. They stopped and stared. I didn't want to look them in the eyes.

Everyone was already gathered in the Security room when we arrived.

Mike was grinning, probably expecting to get his way. I wondered how he'd feel if I exposed his secret to everyone? He was sitting next to Hank. Hank looked up from her tablet, glared at me. Bao was leaning against the wall; she mimicked Hank's expression with near-perfect accuracy.

Then Dalla looked up from the screen she was monitoring. She smiled, wrinkling the soft cocoa-colored skin by her nose ring.

It was a good feeling to not have someone scowl just at the sight of me.

"So." Mike's voice was eager, too excited. "Have you come to a decision?"

I shook my head, leaning my weight on one of the chairs, rubbing my throbbing wound. "I can't."

"It's the only way, Leon," Mike said.

"There has to be a—"

"How about we put it to a vote?" Mike stood up.

"It's too damn dangerous!" I screamed.

"Should we, as a team, be able to help make the decision?" Mike asked, gesturing to the rest of the room.

Bao and Hank nodded.

"I think Mike's right," Bao said.

148

"I need time to think about this," I said, holding my head as I dropped into the nearest chair. I was going to be sick. All I could think about was what would happen to Mike. He was an asshat, but I didn't want his blood on my hands. Maybe that was what he wanted?

"You've had days," Mike said. "And we're no closer to an answer. You have a theory that may be sound, but we must test it."

"We can vote tomorrow—"

"No." Mike's smile faded, then he looked to the others. "We should do it now. Doesn't everyone agree?"

"Well, you already know my vote," I said.

"And you know mine," Mike said. "I'm in favor."

"Me too," Hank said.

"I'm against it," Bao said. "I think Hal may be right about the danger, and we may need more data before we start sacrificing people to science."

Dalla looked at me; her hands trembled. She alone would understand. If she said no, then Mike's experiment would be squashed, at least for now.

"I'm sorry, Hal," Dalla said. "I vote in favor of the experiment."

"What?" My head was spinning. When I closed my eyes, I saw Mike's smiling face getting cut to ribbons. "I thought you of all people would understand my objection to this!"

She nodded. Tears formed in her eyes, drifted down her cheeks. "I do understand. But, we need to know. *I* need to know."

"You have your answer, Leon," Mike said.

I stared at the black plastic floor, watching the reflections from the monitors. The violet dark matter auras on the monitors twisted and bent into obscure shapes when reflected on the floor.

Mike and everyone else droned on about setting things up with Emma. Their voices were barely audible against the strumming of my pulse in my ears.

Things were completely out of my control.

8

The white abyss of The Box was making my head spin. The others had asked to Emma commission it for the experiment, and I was already starting to regret stepping through the doorway. Mike sat across from me in a white chair. The table had been removed, so I could see his fingers twitching atop his knees. He was nervous, or excited, I couldn't tell which. Emma, Dalla, Hank and Bao stared at us from the other side of a two-way mirror.

"I don't like this," Emma's voice buzzed over the intercom. "You're asking a lot of me, Leon."

"Mike's fully aware of the consequences," I said, hoping it was true.

"Oh, I'm quite aware," Mike said. The silhouette of his afro against the all-encompassing white wall was an affront to my sense of place, conjuring up thoughts of heaven or hell or the afterlife. His pale skin looked flushed and his breathing had intensified.

Was this fear, or excitement?

"I want to feel the hand of God," Mike said.

"Excuse me?" I asked.

"I want to experience his angel's wrath, to cleanse me of my sin."

When he said that, I could almost hear my father speaking in my ear.

You know you're going to hell, right?

He stood up from his chair, tightening his fists.

"What the fuck are you talking about?" I asked.

His first punch connected with my jaw, sending me sprawling onto the floor. I heard sounds over the intercom, someone banging at the door from outside. "I never told anyone, not even in confession. So, I suppose now is good enough, if I'm going to meet Jesus." He rushed over and kicked my stomach. "I didn't like it at first, I was so wracked with guilt that I contemplated killing myself. Another sin." Mike crouched down over my body and picked up my head. My face stung like hell. "It's said that if your hands bring you to steal, you should cut them off, and my hands have done more than their fair share. It's so unforgivable that it will follow me straight to hell, because no matter how many times I repent, I know that I'm not sorry." He punched my face with his left hand, then his right. His face was flushed. Something was different about this. I felt empty as he hit me. "My father will disown me when he finds out."

"I don't understand!"

"At first, it started small. I was six. I walked into the local market and stole a bottle of whiskey from behind the counter. It was so easy. All I had to do was wait for the shop keeper to think he was alone so he could use the bathroom. I nabbed it and ran out the door before he realized what had happened." Another right hook to my face, then a left. "But, as I got older, I graduated to other crimes—vandalism, arson, anything to feel that rush of adrenaline before the act. I was even addicted to the guilt that came after. When I became a man, I used my tech skills to create a virus that would siphon off people's pensions. I even stole from my parents. I couldn't help it. I was addicted. I *needed* it.

"Just like you need your monsters, Hal!"

I caught his next punch, sending ripples of needling pain through my bones. The sound of flesh smacking against flesh echoed through the room. "What did you say?"

"I said that you need these monsters to give your life purpose, you need to feel this despair. I've seen it written all over your face since this mess began!"

Going to hell.

"No one needs any of this!" I could feel that familiar fire burn within me, doused once more with gasoline and lit by a stray spark from a burning fireplace within my father's den.

I wasn't sure what was real anymore.

"You do," he said. "You *need* to feel it! Guilt is a drug to us Catholics, isn't it?"

"I'm not Catholic." I shoved my fist into Mike's gut. His eyes went wide with shock and he fell backwards, clutching his stomach. I stood up. "I'm an atheist."

"Is that really what you believe, after all of this trouble with invisible monsters?" He chuckled, rising to his feet in a hunch. "I think you can't face the possibility that your father was always right, that God punishes those who do not fall in line."

I slugged him in the face. He returned the favor. We traded blows. I heard Emma screaming over the intercom, but her words were meaningless to us. Our faces became bloody and bruised as we wrestled in the center of a white abyss. I was on my back. His hands wrapped around my throat. I could feel his anger, his frustration.

My head was swimming, my vision blurring. I imagined that we wrestled in the center of my father's den. Jesus's skull was turning black with rot, worms crawling out his eyes as he laughed at me from within the television. I couldn't move.

"Even *this* sinner is more worthy than you," Jesus said.

"Those heathens on the other side of that wall can't understand, can they?" Mike shook his head as he held me down with his forearm barred across my throat. "Even as they participate in sins that can't be forgiven!"

He kissed me, smearing blood across my lips. The grin returned to his bloodied and swollen face.

"And now I'm guilty of their sin as well," he said, chuckling. "I don't see what all the rage is these days."

"You're insane!" I said, gritting my teeth, trying to find some kind of foothold to get him off of me.

That's when we heard the footsteps. That familiar static filled the room and shifted around us like a cat stalking a pair of mice.

I couldn't tell if I was hallucinating, or if I was really seeing that reality-offending violet mantis shape pace around curiously in my father's den, eying Mike's body with a predator's curiosity.

Emma was pounding on the door. Screaming. She couldn't get in for some reason.

Mike's grin turned into an ecstatic smile. He stood up and opened his arms wide before the glowing form. "Yes, Lord, I hear the footsteps of your angel!"

It opened its arms up, jagged blades spread wide, ready to come down on Mike's battered body.

Behold my angel.

"Take me away from this ruin of Eden," Mike said, spinning around in a circle, beckoning whatever was in the room with us now to kill him. "My flesh is but a vessel, and my soul is—"

It swung its arms down, bringing the blades down in an arc through Mike's body. He fell into several pieces on the floor; a small lake of blood expanded from his ruined pile of severed body parts, a perfect silhouette against the eternal white of The Box. Now it looked like the flesh that had once belonged to Mike was floating amidst that crimson lake. The expression on his face was pure joy, ecstasy of the highest order.

The light had already faded from his eyes. The crimson lake touched my knees, soaking into my jumpsuit. The expression left on his blood-splattered face seemed to say, *Yes, Lord, I accept your judgment.*

Emma was still pounding on the door, screaming for the others to find a way to release the locks. I fell into a daze and the static faded from the room. The vision of my father's den lingered whether my eyes were opened or closed.

I'm still not sure why he did it.

I could still taste his blood on my lips.

9

The shock of seeing Mike die right before my eyes lingered like a cancer that infests the body and corrupts the blood. Mike had hacked the locks on the doors so he could go through with his plan. It felt like it took hours for them to get to me. I wasn't sure what bothered me most: the insane, joyful expression that had beamed from his face, the way he had been so happy to go, or his disturbed laughter as the mantis silhouette had used its blades to slice through his body?

It made me shudder.

We'd gathered in Emma's office. She was projecting the recording of Mike's death on the far wall. The room was silent in its horror.

Emma started the slideshow playback again.

I watched still, animated images of Mike and I sitting in The Box. The details of our conversation were like a hazy mist, like a recording from years ago that'd suffered data fragmentation. The proof was there in the slide-show. Mike's dark matter was jagged, and appeared to have the consistency of bubbling acid, but it was *bright*. My own aura was nothing more than a faint glow around my body.

Until he started beating the hell out of me.

It was like my aura was struggling to come to life, reaching, grabbing, then fizzling like a florescent bulb that's at the end of its life.

It was strange, watching the slideshow play out. Was that really me? Had I really done those things?

I wanted to vomit.

There was a brief thirty or so images where my dark matter aura flared up and flared bright. Like a campfire bursting to life and just as quickly smoldering to embers.

The vents were blowing cold air onto the back of my clammy neck. I felt my breath run hot and rough through my throat when I saw the mantis shape drag itself through the wall into the Box. It drifted up to the very edge of where my dark matter aura had flared. Its violet, featureless head jerked in a staccato rhythm. There was a moment where it looked as though we were looking right at each other.

Then it turned its head and focused on Mike. For a moment, it was as though they had locked eyes—or whatever the creatures used for sight.

My hallucination turned out to be uncomfortably close to what the dark matter camera had recorded of the silhouette. The way it paced Mike's aura. How it raised its bladed arms up...and sliced right through him.

What the hell is wrong with me? I thought.

I couldn't watch it again.

Emma had grown quiet. The other Admins had gathered as well. Hank, Dalla and Bao sat behind me. I strangled the circulation from my hands.

"This is hard to watch," Emma finally said, her voice shaking. Her eyes were heavy and red, and dark patches of inky fatigue painted the skin underneath—a mixture of tears and bleeding mascara no doubt. "And I'm not sure where we go from here."

"It's clear, isn't it?" Bao asked, her voice cold and blunt. "We have to evacuate the colony."

"Yeah, everyone except Hal—" Hank's glare burned my back like the heat from the New Mexico summer sun— "he's the one they're drawn to."

Funny how the narrative changes so quickly, yet stays the same, isn't it?

"That's not very humane," Emma said.

"Not humane?" Hank's voice was shrill. "You know what's more inhumane? Dooming the rest of the colony to death because this asshole gets emotional!"

"It's not like that," Dalla said.

"Isn't it, though?" The chair Hank was sitting in squeaked when she stood up. "You saw the footage, Dalla, it's plain as day. As long as Hal is around, *we're* in danger."

"Maybe there's some way to suppress his emotions to prevent this"—Emma swallowed at the word, as if its very existence at the tip of her tongue offended her—"'aura' from surging?"

"Akio's connected too," I said quietly, the life in my voice all but gone.

"I don't think she is," Dalla said.

"She was there when the camera was first tested," I said.

"And yet, we saw that her aura has always been vibrant," Emma said.

"And no one's died around her," I said, staring at the floor. "Maybe it is just me."

"Even if it is—" Emma put her hands together, closed her eyes. "—I can't say that it'll look too good if we leave Hal here all alone. Our investors would have a fit about the potential lawsuits that would follow. I'm for a more humane—perhaps pharmaceutical-approach?"

"You want to drug him?" Dalla shot up and gesticulated violently at me. "That's not right either!"

"It's fine," I said.

Dalla's eyes drifted to me. Her eyes were childlike in their hurt. "You're just going to give up?"

"Drugging me might be the solution."

"And if it continues?" Hank asked.

"Then you all can flush me out the airlock for all I care. Just be sure to give my father a message once the deed is done."

"Your father?" Emma looked up, her lips drawn tight. "What would you want said?"

"That he can go fuck himself, and I'll see him in hell."

There was a vague sensation of floating. I was beside myself. My mind ever trapped in the past; my face betraying no hint of emotion. I went to and from locations, following Clarence around with only the faintest recollection as to why my legs carried me from room to room.

Somewhat vaguely, I recalled them giving me a cocktail of pills earlier...how long ago had that been? Days? Weeks? I couldn't be certain.

My mind was in a bog so thick that I was in two places at once. The life drained out of me, my soul strained to its absolute limit. Conversations hung barely at the edge of comprehension.

Twisting corridors and sullen students with indeterminable facial expressions that caused no reaction, no emotion to flutter from within the confines of my hardened, husk-like shell of a body, transformed into a single street from my past.

Baker Street, where the asphalt was nearly worn away to uneven patches and gravel from decades of improper road maintenance, where the poor and the downtrodden lived. But, then, the poor and the downtrodden was a great description for all those who lived within the confines of what had once been New Mexico.

I remembered this day. The Sun was beating down overhead, threatening to blister my skin. My friend—what was his name again?— walked by my side, eager to do the thing we'd been talking about doing for weeks. We were going to throw rocks over the wall and see if we couldn't hit a brown-shirt in the face. We weren't sure if there were any more brown-shirts, but we desperately wanted to find out after our teacher's last history lesson.

We lived on the border of what had used to be New America. God's Country as some called it. The wall was just a remnant of a crumbling theocracy, a far cry from the bastion of hope and freedom it had been in the 20th century. They had waged a war against the rest of the world so brutal that it was a wonder that it was still possible to stand on the surface of the Earth without needing a radiation suit.

There were still pockets of them living within the confines of their shattered country, but the rest of the world had largely moved on. Even now, with the scattered smaller countries that had sprouted up beyond the wall to the west, the memory was still fresh.

The Earth was on its way to recovering, some said. There were still the megacorporations to deal with. They had been part of the reason for the great war; their greed knew no end, and even now, with a new generation running them, it seemed that we hadn't learned our lesson.

To give a thing that doesn't live the same rights as a living being is unthinkable. It is a mistake. And yet it is.

My friend's skin...what color had it been again? Brown? Sunburned Caucasian? I wasn't sure. I knew that she often commented on my heritage, asked me what it was like to be Mexican.

It was hard to say what it even meant anymore. After the war, New Mexico had become part of the Californian Republic, along with Nevada and Arizona. So, if anything, wasn't I Californian? I certainly didn't feel like I'd be welcome in Mexico.

My father was one of those people who remembered the war with misguided nostalgia, even believed some of the propaganda that New America's High Priest had spewed before I was even born, the promises of a better world, a *Christian* world. Even when I was a child, when my father recounted these ideas, the glint of wonder in his eyes as he no doubt imagined the heathens of the Earth being burned at the stake had made my skin crawl. It didn't matter to him that he himself wouldn't be welcome beyond the wall in God's Country.

It was all God's will. Even if we were slaughtered or burned away from the face of the Earth by nuclear fire.

Eventually, we reached the wall.

It towered overhead, like the crumbling, decrepit body of some eldritch beast. Its face was littered with patches of crumbling stone, and the Sun's light cast shadows into the belly of the wall, where you could see the inner structure of it.

I had to remind myself that they'd been defeated, that the world was healing. Science was progressing once more, schools and universities were reopening or being built, and the population was recovering, transforming into something different than it had once been. In a few short years, humans would once again be walking the moon, and then Mars would be colonized.

Still, my fear had beaten at the walls of my ribcage, even before it had been determined that we would climb that monstrosity of a barrier. It was not the wall's height that was terrifying; it was the fact that we didn't know what we'd see once we reached the top and peered over the edge.

My memory of the event was so vivid, so real, that I was not entirely sure if my time on Mars was merely a fever dream, an illusion brought on by the terrible heat of the New Mexico sun.

Maybe my mother wasn't dead—maybe there was time to warn her of the terrible future I'd seen?

My skin felt both the stale cold air of Olympus One and the blazing, blistering heat of the summer breeze against my skin. Their simultaneous touch was enough to drive me into madness, to accept both realities as fact.

There was something else in the memory. Something that I wasn't quite sure had happened. If anything had happened at all.

My dirty brown hands found areas of loosened stone, where the wire mesh above the support structure of the wall was exposed. The exposed bits of stone were unstable, still crumbling from a lack of maintenance since the end of the war, but somehow, we didn't break our necks scaling it.

The thing I saw once I reached the top—I knew it was only my imagination, it had to be, there was no way that this had happened—caused my arms to freeze and my grip to almost slip from the edge. My friend was already up, and he gave me a helping hand with a dirty smile. She didn't see what I saw. He was still just a memory.

I wanted so badly to shout to him, to point into the distance, into the blackened hills and the ruined buildings, where violet mantis creatures roamed the streets, hunting. There were millions of them; they lit the blackened, bomb-scarred hillsides like twinkling stars on a cold desert night.

They're here, I thought—perhaps from the one place in my brain not coated in a thick layer of medicated fog. *I brought them here. They'll kill everyone.*

My friend was tugging at a loose bit of concrete, wrenching it free from the wire mesh underneath. He held the chunk in his hand, gave me a wry grin. She couldn't see my terror, he couldn't see them, the damn fool!

I could not speak. I could only look on in horror and hope that they did not see us.

To my horror, my friend wound his small arm up, reached back as far as she could without falling off-balance, and tossed the chunk of cement off into the distance, where it created a small plume of dust that was almost impossible to see from where we sat.

Their featureless mantis heads jerked toward us. I could sense them feeling out, tugging at my atoms, searching for something soft and squishy to cut to pieces.

Every one of them. They could see me. Maybe they could see him too?

The lights moved, like a great mass-migration of bioluminescent jellyfish. They were heading right for us. I could feel my pulse in my ears.

My friend was talking, joyfully pulling out another slab. I was trying to tear my hair out of my head, but my legs wouldn't move. She was either unwilling or incapable of noticing how I was trying to scream, to fling myself off the top of the wall to my death.

I can't see anyone else die! I thought.

The lights came closer. I could see their undefined claws, bleeding together with identical mantis shapes in a glowing mass of marching violet.

The shock tore through my walking, medically-induced coma.

And then I'm aware of the members of my "team." Each of them standing around me with puzzled looks on their faces.

Dalla stands where my mysterious friend is, they meld into one, and I realize that I've been hearing her voice this whole time, confusing it for his, whoever he had been.

There's a new face in the room with us, standing next to Clarence. I don't recognize him, but he has a slight resemblance to Clarence.

I could feel my heart seizing in my chest as the mantis creatures clawed their way up the surface of the wall toward us. My friend's face was filled with glee as he chucked another piece of stone off the wall.

I realize that I've been screaming—my throat is numb from the drugs, but I can still feel it turning to ash. There is a rivulet of blood cascading down the new guy's forehead.

No. Run, run you idiots!

Clarence is the first to notice. The new guy's head splits in half, his brains emptying onto the floor like a spilled bowl of spaghetti. He grabs the boy's body, cradling it as it falls to the floor. I can hear him weeping.

Bao is next. She's saying something, her face twisted in terror. Then she's feeling her gut, there's blood coming out of her stomach. She falls to the floor as Hank comes to her aid.

Dalla screams so loud it echoes down the face of the wall and through the bomb-scarred hills, but it does not impede the slow, methodical movements of the mantis creatures.

She collapses on the plastic floor, clutching her face. A haze of red spills down the front of her body, soaking her coveralls and circling the drain at my feet.

I try to articulate. I try to speak, to yell, in both realities, but it's no use.

The mantis creatures swarmed us at the top of the wall. My friend did not see them. He was cut to bloody ribbons all the same.

Clarence cradles the boy in his arms. Tears dilute the constant flow of blood the way water dilutes oil. It's then that I realize that it's his son he's holding, the one he mentioned to me ages ago, before the medicated fog engulfed my mind.

Somehow, I manage to stand up. The blood on my face isn't my own. I stumble out into the corridor; my feet feel like cement cubes. I'm dragging them as I walk. I'm not sure if I'm seeking help or running away.

Maybe it's both.

All I can think of is Akio. I need to find her, make sure she's okay.

But, before I can, something rattles my brain-cage, and the edges of reality turn fuzzy.

Before reality winks out, I realize I'm drooling on the floor. Students are gathered around me, gawking.

I pity them.

2

I woke up to the feeling of a small lake boiling inside of my skull. I tried to move my hands to cradle my head but found them to be cuffed behind my back. I had the vague impression that I had hit my head on something, or someone had hit me before I lost consciousness. There was a wet, sticky feeling along the right side of my face. Probably blood.

The metal cuffs clanked in the dark as I rattled them.

"Where am I?" My voice was hoarse, hardly recognizable as my own.

I heard footsteps in the dark, pacing around me. "I know what the solution to this problem is."

The voice was familiar, but each syllable was slurred. I tried to push through the fog in my brain, through the pain in my skull, toward recollection.

"It's only a matter of time before Emma gives the order to evacuate."

My mind raced with the implications of an evacuation. There was too much to consider, too many variables. If just one person had become entangled with the mantis silhouettes, then it would be pointless.

I needed to get out. I needed to warn her of the possibility.

"Who are you?" I asked, but it came out in a garbled mess.

Something hit my temple, rattling my brain and tipping my chair over. The pain that washed over my face was instantly dulled by the fire inside my skull. I felt something hovering over my body. Two boots slapped against the plastic floor on either side of my body.

Then, the emergency lights kicked in. Bright red-and-white light flooded into the room, and all at once I know who brought me here and where I was.

I rattled and pulled on the handcuffs. I was lying on the floor of an airlock, maybe even the same one I'd considered flushing myself out of. Sweet irony.

From my vantage point, I could see several open bottles of Dane's confiscated moonshine.

Clarence wrapped his powerful, callused hands around my throat. He didn't so much as squeeze, but I could tell he had more than enough power to crush my windpipe if he wanted to. I could smell the moonshine radiating from each rough breath that he took as he struggled to keep his baser self in check.

"I should end it here," he said. "No one will know."

"Clarence—" My attempt at reason turned into a coughing fit. "—Please—can't let them evac—"

"No more lies!" He applied just enough pressure with his hands to turn my face red. "I'm going to end this."

When he was satisfied that I'd been silenced, he eased up. I could breathe again.

"W-what happened?" It was all still such a blur.

"He was my son," he said, tears welling up in his eyes. "We thought you were sedated." He shook his head. He wiped the tears away with the sleeves of his jumpsuit the same way a child might do after being beaten to a bloody pulp by a bully. "He came to me because it was supposed to be my night off. Emma had me stick around for a few extra hours to make sure the situation was under control. Fucking bitch." His hands fell to his sides; the tears kept coming. "We monitored the screens while you were sedated. You were completely catatonic, or so we thought.

"Then you started screaming. We heard footsteps moments later, and my son's skull…" His fists tightened into blunt hammers. "They all know that you're the key to this shitstorm, but they're all too stuck on their goddamned rules to accept the only just solution."

He's going to kill me, I thought, and I realized that the students who had been assigned to help me stop the deaths on campus, Bao (*clutching*

163

her gut as it bleeds out), Dalla (*holds her face as blood washes down her chest, circling down the drain at my feet*), and maybe even Hank too, were all probably dead. I didn't even know Clarence's son. How many others were there?

"Do it," I said.

He started to laugh. "You'd like that, wouldn't you, you sick fuck? You'd like me to flush us both out that airlock, finally put us both out of our misery!"

"No." I shook my head. "Just me."

He delivered a hard left hook to my jaw. "Shut the fuck up! You don't get to decide how you fucking die! I decide that, do you understand? Do you?"

I nodded.

There was a voice booming over the intercom now: *"ALL RESIDENTS OF OLYMPUS ONE MUST REPORT TO ASSEMBLY HALL H! I REPEAT, ALL RESIDENTS—"*

Clarence's face was twisted into a jagged mess of anger and grief. The pain throbbed from every angle of my face. His head tilted up at the announcement, and a smile of divine knowledge crawled across his countenance.

"I'm not going to flush you out that airlock." He shook his head, wiping tears away with a sleeve again. "I'm going to drag you into Hall H and let your peers rip you apart." He held up my overnight bag. "I'll give them the evidence, and you can share the fate of your precious fucking camera."

"Clarence," I said, pleading. "You're drunk, if you drag me in there to—"

He kicked me in the stomach, knocking the wind out of me. He collapsed on top of me, his eyes wild with drunken rage. *"HE WAS MY SON!*

"He was my son..."

He lumbered off of me. I felt his hands grip at the back of the chair. He pulled me out of the airlock, into an empty corridor as my lungs found new life.

"You're coming with me." Clarence's voice boomed through the corridor over the sirens. "I won't listen to your lies anymore."

The flashing emergency lights passed, one by one, over my line of sight, casting tubular shadows from the overhead atmospheric piping and wiring. Clarence didn't stop, didn't look back at me. The chair's legs scraped against the floor, and the sirens cut the scraping into a strange rhythm that made me dizzy.

I read TO ASSEMBLY HALL H on the wall. It faded into the distance. Clarence wasn't tired, he wasn't even breathing heavy.

To think, this was where my ambition would lead me. This is the price I've paid to peek behind the curtain, to see the things mere mortals are not meant to see. I think I understand now. We were never meant to understand what drove evolution, or the beginnings of sentient life.

Still, I felt a great pang of regret for having paid such a heavy price for something we never truly learned, never had time to research.

It wasn't worth it.

The glass doors to the assembly hall opened. Clarence dragged me inside. There were voices and nameless faces all around me. Some of their stares were hungry.

It must have been the entire west wing gathered there. The afternoon sun shone dimly across a sky of boiling yellow outside transparent walls. Students were still filing in from the two entrances. I couldn't guess how many there were. Maybe thirty people? Clarence laid me flat against the floor, then sat my bag down next to me. I tried to close my eyes. Even as much as I knew it was probably for the best, part of me still didn't want to die. But even closing my eyes didn't shield me from my guilt—I couldn't stop seeing Gila, Wolfrik, Dalla, Bao, Clarence's son and even Mike. I couldn't stop seeing them die.

The auditorium had been a cacophony of noise and panic when he'd first dragged me through the doors. I thought I saw Hank among them, her jumpsuit splotched with blood. Now it was eerily calm. I stared at the ceiling blankly.

The most morbid part of my mind imagined what it would be like for them to tear me limb from limb, anticipating every painful moment. Clarence had said he'd get my peers to tear me apart, and part of me believed he could do it. When in the thralls of terror, a crowd can be led to do almost anything.

"You all know why you're gathered here?" Clarence's voice cut through the silence; a wave of confusion spread through the crowd. Was Akio among them?

"Why?" someone said.

"Because—" I heard Clarence rustling through my bag, digging for it. From the edge of my peripheral vision, I saw him lift the dark matter camera out of the bag. "—Of this. This asshole made a camera that sees things you can't. And it lured things out here. Those things killed my son, they killed Gila Amos, and Wolfrik, and so many others.

"He's the one that caused it. They come when he's angry, or scared, or sad, and they kill people like you. Now he's seen you. Now he knows you. Now you're dead. Dead, unless…"

Clarence held the camera in the air. Their eyes drifted to it.

"There's only one way to stop it," Clarence said. "He has to die!"

A man in his forties with a beard grabbed at my sleeve, tearing it, while others grabbed and kicked and spat at me. The screaming transformed into a deafening choir of unintelligible white noise.

At some point, I felt the arms of my chair shatter, but they still clung to my forearms as I cradled my head from a rampage of kicks and punches and stomps.

Through the chaos, I saw someone rush at Clarence. She shouted something at him, reaching for the camera and pointing at me. I could taste my blood on my tongue. Clarence backhanded her into the crowd. She went limp.

I'm sorry, I thought, hoping it wasn't Akio.

Then, I saw her. Hank came rushing at me, her face twisted into a scowl, dried blood splattered all over her clothes. Her face seemed to say, *You did this.* Something exploded against my left temple, and darkness rang at the edges of my vision. I fell to the cold floor. My head felt heavy.

My sluggish eyes drifted to Clarence, holding the invention that Akio and I had spent so many months, years, developing—the thing that had cost us our friendship—high above his head in his strong, weathered hands; with all his strength, he slammed it against the floor, shattering the casing and scattering the internal bits across the floor in a shock wave. It was strangely liberating, even at the brink of unconsciousness, to have everything I had once hoped and dreamed for shattered and lying broken before me—all at the hands of someone I had once shared a drink with.

There was a metaphor in there somewhere…

XI

I wasn't quite sure if I was awake, or if this was what hell was like. Part of me hoped it was the latter, that it was finally over. I saw only darkness, and I couldn't shake the smell of blood no matter where I turned my head. I heard faint voices echoing around me, like someone had stuffed cotton in my ears.

"His eyes are open."

I was alive. It wasn't over.

I can see Gila wrapped in her towel; she turns around to face me, clutching her throat; she whispers something only for my ears as she collapses on the floor.

"Should we tell him?"

The life leaves her eyes; she's still whispering. I struggle to sit up, to get closer to her bloodstained lips so I can hear what she says, but there's only death and silence when I reach her.

"Let's wait till we know there's no brain damage first."

Wolfrik raises the wineglass to his lips. He stops, blood bubbles out of his mouth.

"Tell me what?" I said. My voice didn't feel like it was mine. "Why can't I see?"

His body splits in half, his pants are already stained red before his body hits the ground. He screams, his eyes are rolling back into his head as he clutches at his own entrails…

"Hal." It was Akio's voice; I could feel her squeezing my hand. "I wish there was an easy way to say this…"

Dalla holds her face in her hands. Blood runs down her face, fills her mouth. She gags, her hands fall limp. Her eyes are replaced by a torrent of ever-flowing blood. She tries to say something to me, but it comes out as a garbled mess.

"Let me guess, I'm blind."

I see Gila die again; this time I can almost make out what she's saying…

I felt her grip tighten. "Temporarily, the doctor hopes."

"It should have been you," Gila whispers…

"Temporarily." I spat. With my vision permanently darkened, all I could see was a never-ending replay of death and carnage. "What the hell happened?"

"You were beaten by a campus police officer and a mob of over thirty angry students…" one of the doctors said. "The exact number is still unknown."

I see the boy who was Clarence's son fall to his knees. His brain spills out of his head and splashes onto the floor like an overturned bowl of spaghetti.

"Why do I smell blood?" I asked. "Did you detain Clarence?"

I could hear them hold their breath and could almost imagine them glancing at each other cautiously.

"Tell me, damn it!" I said.

"We found you there"—Akio's voice was trembling—"covered in their blood… We bathed you, but…"

"You mean my blood, right?" I asked.

"No," one of the doctors said. "Their blood."

"They died, the whole auditorium, shortly after you went unconscious," Akio said. Her voice was shaking; I could almost picture the tears forming in her eyes. "They're still trying to identify them all. The current estimate is in the high thirties."

"All of them?" I barely felt the words ghost my lips.

I saw the auditorium now, the seating area painted red and gray from the sea of death beneath the yellow Martian sky, like Bruegel Jan's *famous painting,* Aeneas and the Sybil in Hades, *and at the center of the mess, there I was, still alive, with Gila, Wolfrik, Hank, Dalla, Davin, Dane, Mike, Bao, and Clarence's son, each of them cut to pieces, their corpses bleeding out next to me, their entrails and bodily fluids mixing with the others into a vortex of pain and misery that was centered on me.*

The eye of the storm.

"The cameras you modified, they caught it all…" Akio paused, her hand leaving mine.

"They were massacred by those things," I said.

"Yes," the doctor said.

"Is Emma still going to evacuate?" I asked.

"She's calling for the colony to evacuate, yes," Akio said. "Olympus Three says they have room for us."

"Are we sure they won't follow us?" I asked.

"We're not sure what 'they' are," the doctor said.

I tried to nod, regretted the action as it only made my head feel worse. "That much is true."

"In any case, there's no way we can investigate further until the evacuation is complete," Akio said.

"They can't evacuate, it won't stop it," I said. "There's only one way to stop this."

"I've looked at the data," Akio said. "And I know what you're going to suggest, but there's simply not enough evidence to suggest that—"

"I know what the fuck I'm saying." I chuckled. "It's really funny, you know. Here I am, unable to see a damn thing, and yet you're the one who's blind. It's sweet that you don't want to admit that I'm the problem here, but let's face facts, Akio."

Silence filled the room. It felt like there was a canyon between Akio and me. If I hadn't been beaten within an inch of my life, she wouldn't have been here. She was here because she felt guilty, even though I was the one who screwed up.

"There has to be another way…" Akio said.

"I'm sorry, Akio, but there just isn't." Tears streamed from my blind eyes; my words caught in my throat. "I tried so damn hard to find another way, but I couldn't. The only solace I find in this mess is that I've ruled you out from the equation."

"You ruled me out?" Akio's voice was a whisper.

"It's either, you're not entangled with them, or you're very fucking lucky." I shook my head. "And you know how I feel about luck."

"I'm sorry I wasn't there," Akio said.

"I was the one who wasn't there," I said. "I was the one who fucked everything up. I was the asshole."

She was making sobbing sounds that tore at my heart. "Say we'll work on it together, say we'll find a way, just don't say what I think you're going to say."

"I tried that, remember?" I said. "Now my team is dead."

"It's out of our hands now," the doctor said. His touch was almost painful on my shoulder, forcing me to lie back down. "And you need to rest."

"Like hell I do!" I shook my head and struggled to sit up, resisting sharp pains in my side, ribs, and hips. "They tried drugging me, they tried to lock my emotions away, so my dark matter aura wouldn't flare…" It sounded like madness. It *was* madness. "But they were still lured to me."

"His stress levels are off the chart," one of the doctors said. "Should we sedate him?"

"Maybe?" Akio's voice sounded uncertain. It was so unlike her. "I'm not sure what to do."

"If I stay here," I said, "you're all going to die eventually, and I can't live with that. At least *you* have to survive, Akio."

"I really don't understand this," the doctor said. "Is it true?"

I nodded, confirming their death sentence. "I thought that destroying the camera, or at least shutting it off, would stop them, that that was the thing that was drawing them out. I was so wrong. I've been wrong about everything thus far, except for one thing…"

"Then how do you know you're right about this part?"

"There's no way to be sure, not really." I paused. "But, I'm not risking anyone else's life. I need to leave Olympus One, I need to—"

"You're in no shape to leave!" Akio said.

"Then you'll wheel my lifeless corpse out into the Martian wasteland!" I slammed my hand into the bed and immediately regretted the action; sharp jolts of pain shot up my arms and traveled through my chest like miniature lightning bolts.

"At least wait until you're better, Hal!" Akio's hand found mine again.

"Get the Admins in here," I said.

"But—"

"Now!"

I heard their frantic footsteps fade into the distance. When I was greeted by nothingness, I felt a violent urge to call them back, so that I wouldn't be left alone to my visions. The corpses in my vision began to multiply to include my faceless doctor and Akio, and still I lived on in the bloody center of it all, still I survived when all I wished for was to join the dead that spiraled around me.

The visions became so intense that I had to be shaken from them when the Admins finally arrived. My breath was short, and I could feel each individual drop of sweat beading above my brow.

"What do you want, Hal?" It was Emma's stern voice. "Your doctor says you should be resting."

"I called you here to stop you from doing something stupid," I said.

"Your task failed, your team is dead," she said. "What the hell else can we do?"

"You can do the only sensible thing that's left to do."

"We're not going to kill you, Hal."

"Don't evacuate yet. Give me a chance to do one last thing."

"I've seen the footage of you standing in the airlock, Hal. If I let you do what you're asking, you'll just try to kill yourself. Milkyway Unlimited has ordered me to evacuate. I can't let you—"

"I don't give a flying fuck what your bosses want!" I quieted down for a moment. "We don't know what caused me to become entangled with these things, so we can't rule out the possibility of someone else becoming entangled either. And if anyone brings those things back to Earth—"

"You're asking me to risk my career, Hal!"

"Better than your life...because you know, if I'm still alive, if I'm still *here*, then more people are going to die."

She sighed. "What would you do then?"

"Send me off in an EVA suit on a walkabout for all I give a shit. Just get me out of the colony, that's the only way to stop this. If you don't take my word for it, then ask Akio to show you the data—"

"I've seen the evidence already, Hal," Emma said.

"Then you have to see that I'm right!"

"If there was more time…"

"There isn't!"

"This is madness." Emma's voice was trembling, her once proud and stern facade eroded. "That's what this is. Pure…madness. Do you understand what you've unleashed upon the world, Leon? I can't sleep anymore without seeing the student body getting slashed up by invisible mantis creatures. I can't even trust my own judgment anymore, because your invention has completely undermined my grip on reality."

"Yes," I said. "People here are dying because of something I created! It's my fault! I woke them up! You have to let me fix it!"

"And what if I don't want you to go?" Akio said. "Have you even thought about that?"

"It's not even a choice!" I pushed myself up and thrust my finger at Akio's voice. "People are dying!"

"And all you have are theories," Emma said. "What happens if people continue to die even in your absence?"

"Then it's an experiment to confirm my hypothesis once and for all," I said. "Send me out in a rover, remote control it if you have to, if the deaths stop while I'm away, then I'm right, if they don't, then you can drag my broken ass back and evacuate us all to Olympus Three."

Emma grew quiet.

"If it works," I said. "You have to promise to dismantle every one of my cameras, destroy them, wipe the hard drives with the image panoramas and videos on them, everything."

"If you send him out there, he won't be coming back," Akio said. She knew me too well. "He'd open up the rover and expose himself to the vacuum before he'd let you bring him back here."

Emma sighed. "Milkyway Unlimited will have other things to say about all this. Wolfrik's son witnessed his father die on a live communication…and all this…it'll spell the end of my career…"

"To hell with Earth and your career!" I said. "They're not here right now, they don't know what we know. Easy for them to sit behind their control panels, sipping lattes, barking orders at us, while we die facing the unknown. You have a duty to protect the colonists here, Emma.

"Even Wolfrik understood that."

She muttered curses under her breath.

"Fine," Emma said. "But, we'll keep constant communication with you."

"Finally," I said. "Someone's making some damn sense."

"Now, Mr. Leon," Emma said. "The doctor says that you need your rest. We'll make the preparations in the meantime."

"Thanks," I said, sinking into my hospital bedding.

Emma left the room, and I could hear Akio sobbing at the foot of the bed.

"So, that's it?" Akio said. "You just want to go off to die?"

"If my theory is wrong, they'll bring me back," I said.

"And I already know that you're not going to let that happen," Akio said. "We both know you're too damn stubborn for that! I can hear it in your fucking voice, you've given up!"

"And why the hell shouldn't I?"

"Because there's still hope!"

"Where? Where is this hope you speak of? Cause I don't see it, or maybe you've forgotten that I was beaten blind by an angry mob? Maybe you forgot that countless people I know were killed because of something I created, and then even more died while I lay unconscious on the floor, my curse to be *lucky* enough to be mistaken for a corpse!"

"We."

"What?"

"We created that thing together."

"It was my idea. My fault."

"But I helped. Without me, you would have never been able to complete the design."

"Small comforts."

"Fine!" Her feet slapped against the floor, carrying her to the doorway. "Wallow in your own self-pity. I won't have any part of it."

Then she was gone, and I was left alone with the spiraling corpses of the auditorium.

Now Emma Williams and Akio were among the dead…

It was a constant struggle to hold onto what was left of my sanity. I choked down the urge to start laughing.

2

The sounds of panicked students' footsteps speeding through the corridor rushed by my ears as they wheeled me to the hangar. How many were left in the colony? The estimate of how many had died in Hall H had risen to the low forties. That left just under sixty people left alive. The bits of conversation I overheard told me that there were rumors that Milkyway Unlimited was rescinding their evacuation order in favor of quarantine.

I hadn't heard from Akio again since she'd stormed out of the infirmary. I hoped she'd stay away. I'd caused enough trouble in her life.

My vision was still gone, and with each new name that I heard called out, my imagination approximated what they would look like swirling among the dead.

My left leg was broken in three places, my right arm fractured, and I had three broken ribs. I'd told the doctors to break my casts so I could wear the EVA suit, that I'd tough the pain out somehow. I didn't need vision to be able to tell what their reaction was to that request.

One of the doctors fed me some morphine before stripping my clothes off and helping me into the EVA suit. Maybe it was the drugs talking, but I'd never noticed how scratchy the cloth armor felt against my skin.

"Up you go, watch your step, Mr. Leon," one of the faceless men said. This one's name was Jim.

He helped me into the rover's cabin, and another person helped strap me in.

"Just yelp if it's too tight," he said.

"Funny," I said.

If Emma was there, she was keeping quiet. After what I'd said earlier, I couldn't necessarily blame her. I was waiting for them to close the hatch and send me on my way; they were babbling about who was going to run the remote controls for the rover when I heard her voice.

"Get the fuck out of the way," Akio said. "I'm driving."

She didn't say much else. There were sounds, arguing, ruffling of clothing and clanking of machines and the alarms for depressurization.

She settled into the driver's seat next to me; her breath was short. I could almost hear the steady pounding of her heart through her EVA suit.

"You don't have to do this," I said.

"Shut up," Akio said. "I'm not going to let you kill yourself for nothing and that's final."

"I hoped you wouldn't try to stop me," I said. "I've caused enough—"

"Stop. I've made up my mind. There's nothing you can say to convince me to stand by and watch you throw everything away."

I felt the rover moving forward, heard people talking over the intercom with authority. Akio got quiet again. The ride got bumpy, and I knew we were outside.

"What made you decide to do it?" I asked.

She sighed. "The fact that you're basically a cripple."

"That's harsh."

"Well, I couldn't live with myself if I let you go off alone…"

"I'm sorry…" I swallowed a lump in my throat, forcing the words out. "For the things I said before."

She gasped. "I don't think I've ever heard you apologize for anything."

"You should have been around the last few days, then. I've done a lot of apologizing."

"You remind me so much of my grandfather." She laughed.

"I hope that's a compliment."

"He was the founder of the research and development company that my father inherited when… He had so many responsibilities, but he always made time to conduct his own research. The company was responsible for the weapons that ended the war. He always felt guilty for that, despite how so many people praised him for helping end the worst war in history—the idea that he'd created something that had caused the deaths of so many people just wasn't something he could live with. He devoted his life to helping people after the war, making biomechanical prosthetics, donating to charity, fighting for human rights in the war-ravaged and collapsed remains of New America, and creating the basis for the food we eat out here on Mars. He was often regarded as a stubborn and rude man, but I knew him better. I used to visit him when school was on break, my parents would fly me out to Tokyo to his company's headquarters, and he'd make time for me."

"What happened to him?"

"I loved my grandfather, but his guilt eventually destroyed him. It ruined his marriage, and he nearly bankrupted his company fighting his crusades against the evils of the world. He jumped to his death from the top of his own building."

"I see…"

"I couldn't be there for my grandfather when he faced his demons. I don't want the same thing to happen to you."

We were quiet for a while. The visions continued, influenced now by the bumpy climb up Olympus Mons. But, several hours into our journey, I began to see something, a red-and-yellow blur. My eyesight was returning, just as the doctors had said it would.

"I can see," I said.

"Really?" Akio said.

"Not much more than a blur, but I can see."

Akio waved her hand in front of my eyes. I couldn't tell her fingers apart, but I could see the motion.

"Yes, I see that."

She jerked her hand back to the wheel and screamed, "Shit!"

I heard her draw in a deep breath, then jerk the wheel hard to the right; I felt the rover's weight shift in my broken bones. My teeth clenched. The rover tumbled several times. Akio screamed. The kaleidoscope of colors and spinning shapes made me vomit. I could have sworn I saw the ground crack open and swallow us whole. Akio was still screaming, cursing, but the rover was still in one piece.

"I can't stop it!" she said.

"What the hell happened?" I gripped the arm of my seat tight with my good arm.

"I don't know! The ground gave out, and we started sliding down this tunnel!"

"Tunnel? Try the emergency thrusters, point them forward!"

The emergency lights came on, lighting the cockpit a deathly crimson. Error sounds buzzed from Akio's console. "They won't come on!"

I could see a steady blur of shapes through the windshield, and grinding sounds echoed from outside as Akio locked the brakes in vain.

"Comms?" I asked.

"Nothing but static!"

I sank into my seat, sticky from my vomit. "Maybe this is it…"

"I love you—"

A crashing noise, vibrations tearing through the hull, scraping sounds, screaming, static, glass shattering, blood rushing to my head, and finally, sweet nothingness.

I wouldn't have been able to say it back anyway…

XII

I inhaled fire. It filled my lungs and spread through my broken limbs in cascading waves of pain. I felt like I was floating. There was an oppressive pressure coming from above, pushing me further and further into the abyss.

The cold embrace of death, perhaps?

I didn't have the strength, or the will, to open my eyes. For the second time in so many days, I asked myself if I was in hell — if I'd been judged and found guilty. There was no guilt. No fear. Only sweet relief that it might finally be over.

There was a ringing in my ears. Then, the crack of sparks dancing. Hope ebbed, and my eyelids fought against the intense pull of gravity.

The sweet feeling of relief drained from me in the mere instant of seeing blurry, blinking red lights inside the twisted cabin and was replaced with an all-encompassing dread. The floating feeling I'd experienced evaporated, replaced by a fever that constantly battled with the chilling embrace of my own mortality.

Death's icy hand caressed my skin, and I shivered. All my injuries seemed to be sounding off at once. The stab wound I'd suffered at the hands of one of my peers — what was his name again? It seemed so far away — the numerous head injuries, my broken arm and leg, my ribs, everything calling out to me, begging me to make it all stop. I wished I could answer.

What would it take for it to end?

Maybe if I just lay here, I'd die eventually? Maybe I could just let it happen? Accept the embrace. Let the abyss take me.

I pushed through the fog in my brain. There was something I was forgetting. Something urgent. I needed to do something, check on something. What was it?

Akio.

I struggled to sit upright, and my screams rang off the cabin walls, coming back to my ears as if they weren't my own. I sat there for a moment, zoning out, squinting at the blinking lights; it seemed like my vision had finally returned to normal.

How long had I been unconscious?

I scanned the cabin for Akio. Two stalagmites had pierced the hull on the right side of the cabin, metal twisted and stretched up the pointed rock, sparks dancing across the console erratically. Akio was still in her seat. Her chest rose and fell; she was alive; the stalagmites had missed her by mere inches, impaling the right side of her chair and pushing her harmlessly off to the left.

The impact with the hull must have happened so quickly that the cabin didn't have a chance to depressurize. How much atmosphere was left in the rover? By all rights, we should have been dead.

"Akio," I said. "Akio, wake up!"

The front windshield had several long cracks in it, and I could see violet lights in the distant reaches of the tunnel beyond. My instinct to survive pushed the obvious questions to the side. I struggled to get closer to her but couldn't move my good leg. I looked down to see that my chair had capsized in the crash and pinned my leg in place. Another stalactite had come out from behind my chair, pushing the metal supports and spine of the chair forward—bending it over my leg. I tried to wriggle my toes and flex the muscles in my leg, succeeded, which meant my "good" leg wasn't broken. My foot was caught on the harness strap; I could feel its tensile strength being tested every time I tried to pull free. I tried to reach my good arm out to Akio; my fingertips grazed her sleeve. She was just inches out of my reach.

I called her name till my throat was raw. I felt a coughing fit ripple through my chest. My back arched up off the floor of the cabin as my body attempted to force my lungs out through my mouth. Saliva and blood sprayed into the air, came back down and danced on my lips. I tasted iron. All the noise I was making, and still, she didn't wake.

I allowed myself to collapse on the uneven metal floor, breathing heavily. The air felt like it was thinner, probably a combination of the hull being shredded and my own broken ribs stabbing into my lungs.

The atmosphere was likely still leaking out. Whatever luck we had would be running out soon.

I looked around again for anything that might help me get free; one of my chair's arms had broken off and was lying free on the floor several feet away from my good arm. I reached out to grab it, but it too was out of my reach. I groaned, my shattered ribs mounting their protest, as I attempted to shimmy my back over toward it, closing the gap. My fingers found the broken piece of chair and I was able to finger-walk it toward my armpit.

I cradled it in the palm of my hand and poked Akio with it like a child might poke a dead squirrel with a stick. It's been so long since I'd seen a squirrel. Three nudges and she was still unconscious. Finally, frustration won out and I smacked her with it. She yelped and sprang forward, snapping back into the chair like a rubber band.

"What the hell was that for!" Akio said.

"Take a look." I gestured at my present condition.

"Shit!" Her eyes darted around the cabin, assessing the damage. "How are we still alive?"

"That's a good question, though I feel a more pressing one is, how the hell am I going to get out from under this damn chair?"

Her eyes opened wide; she unbuckled her harness and rushed over to me. "Can you move your leg? Is it broken?"

"It's not broken, I think it's stuck on one of the straps from the harness."

"How did it come loose? Those things are made from Kevlar…"

"I probably took it off while the chair was ripping itself from the hull."

"Okay." She looked around herself. "Cutting the strap won't work, the material's too strong. I need something to wedge underneath the chair to prop it up…"

She tried pulling a metal beam from one of the control ports loose; the bolts had already been damaged in the crash, so they snapped right off. The beam was about the length of her leg. She wedged it between the floor and the chair and pressed her weight down on it. The chair lifted into the air, and I was able to untangle my foot from the strap and withdraw my leg. Akio sighed and let the chair crush down onto the floor.

"Okay," she said. "Now what?"

"Is it just me, or is the air getting thin in here?"

She took a deep breath. "Damn it."

"It is, isn't it? And here I thought it was just my lungs getting perforated by my ribs."

She nodded.

"We need to get out of here, where are the helmets?"

She panicked, rushed and found our helmets, handed me one. There was a small dent in the metallic frame at the back of it, and several dings in the glass that might prove problematic if I took an unexpected fall. I fastened it around my neck and listened to the suit pressurize itself. Akio did the same, and we searched for a way to exit the cabin. She handed the beam to me to act as a cane, but I had a better idea. I grabbed for the straps on her chair, disconnecting them at the maintenance links, then wrapped them around my leg and the beam to create a splint. I tested my weight. The pain was excruciating. I gritted my teeth and managed to stand upright.

Akio shook the handle and tried to open the left hatch several times, but it wouldn't budge. "The frame must be too bent."

"Try the emergency release."

"Right."

She bent down and opened a compartment inches from the hatch, pulled the red lever inside; the hatch gave a loud pop as the near vacuum outside instantly sucked the pressure and air from the cabin, and the door was dislodged from the rover's frame. There was now a small half-foot opening to the outside tunnel; the rest of the hatch was still lodged in the twisted frame. I pressed my weight against it and waved her forward.

"Ram it," I said.

"Are you sure?" Akio asked.

"No, but do it anyway."

She rushed the hatch again, tackling it with all the force she could muster. We tumbled forward on the hatch together, my teeth rattling, and my limbs protesting by shooting continuous waves of pain through my body. When I looked up again, we were lying in the middle of a dark tunnel filled with blackened rock.

When the pain finally subsided—my eyes rested on those violet lights I had seen earlier, blinking in the distance. The light seemed to ripple and cascade on the rocks, almost like an aurora reflected off an ice cavern.

"Do you see that?" I asked.

"See what?"

I struggled to my feet, leaning on the far wall for support. "Those lights in the distance."

Akio let her eyes adjust, squinting at the lights. "What the hell?"

I was mesmerized by those lights. The way they brightened the pitch dark of the lava tube with a caress of violet light. There was something else. A tiny impulse at the back of my brain, compelling me forward. I started limping down the tunnel. "Let's check it out."

"Shouldn't we find a way out of here? I don't like this."

"Can't you feel it? It's calling to us." I shook my head. It was something I couldn't put my finger on. A pull. "Besides, I can't climb up that incline with a broken leg anyway."

"Are you feeling okay, Hal?" Akio's eyes were full of concern, standing at the top of the incline, looking down on me.

I turned from her and continued walking down the incline of the tube.

The pain was almost manageable thanks to the downhill slope; I took special care not to put too much weight on the bad leg. Akio followed closely behind me, probably after realizing that I wasn't going to give up. She grabbed my good arm and pulled her head underneath to give me support, then smiled when our helmets clanked together.

"I guess we're going down, then," she said.

I smiled. "I did tell you to let me go, didn't I? Are you regretting it yet?"

She shook her head. "Don't be stupid."

The reflections from the violet light transformed before my eyes, and at first, I almost thought they might have been bioluminescent forms...but, as we approached, the lights gave hints of inorganic structures, smooth geometric shapes, and processed metal.

A strange sense of awe and dread spread through me, and judging from Akio's expression when we exchanged looks, she must have been feeling it too. The geometric forms became more and more distinct and detailed. Strange, rhythmic grooves etched in blackened metal that seemed to have the same surface qualities as ice. I wiped my glove across the surface and confirmed that there was indeed some kind of condensation on the metal. Perhaps from an atmosphere being produced further in?

Akio and I gave each other a long, eerie look.

For years humans had speculated on how deep the lava tubes within the volcano ran, but no one had ever dared to explore them more than a few yards, and typically only with drones. I could not guess how deep within Olympus Mons we were. The interest had always been in the northern hemisphere, where subterranean ice was most prominent. There just wasn't any known profit for exploring the inside of Olympus Mons if there were no resources readily available.

If we had only known that the remains of a billion-year-old alien race were down here.

The sound of our breathing was white noise in my ears when we came upon a massive oblong-shaped door at the end of the tunnel; monolithic pillars cascaded up to it, betraying impossible weathered shapes that looked all too familiar to me. The walls were embedded with ancient lights of an unknown technological origin and composition. It was almost as if the lights were part of the wall itself. The violet light seemed to follow us as we walked. The metalwork here was nearly pristine, which was a stark contrast to the monoliths, almost as if they had been broken on purpose. Even with the damage, I could still make out the shapes on most of them: four arms, a large bulbous head, and a pear-shaped body that stabbed down into a set of indistinguishable legs.

"The silhouettes," Akio said.

I nodded. "They weren't animals after all."

"Hal…" There was a worried look in her eyes.

"What?"

"We know that something hit Mars, right?" She caressed the leg of one of the statues. "And if they migrated beneath the surface…"

I swallowed a lump in my throat. "Then, what wiped them out?"

She nodded.

"Maybe there's answers inside?" I gestured my head toward the door. "Help me get up there."

Akio helped me limp up to the door; I placed my glove upon its surface. There were strange carvings in the relief. I traced my finger through a few of them, great circles and jagged edges that reminded me of Native American cave paintings for some reason.

We were startled by vibrations in the ground and stumbled back to see that the circular door was sinking into the wall. I winced, the vibrations causing aches to bubble up within my bad leg; I could almost feel the broken bones vibrating and sliding around within my flesh.

"Oh wow," Akio said.

There were more lights inside, blinking and dancing in a pitch black-darkness—what I assumed was a corridor. Violet and blue and red neon things, geometrically lining the walls in jagged corners and perfect circles, but the light did not travel far. The floor was cut from some kind of stone, but it hadn't turned red like the surface of the dead planet had. Cautiously, we moved forward, keeping our breaths controlled and our steps as quiet as possible. For even in our wonder, there was an unspoken fear of what could be lurking in those depths, whether it be physical or incorporeal.

Broken statues lined the sprawling labyrinthine corridors, their faces and limbs cut and smashed about the floor. The rubble looked as fresh as if it had happened only yesterday, and maybe it had. There were metallic doors, some like the one we had entered from, and others tall, rectangular shapes that fit into the walls of the corridor without any rhyme or reason, no architectural logic. Perhaps they were rooms, dwellings that the Martians had once called home. I wondered if we'd find personal items, beds, terrestrial things, inside them, were we brave enough to look inside.

I limped on through corridor after corridor, Akio supporting my weight. With each step we took, more geometric lights came to light our path. We had taken three right turns, and one left, before it became clear that we were being led somewhere.

"Let's turn back, Hal," Akio said. "Let's go back to the rover, and just—"

"The rover's trashed," I said. "We can't use it for air anymore...like it or not, this is our only option."

"But, where's the light leading us?"

"Good question."

We tried veering off course from the lights several times, and each time they guided us right back to where they seemed to want us to go. It was a crazy thought, a theory, but it was almost as if it had a psychological hold over us. To look into the lights was to be mesmerized, entranced. Maybe they played tricks on the mind, resulting in some kind of hypnotic state of suggestion in the subject?

Maybe my fever was just melting my brain cells. My forehead was drenched in sweat, my head swimming. It was slow torture, feeling sweat drops bead and drag across the surface of my face.

An itch that couldn't ever be scratched.

Those hypnotic lights led us deeper and deeper into the mountain, a progression that felt like it took years thanks to my broken leg and the strange buzzing feeling that echoed in my brain. My feet felt like they were blistering within my suit. I wanted so desperately to stop, rest for a short while, gather my strength. But something inside me told me to keep pushing, to ignore the pain, just a little further. I looked at Akio briefly and I could see the same frightened determination wrought across her face.

When the lights finally stopped at the foot of another circular depression in the wall, it felt like a hold had been released from me. The circular depression was very much like the door that we'd seen earlier. The lights turned a deep and vile crimson.

Vibrations spread through my bones again; Akio held me tight as I collapsed forward, gritting my teeth. The door faded away into the darkness, and the crimson light spread to fill another corridor, one that was smaller and smoother than the others.

Akio helped me struggle back to my feet.

"Should we go in?" she asked.

"What other choice is there?"

She shook her head, but took a deep breath. We limped forward; our boots scraped and echoed and reverberated through the tunnel. The crimson light stretched farther and farther, until the tunnel opened up into a large spherical room.

The door closed, its edges fading until it looked like any other part of the wall. White light traced across the walls, starting from the farthest part of the wall across from us, forming more symbols and markings, and ending at our backs. White hieroglyphics lit up beneath our feet, following from the place they had stopped on the wall, and finished across the path at the center of the room. There, a large, transparent, membranous object lit up before our eyes. It seemed to glow from within, pulsing, orange and then to white, as if it was beckoning us toward it.

I limped forward, practically dragging Akio's dead weight with me.

"No," she said. "Don't, let's leave, let's leave, I can't—"

"There's nowhere else to go," I said, having finally reached the center of the room—Akio's hands gripping and strangling the life from my waist.

I felt compelled to reach out and touch it.

"Don't do it!" she said.

It was too late. I laid my hand flat on its surface. Even through my glove, it felt hard to the touch, not unlike glass. My hair stood on end. The membrane pulsed, blinding me with a brilliant pulse of white light, and I felt a strange sensation from within my gut trace its way from my groin to the tip of my skull.

I felt lightheaded; I could feel my pulse in my ears. The light faded, and I stumbled back into Akio's arms.

Her lips were moving, veins popping out of her temples, but I couldn't seem to make out what she was saying… Sleep seemed like such a great idea…I closed my eyes…and for the first time in days, I felt at peace…

XIII

The first thing I noticed was my hands. They weren't hands at all, but four strange twig-like things that ended in sharp hooves. I looked around myself, expecting to see that strange spherical room filled with unintelligible glowing symbols, but, instead, found myself in a large open field covered in long, flowing pink grass. I stretched my head up to see a brilliant blue sky surrounded by dark crimson and rusted orange rock formations.

There was a strange, distorted riffing sound that seemed to fill the entire field. I caught a glimpse of a small, multi-limbed insect, flying from plant to plant in what I assumed was the Martian equivalent of pollination. There were thousands of them, which was where the sound seemed to be coming from. It was almost soothing, in a way. Like a chorus of a thousand electric guitars, strumming in an unending hypnotic pattern.

A large hairless beast ran across my field of vision, causing the ground to vibrate around me. It stopped briefly to regard me, standing on all fours. Its large bulbous head was covered in eyes, and thick scales ran down its skinny, toned, body. There had never been anything quite like it on Earth, at least, nothing within our fossil record, anyway.

Was this Mars that I saw? Some ancient recording or invasive virtual reality program? Maybe it was none of those things. Maybe I was dead, and the sights before me were just the result of the neurons in my brain slowly dying.

If that was the case, what would Akio do without me?

I took a step forward and noticed that, not only was my leg not broken anymore, but my legs were not unlike a bird's foot. There were no muscles; instead, I could feel tendons lifting and pulling my legs forward. My feet were not feet, but, yet again, sharp hooves that could stab into the ground for better stability. I tried to move my tongue around inside my mouth, and found that it wasn't there, but somehow I could feel my teeth, grinding against each other. They were long, flat things, arranged in rows, perhaps to chew plants and other forms of vegetation. Was I an herbivore?

Somehow that felt right.

I sprinted across the field and felt the wind in my fur, scaring the strange animal off into the tall grass. Soon, I was over the next hill, approaching a large series of towering rock formations; but as I got closer, it became apparent that they weren't rocks, but a sprawling skyline, a city of silver and red metal perched atop orange cliffs.

The towers stretched up into the sky, taking full advantage of the low Martian gravity. There were great spirals, ramps, and statues not unlike the ones Akio and I had seen in those tunnels beneath Olympus Mons. These statues were full and complete. They stood tall, and proud, and bore the weight of the support for each tower. There were no roads; tall grass and vegetation stretched from building to building, vines wrapped about the bases of towers, and trees grew in harmony with construction.

"We've waited for someone like you for a long time." A voice echoed through the empty city, and I turned to face a creature wrapped in drapery, clutching a long, gnarled staff with two of its wiry limbs; long twisting tentacles wrapped about the staff's length, coming from within the sharp ending hooves at the end of each of its limbs.

"Who are you?" I asked. The words were strange and distorted coming from my inhuman mouth.

"A memory. One left over from those that lived so long ago," it said. *"Long before you, before the cataclysm robbed us of everything we held dear."*

"Why are you talking like the village elder in some cheap *Battle for Drogon* knockoff?"

"You chose this voice." The creature grinned. *"We probed your mind for what an elder sounds like to humans and settled on this. Is it not a satisfactory choice?"*

"You probed my mind? So, you're probably some kind of artificial intelligence then."

"Is it satisfactory?"

"I guess it doesn't matter, carry on."

"We require one last bit of consent to access the rest of your memory."

"Consent?" I shook my head. "How do I do that?"

"Tell us how is it you came to find this place."

"I—" I stuttered. "I don't know where to start."

"Take your time."

We sat in silence for a time, while I ran the events over in my head. Finally, I started to speak. I explained everything, the dark matter camera, Akio, the deaths of Gila, Wolfrik, Adams, and everyone else, in exhausting detail. I spent the most time explaining the mantis shapes, and my recurring nightmares. I hadn't told anyone about those yet. It was therapeutic in a way.

"The diorama in the dark matter web only hints at the cataclysm you speak of. What happened?" I paced around the creature, taking notes on its anatomy. I couldn't help myself.

"You will live it as we lived it."

"What the fuck does that mean?"

The creature shook its elongated head; its four eyes regarded me with slight indifference. It turned around and ascended the hill that led to a large tower. It twisted its head at me and gestured with its staff for me to enter.

"What is this?"

"It will become clear."

"What will become clear? Your history? The cataclysm?"

"Most things." The creature sighed. *"But not all."*

"Okay, *now* it's getting annoying."

The creature focused its gaze forward and placed its tentacles on the wall. Geometric green lights appeared around the points of its appendages and wrapped around a large rectangular section of the wall. The wall collapsed inward; the creature disappeared into the darkness. The doorway stayed open, but I hesitated to enter.

Was this real? Once again, I imagined myself dying within the confines of my own space suit, Akio pleading with me to somehow come back from the dead so she wouldn't have to die alone when her oxygen supply finally ran out.

"It doesn't matter," the creature said from within the darkness. *"If you were dying, none of this would matter."*

"Are you inside my head?" I asked.

"You let us in when you touched our skin."

"When I touched that thing in the middle of the room?"

"Yes."

There was a slight breeze, and I felt as though the darkness was beckoning to me. Cautiously, I made my way inside, where the creature was waiting in the center of a glowing circle.

"We have assessed your memory, and compared your culture with ours."

"Is that right?"

"You are still very much in your infancy, and still rely on the consumption of the precious resources of your world to survive."

"We've gotten better about that, though. We made it here before we blew ourselves up—*despite* our *best* efforts—didn't we?"

"You could have been much further."

"Well if you're so damn great, why aren't you here now?"

"A part of us is, and now it rests within your mind, so that you can tell our story and prevent such a cataclysm from destroying your world."

I sighed. Even in this world, this fantasy, I felt exhausted. "Please, tell me."

"We were at harmony with our world, with the beasts of all things, of the sky, of the sea, and of the land. We developed great technologies and science that helped cure diseases, we ruled this world with strength and dignity, and eventually reached for the stars. We traveled to each world, except for yours, for fear of what our presence there would do to the emerging beasts that roamed those lands."

"Dinosaurs, you're talking about dinosaurs, right?"

"We *do not know this word, but searching your mind tells us that there are many gaps in what your science calls the* fossil record. *But perhaps there is some truth to your assumption.*"

"So, there's no telling how old you are?"

"We *have kept careful track of the progression of revolutions around what you call the Sun. It has been exactly seventy-two million revolutions, sixteen seasons, and thirty cycles.*"

"A revolution is what we call a year?"

"*This is correct.*"

"So then, I'm assuming that a season is what we would call Winter, Spring, Summer, and cycles would be our equivalent to days or Sols?"

"*You are correct. We remember a time when ours was a strong race, who came to fill our whole world. We established places of research on other worlds in this system and tried to learn all we could.*"

The darkness gave way, and I saw the globe of Mars below me, blue and green, rich with life, as they would have seen it in their age—dangled invisibly against the backdrop of an infinite blanket of stars. It was so much like Earth, and yet it was different all the same. One key feature that I noticed was that Valles Marineris, the blackened shadow of a canyon that cut across Mars' belly, was strangely absent from the vibrant blue and green and cloud-covered world that I saw before me. In fact, there were many familiar regions that seemed to be different, or completely missing from the planet. I reached out with my arm tentacles, hoping to caress a world that was both out of reach and out of time. It made my heart ache to know that there was so much we didn't know about even our own solar backyard.

Great pod-like ships left the atmosphere for other worlds. One found its way to the moons of Jupiter, another to orbit Saturn, and another studied the Sun and Mercury.

"*Then, after many revolutions, our way of life was threatened by the coming of a great comet.*"

To say the comet was massive was an understatement. Jets of plasma shot off it into the depths of space, creating what looked like a terrible star. From the surface, the comet looked as though it split the heavens in two, creating gigantic electrical discharges between the two bodies.

I saw smaller creatures cowering at the sight of the comet, their parents cradling them close with their tendrils. Some went mad as it approached, growing larger in the sky Sol by Sol. Some worshipped it as if it was some kind of God, organizing cult-like congregations to gather at the edges of cliffs where they would then commit suicide by jumping off.

We were so much alike.

"We didn't know where it came from. Our science was helpless in trying to divert it or destroy it. Then the day came when we lost all hope."

"Wait. You're telling me that even with all of this amazing technology, you weren't able to even divert its course?"

"Can you move planets or moons?"

"No, but, we—"

"We lacked the ability. Now silence."

The comet bore down on the planet. Herds of these creatures stared up at the white comet in the sky as it ignited the atmosphere. The ground cracked and shook with such force that the creatures were tossed to their backs. Some were flattened by falling rocks and shifting land masses; others fell to their deaths when the ground opened up and consumed them whole. It had impacted, and there was a wall of fire and death on the horizon that I had only thought possible in movies. A wall of ash and fire towered into the heavens, spreading across the entire northern horizon. It was slowly creeping toward my vantage point.

"Those of us that were not killed by the initial impact ran for cover, with little success."

I saw visions of them hiding in tunnels, like the lava tubes beneath Olympus Mons, and then I saw those same lava tubes filled with fire and ash. The dead lined the walls of the tunnels, like one gigantic mass grave.

"All those who stayed behind on our world perished in the cataclysm." Pod ships descended through the ruined and ash filled atmosphere, returning to the world they had abandoned. *"What was left for our people was a lifeless shell of its former glory."*

"You survived down there...inside Olympus Mons."

"*We were unable to survive on the surface anymore, and the impact destroyed our magnetic field. The clouds and ash that hung over the planet would have lasted for hundreds of revolutions had the solar winds not blown the atmosphere away to dwell among the stars.*

"*Those of us who were spread across the stars felt an urgent duty to return. When we did, our hearts could not take the devastation the comet had left in its wake. Gone were our fields of grass, the animals, and our great sprawling cities. We built machines underground to produce artificial atmosphere and grew crops and brought the animals that we had taken with us to live among the stars down below the surface, where we constructed great cities. For a time, it was enough to keep our species alive.*"

"But, the mantis creatures I've been seeing, the ones that I awakened, they started killing your people inside the tunnels. Didn't they?"

"*Yes. We believed these were born from the great trauma that our people had felt upon facing its own extinction.*"

"I see." I paced back and forth, the way I would in my human body when attempting to process a thought. "So, the same event that caused the impact of the comet to be recorded in the dark matter web here, those emotions also created a new kind of life form."

"*Except, all that this creature knew was pain and despair, anger and dread. We had machines much like the one you describe, which could see the binding energy of the universe, and when we activated these machines for the first time after the cataclysm, we saw them, and then they saw us. We were bonded. And they did not love us.*"

"We would call that quantum entanglement, where defining the state of one particle determines the state of another. Except, these creatures, they must use that as a means of determining what exists here in our dimension."

"*Be careful with your assumptions. You assume you've unraveled a great mystery by seeing these images, but the mystery is one that not even we could solve. Much is unknown about these beings. We were driven to extinction quickly by them. We decided to make this record of our history with the hope that one like you would discover it, so that our voice would not be eternally lost.*

"But, we know your mind, the constrictions it places on what is possible. Know this. There are things in this universe that are older than us, than you. Things that are not bound by the confines of time and reality, that do not need space to live, that see us as mere specks against their vastness, their brilliance."

"Wait, is there more history here?"

"Yes. It is waiting for you to discover, should you survive."

The room became as white as the Sun's surface, and I heard a familiar voice calling to me…

XIV

I woke in Akio's arms, tears dripping and pooling in her helmet.

"Akio?" I said.

"Hal!" The anguish faded from her face.

"How long was I unconscious?"

"Unconscious?" She shook her head. "You flatlined for five minutes! I patched into your gauntlet—tried beating on your chest to start your heart—nothing worked! I thought I *lost* you."

I sat up, my broken ribs protesting once again; the room had gone dark. "The lights are gone."

"They shut off before you came back."

"It seemed so real…" I placed my hand on the glass that separated my body and the environment beyond. "I saw their society, their cities, talked with an AI program left over since their race went extinct."

"What?"

I struggled to my feet; Akio quickly stood up and helped me. "My gauntlet, I need you to turn on the flashlight."

My gauntlet's screen illuminated her face, and the glove on my hand lit up with brilliant white light. I clenched my fist and aimed the light at the center of the room, where the strange membranous thing had been. It was gone now, replaced by an empty void, a hole in the floor.

"I'm not imagining things, right?" I asked. "There was a thing in the center of the room before I collapsed, right?"

Akio nodded and turned her own flashlight on. She shined it on the walls where we'd seen the strange glowing hieroglyphic symbols earlier. Her light showed only a smooth black wall, slick with condensation. "The symbols we saw are gone too."

"I think we should go down that hole. While I was unconscious, I saw things. I thought it was some kind of virtual reality, but now I'm thinking that thing in the center of the room was some sort of living computer. I think it passed its knowledge on to me."

"Have you ruled out the possibility that it was your brain cells committing suicide?" Her sarcasm was screened by fear, concern.

"That was my first thought."

"Go on…"

"Well, in the dream, or whatever it was, I talked with one of the creatures that lived here over one hundred and forty-four million of our years ago. It told me that once Mars was a lush and green world, but that changed when a giant comet slammed into the surface and destroyed their magnetic field—destroyed everything. Those who dwelled among the stars, they returned, came to live down here, building machines to produce atmosphere and herd animals and livestock to preserve themselves.

"They were eventually wiped out by the very dark matter creatures that we've been dealing with, and I believe they had devices like the one we built to observe the dark matter web around them. If that's the case, we can find one and use it."

Her eyes narrowed. "Interesting. It must be an artificial intelligence then."

"That's my best guess too."

"And it's trying to help us?" If there was doubt in her voice, it was written on her face.

"Near as I can figure."

I started limping toward the hole in the floor.

"Before we go spelunking," she said, "what about air, what about food?" She held up her gauntlet and pointed to her air tracker. The bar was over halfway depleted.

"Right, at the very least, we'll need to find the machines that control atmosphere and turn them on. Problem solved."

"How do we know they even breathed oxygen like we do?"

"We don't. But, I have a hunch."

"Hunches aren't going to save us, Hal…"

"Well, they're all we've got right now." I turned back around, continued limping over to the hole, and prepared myself for whatever fate might await us.

Akio grabbed my arm. "Are you sure about this?"

I nodded. "Jump."

I stepped off the ledge and allowed myself to fall down the hole. The descent was short, only a few meters; I hit a curve, slid down a long twisting pipe, and was tossed out, tumbling in darkness. Waves of fire engulfed my limbs and my screams scorched my lungs, fogging up my helmet. I heard Akio calling for me from above. I stifled my screams by clenching my teeth so hard I feared they would shatter. The bandaged wound in my side screamed—it felt like tiny, microscopic hands were reaching out from inside me, spreading the wound open like a damaged zipper belonging to a tattered and beaten pair of jeans. I focused, trying to lock the pain away, and bit my lip as I stood up.

With my good arm, I grabbed at my broken one, aimed it and my flashlight in front of me.

I was surrounded by blackened floor and walls, the shape one might assume the inside of an old-timey water tower takes. A dead end. The floor was littered with small grooves, possibly symbols, which seemed to have been etched into it. I saw echoes of Akio's light above, near the mouth where I'd been shot out.

"I found the bottom," I said. "You'll be fine if you jump, but there's nothing else down here."

"Are you okay?" she asked.

"No more broken than I was before."

"Smart-ass. All right, I'm coming down, stand against the wall so I don't hit you."

I nodded and slid against the far wall.

Seconds passed and I didn't see Akio jump.

"Akio, what's going on?" I asked.

She shushed me and whispered, "I think I hear something."

"Hurry and jump, if it's one of them it already knows you're there." My aura must have flared when I came back from flatlining. Damn it.

I shouted Akio's name; my blood ran hot. Then, silence, my heart thundering through my chest.

I can't lose you, I thought.

I imagined it moving about the room above, slowly, deliberately, circling around Akio, considering her dark matter aura—stretching its glowing, violet blades high above its featureless mantis head.

"Akio!"

I heard a bloodcurdling scream over my comm and saw a large mass fall to the center of the floor. I limped over to her side as fast as my broken body would allow me to.

"Akio!" I grabbed for her hand, squeezed it. *Please be okay.* "Are you okay?"

I saw that she was still breathing. My heart calmed.

She shook her head, cursing; there was a faint wisp of oxygen trailing from her left arm. It was a gash that slashed across part of her sleeve, and I knew what it meant. She was fucking lucky. I held down on the breach in her suit and reached for the adhesive gun on her hip, but it wasn't there. I grabbed my own instead and sealed the tear. Pressure filled her suit; she breathed deep, her eyes were wide, she looked at the gauntlet.

"What happened?" I asked.

"Okay," she said. "If I had any doubt before, I definitely believe you now."

I sighed. "You still doubted me?"

"No, but shut up." She glared at the information on her gauntlet. "I lost a lot of oxygen because of that invisible shithead."

"Damn it," I said. "Can you stand?"

"I think so…" She got to her feet. "It's not going to do me much good if you're right about them being entangled with you, if it isn't already here."

"Then we need to find a way out of this hole." I imagined the mantis silhouette hovering above us, watching the dim light that was Akio drifting away. Would it follow? How would we know?

"Agreed." Fear painted her face into a worried scowl; her eyes drifted around the room, scanning it for any hint that might lead us to finding a way out—or invisible predators.

I bent down low to the floor, gritted my teeth, and ran my hand over some of the grooves.

"What are you doing?" she asked.

"When we got here, I ran my finger through one of these grooves, a symbol of some kind, and then simply touching that membranous thing allowed me to connect with the AI. Maybe that'll have an effect if this is a trapdoor?"

"What if this place doesn't have any defined shape?" The fear was still present in her voice, but it had diminished slightly. She was doing exactly what I was doing, focusing on the task at hand to keep herself from self-destructing.

I'd tried several combinations, but nothing had happened yet. I had to stop; the pain in my broken leg was getting to be too much.

"Let me try," Akio said.

She helped me up, then bent down and tried a few combinations. She traced her finger through a circular groove and down a set of symbols; she cursed when light traced around the exterior portion of the circle, illuminating our boots, and creating clear divisions in the carvings, like a segmented maze. Part of the floor fell away, creating a staircase that faded into darkness. It was like reality itself was warping before our very eyes.

Akio rushed down the steps, and I limped after her. The way behind us closed, but we kept walking. The lights returned to guide us once more, casting geometric shapes in the floor and walls.

Still, I imagined that our mantis friend stalked us through the walls. Slowly drifting toward Akio from behind.

The worst part was not knowing if or when it would happen, and being powerless to stop it if it did.

We twisted around corridors, through bends and turns. My feet were so numb I could have sworn they'd crumble to dust if I took my suit off. Finally, we emerged from the hallway into a large dark room. The path behind us slammed shut with such force that I felt it vibrate through my bones. I gritted my teeth.

I scanned my light through the darkness, Akio doing the same.

It looked like we'd entered a massive spherical room filled with dusty tables that reminded me of a laboratory. It was at least four stories tall by human standards.

For the light to lead us here, when we'd just been talking about using their machines—was the AI still in my mind?

I limped over to a table on my left. Akio helped me ease down onto one to rest. The tables were curved, cascaded up several levels, and were joined in the center of the room by a single staircase and a large damaged statue that was clutching a thin staff with its tentacles. There were several items on the table; one of them was a large, oval-shaped helmet that had an opening on the bottom. It was remarkably intact, save for a single crack that ran along the right hemisphere of what I assumed was the visor. I peered inside, and saw that there was no face shield, unlike our helmets, but a large glass plate that fixed over the creature's eyes to project an image. This must have provided some protection to them in harsher environments.

Not enough to save them, I thought.

"Are these parts of a space suit?" Akio asked.

"Not sure," I said. "If they had machines like our dark matter camera, even if they're built into a helmet like this, we should be able to recognize similar components."

"Then what?" She leaned against the table, toying with some kind of tool haphazardly. Now that I was sitting down, I could see how much she was shaking. "Even if we can see them, what good will it do?"

"We'll, at the very least, be able to stay ahead of it until we can turn the atmospherics back on. Remember how slow it moved in on Mike? If we keep moving, we might outrun it…if it's still after you…"

"And then?" Her eyes locked on mine. Her very soul looked tired. "I don't know how long I, or you, can keep this up."

"I don't know, either…" I wanted to rub my fatigued eyes. Wanted to wipe my sweat-drenched brow, my face, or submerge myself in a cold bath to ease my fever as my mother had done when I got the flu as a child. "Maybe we'll just sit down and have a chat with them?"

She chuckled, smiled at me. "You're not scared at all?"

Even in the darkness, surrounded by a suffocating air of dread—even in this self-aware tomb of a maze—there was warmth in her smile.

"I'm terrified," I said quietly. "The pain is constant, it's all-encompassing. I feel like I'm losing my mind."

Her hand caressed the glass of my helmet. I could almost feel her. I wished I could peel the suit off. The tool was still in her other hand. I nodded at it. "What do you think it is?"

She shrugged. "A paperweight?"

I held my palm out for the tool Akio was holding, and she dropped it into my hand. The tool, which I had originally guessed was a cutting device of some kind, had a soft depression at its end, and a small hole in the center at both ends of the stick. Either one could have been a button. After several long moments tinkering with the thing, I couldn't get it to respond.

"Maybe it's broken?" Akio said. "I mean, this stuff's millions of years old."

"But, wonderfully preserved...I just wish there was a way to ask what works and what doesn't!"

Akio and I almost shouted in unison at the mantis-like shadow that resulted from the sudden brightness behind us. I jerked around quickly—regretted it—and discovered that a luminous geometrical star shape had formed in the center of the floor. Lines and glyphs traced across the floor, bled to the walls, and reached the ceiling, like a darkened room lit only by an illuminated pool.

The helmet and the device I was holding lit up in my hands.

"Looks like you got your wish," Akio said.

"How about that." Was the AI still watching us? Was that what seemed to respond to our need? If so, how could we communicate with it?

I turned around and tried the button on the side of the stick; a small sliver of yellow light extended. The tool appeared to be creating a blade of hard light—a feat human scientists still could not master.

The hard light tool cut through the side of the helmet with ease, and I was able to pry it open to get a look at the interior bits. What I saw was a mix of the expected and the unrecognizable. These creatures, whoever they had been, were far and above us. To think that they hadn't been able to prevent something as crude as a comet—even one the size of a moon—from bringing ruin upon their world. What hope did the human race have?

Our dark matter camera had utilized a modified interferometer to track subtle changes in the atoms using two beams of light, comparing them to how atoms would have behaved if interacting with dark matter clusters. Then it would take that data and render it as a 3D image, overlaying it on top of a panoramic shot.

I could see several components in the helmet that appeared to be small magnifying glasses, or mirrors, or both. Perhaps a miniaturized version of the same concept?

"That looks nothing like our machine," Akio said.

"Thank you for stating the obvious," I said.

"You looked like you were having trouble."

"I don't even know how we can use this."

She snatched the helmet out of my hands and peered inside. "Let me take a look."

I watched her squint at the helmet for several minutes, until she finally reached inside and ripped out several bits and pieces.

"What are you doing?" I asked, only slightly panicked that she was ripping apart a million-year-old antique.

"The interferometer is very small, but it's there. Maybe we can patch this thing into our suits somehow?"

"Oh, sure, just a matter of a simple software update!"

"Sarcasm won't help us here." She rolled her eyes. "Besides, what else are we going to do?"

I let my weight press against the table, taking the pressure off my good leg. "How're your oxygen levels?"

"Below fifteen percent."

I sighed and checked my own. "I'm sitting at just over fifty percent. If we had an oxygen cable, I could hook you up to my air supply."

"Then we'd both die quicker."

"Better than dying alone."

Akio grew very quiet; her eyes quivered and I looked away, staring at the glowing glyphs on the ceiling, walls, and floor.

"Hal," she said. "What if we don't get out of this?"

203

"Thought hadn't crossed my mind," I said quietly.

"Don't give me that bullshit, answer the question."

"Then we die. What is there to say? The world keeps moving, maybe Olympus One survives, maybe it doesn't, maybe someone stumbles upon us and discovers what happened, maybe they don't."

"You don't care?"

"Let's just focus on the task, Akio."

"No, damn it!" Akio lifted the helmet above her head and tossed it at the floor, causing both halves to roll to a stop. "This matters! You can't just keep locking your feelings up, expecting people to believe that you don't give a shit!"

"You're right." I sighed. "I'm just trying to keep us focused, keep us set to the task. I don't want either of us to die here…" My eyes focused on the finger-shaped smudges that Akio had left on the glass of my helmet. "I care."

"Was that seriously so hard to say?"

I shrugged.

Her eyes drifted to the dancing light within the glyphs on the floor.

"Now, you've got less than fifteen percent air left," I said. "Let's get to figuring this out."

I watched her pick up the helmet's two halves and peer down at the pieces she had removed. "The mirrors and magnifiers are all here, they're made of a kind of material I can't quite place, but if we open up our gauntlets, we should be able to create a kind of detector from them and use the front of the gauntlet to aim the camera."

"We can feed the image back to our HUDs directly then."

"Right, but that could take hours, and we don't have it."

I forced my weight off the table, trying not to wince, and limped toward the star of light that danced in the center of the floor. "Then you'll have to work as we walk."

"Where? The place is sealed up."

"I think you're right about this place having no definite shape, at least to a certain extent." I grinned, gesturing with my good hand at the lights around us. "If *our* bodies contain *our* brains, then this *place* is the AI's *body*. It's been talking to us this entire time, guiding us to safety."

"You call it what you like, but I feel like we're being led around like mice in a maze."

"We are mice compared to them."

"That's what I'm afraid of…"

"There are things older than us in this universe, older than time, older than space."

"What?"

I shrugged. "Just something I heard in a dream."

I stood there, in the center of the star formation. Akio went quietly about her work with her project, leaving me to ponder on how I could get the AI to answer my commands. In the dream, they had known my language, and every time we'd been in trouble leading up to this lab, we'd found a new opening at the last second, almost as if this place was listening to us.

"We need a way out," I said. "Show us the path to the atmospheric systems so we don't die."

The lights kept dancing. Nothing happened.

"Maybe you're wrong," Akio said. "Maybe all these lights we've been seeing are all in our heads and we're slowly dying?"

"Very funny. Be quiet, I need to think."

She stuck her tongue out at me. "Screw you too."

"Each time a doorway opened, we used our fingers to trace one of the glyphs on the wall, or the floor. Maybe that had something to do with it? Maybe touch allows it a direct link into our minds?"

I struggled to bend over, moving my leg into an awkward position to lessen the pain from my broken ribs, and placed my finger on the floor. I traced a line through one of the glyphs.

The lights kept dancing. Nothing happened.

"Well, there goes that theory," Akio said.

"It doesn't prove anything," I said. "Maybe I need to be thinking of what we need before it knows how to respond?"

"Maybe you need to do both at the same time. I think that's how it worked last time." I heard her let out a heavy sigh. "Or, maybe it just doesn't fucking work?"

"Maybe you're right?" I focused on getting to some sort of atmospheric control unit as I traced the glyph with my finger.

This time, a darkness appeared to grow from the ceiling above me to the star in which I stood. I could feel vibrations in my feet, and part of the floor melted away, creating a staircase.

"Got another sarcastic comment for that?" I asked.

"Yeah, how about, '*Hah! I was right!*'"

I sighed and waved Akio down the staircase. "Yes, you were right."

She passed me by, looking over her shoulder at the now darkening room. Her laughter and sarcasm. The brief relief of normal conversation. All a mask. I followed her into a twisting corridor. The multicolored geometric lights returned, dancing, twisting, turning, and guiding us around corners, through another spherical room filled with dead alien technology, and through a massive arched doorway that a shuttle could have flown through.

The lights stopped here. They hovered, circling, waiting, several feet in front of us. We stopped and peered out at a vast bridge that seemed to stretch into a wall of black so total that my eyes imagined that it continued on past the horizon. The bridge had no rails, nothing to keep you from falling off the edge. There was nothing but darkness on either side of it. Akio and I stood there at the arched doorway, shining our tiny lights into the abyss. Our beams of light touched nothing but darkness.

Some ancient, eldritch fear clawed at my heart.

"I think it's telling us to cross it," Akio said. She sounded like she was out of breath.

All I could do was nod and follow her as she began what seemed like a long journey across that massive thing.

I stopped briefly and shined my light off the edge. The abyss had no end, but the bridge seemed to be supported by a megalithic piece of molten rock.

"This must be one of the magma chambers," I said. "Long dead, just like the planet's core."

Akio stopped, holding her devices close to her chest, probably fearing how screwed we'd be if she were to drop them. "How big is it?"

"No idea."

We pressed on across the bridge; the darkness in the distance played tricks on my eyes. Sometimes, it was like being blind again. I could see shapes, wraith-like things that dashed and stalked us, waiting for the time when we would be most vulnerable.

And, sometimes—when I stared too long into the dark—I would start to see the auditorium where I had been beaten and battered. The blazing, hellish, yellow Mars sky just outside the transparent wall. The bodies of the dead still swirling around me, their dead hands reaching to pull me along with them.

Each time the vision took shape in the dark, I had to focus on Akio to stop it.

She would be amused to know that, in a way, here in this shapeless alien city, she was the anchor for my sanity.

I couldn't help the constant feeling of being watched. Part of me didn't want Akio to finish with the dark matter camera, for fear of what it might find waiting in the dark.

The bridge seemed to stretch on for miles, and the pain was so great in my good leg that I was forced to put equal weight onto the splinted one. Akio helped me when she could, but I got the sense that she was too tired to even shoulder my weight anymore.

When I saw the arches at the end of the bridge, I had to make sure I wasn't seeing things. There was a large gate at the end of the bridge, beyond the arch that marked the start of another long-dead lava tube. Two statues stood at either side, cracked and faceless. If there was a door to this tunnel, it was already open by the time we reached it. While the walls were naturally rocky, the floor was composed of the same slick black substance that we'd seen in the other sections of the city. Those geometric lights returned once our feet left the bridge's surface, led us under the arches, through the gate, and into the lava tube.

The path stretched on, and the geometric lights kept ahead of us, casting shadows in every direction, like eager puppies leading their master to a bone. Akio was still fiddling with the helmet and her gauntlet when we reached a dead end. The end of the tunnel stretched up, meeting a wall hundreds of feet tall. I shined my light up at the wall, moving it up the surface until the circle of light illuminated a large oval-shaped glyph in the center of the wall with three jagged lines slashed through it.

"What is it?" Akio asked.

"Maybe a door," I said, limping up to it.

I placed my hand on the wall and closed my eyes, holding that same need for oxygen at the center of my thoughts. I kept it there for several seconds before I finally felt a tremor erupt through the stone. The symbol in the middle of the wall lit up bright, segmented, and sank into the depth of the wall. A slim division was created between the two halves of the door, and they slowly fell away to reveal a dark, monstrous chamber. My flashlight played tricks with shadows; there were giant, textured, spherical shapes, connections, tubes, and smoothed rectangular things inside that chamber that seemed to stretch on for the length of a football field.

I limped on inside, and Akio came after me reluctantly. The glyphs led me to a set of steps that had been blanketed in darkness. The light danced up to an array of transparent globes and tables where it hovered like an arrow on a GPS that says 'You Have Arrived.' Perhaps this was the Martian version of a console?

I took one step at a time, limping up the blackened staircase in a way that would be least painful to my tired broken limbs. My hand came to prop the rest of my body up when it met the table's edge. It was a reflectively smooth surface, colored like obsidian, and yet it also appeared textured at first glance. I caught my breath and tried to "think" the transparent globes and the table to life. I closed my eyes and focused, shutting out the constant pain in my limbs and chest.

I saw the globes come to life with light and strange hieroglyphs that scrolled up and down the surface. The table came to life as well, segmenting into large geometric shapes that looked like a keyboard that had been sliced up into a jigsaw puzzle. It made me think of the tentacles that came from the stubs of the creatures' arms in the dream, and I imagined one of them standing before the console—its tentacles dancing across the surface of the table with careful timing and dexterous, slippery movements.

Turning back to Akio, I saw that she was putting her gauntlet back together. "Is it ready?"

"Almost," she said. "By the way, my oxygen levels are down to three percent, so, no pressure or anything."

I faced the globes and placed my hand on the console again. This time, I closed my eyes, and focused on thoughts that led to our lungs being filled with breathable air and the halls of the great sprawling alien city being filled with pressure and atmosphere.

"Hal, look!"

My eyes opened, and I saw Akio's hand in the corner of my vision, pointing at the large spheres and smoothed rectangular shapes.

They were covered in glowing hieroglyphs, revealing large mechanisms, metallic and industrial-looking, which started to turn and send vibrations through the whole chamber. Each apparatus began to move, until the chamber was a cacophony of vibrations and moving parts, like the biggest damned engine I'd ever seen.

I could see the outside temperature reading on my HUD steadily climbing above freezing, and white clouds of vapor shot from large newly formed vents above us. This alien city felt like a living plant and a computer all the same, growing what it needed and destroying what it didn't. What would it do with us once we had fulfilled our usefulness?

Akio placed her hands on the latches of her helmet. "One percent. Guess I have no choice."

I nodded. My heart rate accelerated, displayed to me as numbers on my HUD.

She unlatched her helmet and closed her eyes, as if she was accepting her fate, whatever it might be. I saw her eyes open wide as she inhaled deep the atmosphere that had filled the chamber.

A smile cracked across her face, and she took a few more breaths. "It worked."

I unlatched my own helmet and placed it on the table. The air tasted somewhat strange, and stale, but after being trapped within those tubes for millions of years, who could complain?

"There is one problem," I said.

"Yeah, I thought of that too. Who knows what kind of microbes and viruses are in this air?"

"Death or slightly prolonged death? Can't be helped."

She nodded and closed the hatch on her gauntlet, then replaced the screws. "It's time to test this thing."

"Can you link the feed up to my HUD?"

"I will, just give me a minute."

Soon, I saw the images roll in from the dark matter camera on her gauntlet. The web was vibrant here, with fluctuations and changes, but there were no strange shapes here that we could see—except when her camera panned across my body.

My dark matter aura was bright. Luminous. My heart began to hammer through my chest. There was worry in Akio's eyes.

Was this a change in me that would be permanent, or would we be able to flee this room before anything happened to us? Whatever the case, it was only a matter of time now.

She moved her arm in a sweeping circle, and I heard her gasp. I saw shapes in the violet web that showed on my HUD, creeping mantis shapes, waiting at the edges of the room as if they hadn't noticed us yet. And I knew that they had. What irony that would be, to be saved only by our own ignorance of the things that waited to kill us.

Then we heard clear sounds, rustling in our ears like the crumpling of nonexistent leaves, that drowned out the thrashing and rambunctious sounds of the machines around us. Our backs came together, and the sounds seemed to surround us. The images coming in on my HUD reflected this: the strange, praying mantis-like shapes, creeping toward us, like creatures animated by stop motion.

"What are we going to do?" Akio asked, her voice quavering.

"I hadn't thought it through that far," I said.

"Well, think, damn it!"

"Okay, okay." I ran my hand through my stringy, sweat-stained hair. "In my dream, the creatures had only appeared after the comet hit the planet. Presumably, the Martians had had the technology to observe the dark matter web long before the cataclysm sent them down here, but they'd only had trouble with the phantoms after."

"So, the impact caused them to appear?"

"Or, it created them."

We started to move away from the dark matter phantoms, backing down the stairs as they advanced on us. There was a small area of violet web that appeared devoid of them, so we moved in that direction.

"If that were the case," she said, "why don't we see them on Earth?"

"One of two possibilities." I said. "One, they don't exist on Earth's dark matter web, or, two, we haven't noticed them."

"Okay, so, why are they attacking us?"

We found our backs to the massive wall, the phantoms slowly closing the gap. "Why does any predator hunt?"

"To eat, usually..."

"To survive." There was a kind of knowing when the words escaped my lips.

"What?" Akio's eyes were wide, her face stricken with stress and terror. "What is it?"

"I think I know what created them."

The phantoms were just meters in front of us; I touched my hand to the wall and felt it collapse again. We stumbled back into the corridor and continued to back away from them.

"Think about this," I said. "The recordings in the dark matter were probably caused by some kind of trauma that the Martians felt when they were faced with extinction; that emotional stress had a direct effect on the dark matter web around them as they were killed."

"Okay," she said. "So, you're suggesting that these things were created in that same event?"

"Right! And, what if those same emotions, the fear, the anger, the unconscious desire for survival, what if that was what created these things?"

"So, their first moments were born from these emotions..."

"They were born only feeling the intense need to survive at all costs, and so they still continue like this, destroying everything around them, because they've never known anything else, and everything is a threat."

"So, nice theory and all, but how the hell does that help us?"

"Remember when I said we should sit down and have a conversation with them?"

"You were joking, Hal!"

"And I'm not joking now."

"You want to fucking talk to them?"

"Communication is the only thing that's going to save us. We can't hurt them, and that won't stop them from killing other visitors to this world who are unlucky enough to catch their notice."

"Yeah, but how?"

That was a problem. We were being forced to back away from them, down that long tunnel, and eventually we'd be forced to confront them, or risk the little remaining air in our suits in the magma chamber, where there would be no atmosphere from the rest of the underground city.

What could I do to communicate with them? Did they even have a language? I guessed that they simply existed in a state of constant stress, watching the replay of their own doom again and again.

We backtracked across the blackened floors, past arches, darkened rooms, faceless statues, and eventually found our backs against the gate to the bridge beyond, now sealed. The phantoms approached, unrelenting.

I closed my eyes and limped forward; Akio seized my bad arm, sending waves of pain into my chest. "Don't do it, Hal, we'll think of something else!"

"No." I wrenched my arm free of her and gritted my teeth through the pain. "I have to do it now."

I limped before the approaching phantoms and struggled into a crouch, placing my hand upon the floor. Hopefully, the city's AI would feel my touch, my thoughts, and find some way to help us.

If only the phantoms could see what we saw, could see what they were doing to us. I dug up the memories of Gila and Wolfrik's deaths and replayed them in my mind's eye; I watched Gila's throat open up and spill its contents down her chest as she fell face-first onto the exercise mat; and Wolfrik's body once again split in two, his torso went one way, his legs another. I focused on the expressions on their faces, forever burned in my memory. Gila's eyes white and wide, her innocent smile lost forever, the life fading from her face. Wolfrik's dull downcast eyes, a frown and a longing in his eyes. What he longed for, I couldn't say.

Probably home.

I opened my eyes to see that the mantis figures had stopped approaching several meters from me. I stood up, holding my good hand out as if to hold them at bay.

Perhaps, somehow, they had heard me?

The phantoms seemed to be pacing around me. Akio found herself at my side, helping me to my feet.

"Why haven't they killed us?" Akio asked.

"Maybe we're getting through to them?" I said.

My heart rate was well above one hundred and fifty beats per minute, my blood pressure spiking. Finally, one of the phantoms moved forward till it was standing right in front of Akio's face. Sweat beaded and created rivulets down her brow; her lips quavered.

"It's in front of me," she said. "Isn't it?"

I nodded. Hope reached its apotheosis in me, and I dared to speak directly to the phantom. "Can you understand us?"

There was no reaction. It did not move. Akio's nervous brown eyes met mine. She was beautiful. I'd forced myself not to see it before for selfish reasons. "I want to run, Hal. I don't want to be here anymore."

"Trust me, it'll be fine. Talk to it."

I envisioned us surviving, leaving Mars, maybe settling down somewhere in the countryside together, having kids.

The whole deal.

Akio's cheeks quivered. She opened her mouth. "We...we mean you no harm—"

It was such a pleasant fantasy. I thought of us growing old together, our children growing up, marrying—or not—and having kids of their own. They'd comment on how their mother and father constantly argued, constantly teased and prodded at each other, but that, for some odd reason, they loved each other.

"Akio," I said. I saw a fire alight in my gut; my aura, as bright as a star in the video from her gauntlet. "I—"

Then she screamed; I stumbled backward; something wet coated my face, and I could taste iron on my tongue.

It was as if something snapped inside my brain, and I saw before me the truth of the creatures, the things that I had called mantises. Phantoms.

I focused on the one in front of Akio.

It was a monstrous thing, covered in eyes, with four bladed scythes for arms and long, amorphous and thin, segmented wiry legs that looked like they were covered in a sick, oozing ink, bleeding onto the ground, becoming one with it. There was no mouth to speak of, just a black orb covered in more eyes. One of its blades was lodged inside Akio's chest. It swiped with another blade and stabbed at her throat, red liquid spilling from her mouth and mixing with her tears.

I was screaming, yelling; the image projected from Akio's camera showed my dark matter aura dimming, like a candle being snuffed out.

She fell to the floor, lifeless. Her last words were a garble of nonsense that will haunt me till I draw my last breath. I stumbled back, tears in my eyes, attempting to limp away. I could see the phantoms moving toward Akio's corpse. I scooped up my helmet and fastened it on my head, felt the pressure fill my suit. I didn't want to die.

The coward that I am.

I found the wall and started to pound on it, to scream and thrash about wildly. Something had snapped inside me, and I lost all reason. I swiped at my back with my good arm, hoping to maim any phantom that came too close to me, while I fell into a painful crouch and cried myself stupid.

I was wrong.

I was wrong!

I felt the vibrations from the door opening, and, as soon as there was a gap large enough for my body to fit through, I was sucked out onto the great bridge that joined the two sections of the city by the force of depressurization.

My broken body tumbled across the bridge, coming to a sliding, grinding stop near the edge of the abyss.

The gate closed behind me.

I crawled for a while, and somehow found the strength to stand and limp. Surely, the phantoms would find me, surely they would end my life?

The darkness of the dead magma chamber called out to me, taunting me with familiar faces. Gila, Wolfrik, Clarence's son, Dalla, Mike, and now Akio at the center of my vision. Their heads whirled about me as I limped on like the coward I was. Akio's head seemed to dangle on violet strings that wrapped about her throat, just above where she'd been cut. Her lips were turning purple, her eyes cold and dead and accusing. Her mouth filled with blood, she smiled down at me, as if it say, *Soon, Hal, soon you will join us.*

Blood came from the mouths of Gila, and Wolfrik and Clarence and Dalla as well, until they were filling the magma chamber's unknowable depths with rivers of it.

"Your invention killed us," Gila said, her eyes turned white, flecks of dried blood flaking from her dead lips.

"Tell me, Geraldo," Wolfrik said. "Why is it that you do not seem to believe in procedure, or safety?"

"You missed out, buddy boy!" Akio said. Her smile—wide and drunk. Her teeth—full of blood. "I woulda fucked your brains out!"

"If I would have known knowing you would have ended my life, I would have stayed clear of you," Gila said.

"You betrayed me," Dane said. "You murdered me with your anger."

"Your father was right about you," Wolfrik said. "You are a disappointment."

"I was your friend," Dalla said, her eye sockets oozing a constant stream of blood. "And look where that got me?"

"I felt the hand of God," Mike said at last, his grin as obnoxious as it had ever been when he was alive.

"Why don't you join us for a salad?" Gila said, laughing, gurgling, drowning on her own blood.

"I wanted to know what it's like to fuck in no gravity," Akio said. "Now I never will."

"You took Gila from me," Dalla said. "I never forgave you for that."

"I experienced his angel's wrath," Mike said. "It cleansed me of my sin."

"It should have been you," Akio said, her once-purple lips turning black from the ever-flowing blood. Her smile faded, her eyes turned a

215

milky white. "But they will find you soon enough, and when they do, you'll join us here. A hell fitting for us all."

I started to laugh; steam filled my helmet, fogging it up. I was so far gone that I hadn't even noticed that Akio's gauntlet had stopped transmitting to my HUD. I passed through the archway, exiting the bridge and leaving behind the heads of my fallen friends. Their voices echoed through the tunnel behind me.

My oxygen levels were below twenty-five percent now, and yet I yearned to be outside, to be away from this ancient hellish, subterranean city.

After what seemed to be hours of walking down darkened hallways aimlessly, I collapsed on the floor. My laughter did not cease. I felt light trace around my body, and the floor begin to vibrate, then, when I finally rolled over, I could see that I was on some kind of platform, rising slowly up one of the magma tubes.

The pain in my limbs overtook me, and the toll from the efforts and stresses I'd suffered from the day finally reared its ugly head. I felt my eyelids close, to relive the nightmares again and again, until I woke, or expired from a lack of oxygen.

I didn't care which.

XV

I woke to hellish yellow skies and waves of dust clawing at the soft red sand around me. The platform was so thick with it that it covered every hint of the city that I had just been inside.

My HUD told me that my oxygen levels were down to fifteen percent. I struggled to my feet, aches and pains spreading wildfires through my body, but by now I was growing used to the feeling. At least I still felt something, unlike those who had been close to me.

The momentary madness that had gripped me seemed to have passed, but the memory of seeing Akio die before me clung to my heart like a vice. My tears were raw, and they were like razors cutting into my flesh.

There wasn't enough oxygen for me to limp anywhere significant, yet I didn't want to just sit there and wait for the end to come.

I started to limp in a random direction. So much had happened in such a short period of time. Maybe all of my theories about the phantoms were wrong, maybe they had been here all along, a race of beings far more ancient than either of us, Martian or human. Maybe their motives were unknowable, and maybe I had gazed upon their true form. My skin still shudders when I think of it.

Perhaps when the Martians and I had peered at them with our machines, assuming in our own arrogance that our place was as significant as their own, it had made them angry?

In any case, others who came this way should be warned, should have a log that told them not to venture into the twisting magma tubes and that ancient Martian city, with its unknowable chambers and depths.

I opened up the log file in my HUD, struggling with the gauntlet on my bad arm.

"This is Hal Leon," I said. "And this is my final log. It's my hope that anyone who finds this will take it seriously, and not venture to the city below. There are some things that science should leave well enough alone."

I cleared my throat, stopped, catching a glimpse of the golden orb of the Sun through the raging dust clouds. It made me sad that I'd never see another cobalt sunrise again. I thought back to just days ago, to the walkabout I'd taken just before the madness. I thought about the sunrise. I'd had my whole life ahead of me then. If only I could go back to that time, to warn myself of where my foolish arrogance was leading us.

"Sunrises on Mars are always strange to behold," I said, remembering the cobalt haze and the white-hot globe of the sun. "I watched a small white globe cut through a cobalt-blue haze over Olympus Mons, cascading its light dimly across the red planet's dusty surface…"

By the time I finished recording the log, my oxygen levels were down to two percent. It was only a matter of time now. A dust storm was rolling in.

I sat down, too tired to keep moving.

Maybe I'd die in my sleep…

XVI

*T*here's a murmur that vibrates through my broken ribs, a constant, strumming thing that wakes me from the fiery pits of hell.

I inhale fire.

I sit up. My head feels like it's swimming in a familiar medicated fog. My eyes focus from a blur of crazed faces, people I once knew, and one that I loved, then to a cold metallic container. Beds, there are beds in here, with straps and instruments.

Where am I?

"He's awake." *A voice echoes off of metal walls.* "Someone go check on the patient."

I'm in a sickbay. How am I not dead?

A man in a blue-and-black jumpsuit, with a name tag that's too blurry for me to read, comes in and checks the instruments next to my bed. I notice that my arm and leg are done up in casts, my body is wrapped in bandages.

"Mr. Leon," *the man says, and it causes panic to come surging through me. I struggle to get up, to see where I am, but I'm tied down to the bed.* "I wouldn't do that if I were you. We're just about to take off."

Take off? I try to speak, but it comes out as spit and saliva. How long was I out?

Why am I not dead?

"Right, you're probably wondering what happened to you," *he says, chuckling. Fucking asshole thinks this is funny.* "They found you out there on the slope; your air was depleted, but they got you back in time to slot you up in the infirmary. You were nearly dead, Mr. Leon."

You should have let me die.

"They're saying that you're a hero, though." A what? I want to strangle him, shake him stupid. "The deaths stopped for some reason. Whatever you did down there, it worked."

Down…he means the city…

"They're going to send an expedition down to explore the city sometime within the next couple of months, as soon as the supplies have been allocated."

No! You can't do that!

My voice fails me again, nothing but garbled consonants and spittle.

A look of pity spreads across the man's face. He checks my vitals. "You're agitated." He turns a dial on the console next to my bed; I feel lightheaded. A cooling sensation fills my brain, silencing my panicked thoughts. "In just six short months, you'll be on Earth again, where you can heal properly."

He pats my arm as sleep takes me, drowning my anger and my fear.

Oh, god, they're taking me back.

You can't take me back!

They'll follow me!

2

I'm sitting on the wall bordering what was once New America. The friend I once had is staring forward, holding another chunk of stone in his hand. He's staring forward, his mouth agape. I can't tell whether he's afraid, or in awe.

My eyes drift over to where he's looking.

"You never believed me about the ghosts," he says.

There they are. Thousands of blackened mantis creatures, with reflective skin the consistency of tar. Their sickening eyes open and close as they prowl the ruined landscape, through broken and shattered buildings and bomb-scarred hills.

Tears dampen my cheeks. I knew this would happen. Maybe it was inevitable?

Then, I see something else. It rests just above the edge of the hills, above the skyline of ruined buildings and a rusting cell phone tower.

The atmosphere washes the obelisk out. It spires up and up, into a jagged point. Its edges are like molten glass, constantly shifting.

I can see an eye with too many pupils open from within the obelisk, and mouths, great, black-yellow teeth that fade in and out, like a broken television that's changing channels too fast.

I can see that the land is changing: there's an ink-like substance that covers the ground and the buildings like spiderwebs, all tracing back to the obelisk that is there and not there—the thing that will be, the thing that is coming.

There are things older than us, older than time, older than space.

I grip for my friend's arm, but it's not there.

I look over and it's Akio standing next to me. There are holes in her chest; her eyes are black.

"You will be our vessel," Akio says. "We shall spread to the stars and devour all that rests in our path."

She opens her mouth; black ink spills down her once-beautiful lips, down her chest, until it's coating the wall beneath me.

I can't let this happen!

I will not be a vessel!

It takes all of my effort to push myself off of the wall.

There's clarity in a free fall.

This was the answer the whole time.

Here's something you can't do, father.

The ground rushes toward me—

3

I inhale fire.

Where am I?

I see beds and a cold metallic chamber, and I realize that I'm on the transport vessel still. The memory of the dream is still fresh.

I squeeze my good hand into a fist. The medicated fog still persists, but I can move. The straps. I have to undo the straps.

Somehow I slip my hand out of the bed. I undo one of the buckles. For some reason it makes me think of my mother in hospice.

First belt is done; now for the hard part. I try to sit up, and it's like I've got broken glass in my midsection. I grit my teeth. I remember Akio, I remember Gila, I remember Wolfrik, I sit up and tear off the last two straps.

Now I'm trying to stand. The cast helps, but I have to use the wall for support.

This ends now.

I will not bring those things to Earth.

I've found my way to the door. It's locked. The security code is a joke; I hack it with ease. The door opens. The hallway has a transparent wall. I can see Mars in all its hellish crimson glory, sandstorms ravaging part of the northern hemisphere. We still haven't broken orbit.

I flip Mars off and continue on down the hallway, through the next door. There has to be an airlock somewhere on this fucking ship.

The next door opens before I have a chance to get there. It's the man from earlier.

"What are you doing—"

I clock him across the face with my bad arm. The extra weight from my cast adds to the force, bouncing his head off the glass. His body slides off the curved glass into a puddle. He's bleeding from the nose, but he's alive. I take his tablet and some keycards in his pocket. He'll be fired, most likely, but it's a small price to pay for saving the species from extinction.

I find the airlock.

The security card that belonged to O'Brien opens it. I take a deep breath, close my eyes, and stagger inside.

My head is starting to feel a little clearer.

I close the hatch behind me with a press of a button.

There's pounding now. Footsteps reverberating down the hall. There isn't a moment of hesitation left in me. They're rushing to open the hatch as I press the button.

The air is ripped from my lungs, my body is sucked out into space. The first thing they ever teach you about space is not to hold your breath if you're blown out an airlock, so your lungs don't expand and rupture. The second thing they teach you is, you won't have long to live.

My body is spinning. I can see men and women, people I don't know, pounding on the airlock, screaming. They can't understand that this is the best possible outcome.

They can't understand.

My skin feels funny, like it's expanding. It won't be long now.

Something's bubbling on my tongue. Air evaporating.

Darkness at the edge of my vision.

I see something inside the airlock. I fight to see what it is, just a moment longer before death's embrace.

A black silhouette rises up behind the men and women who are screaming at me from the airlock hatch. It spreads its blades out, like a butterfly opening its wings, ink drips off each of the metallic blades, eyes open all over its body with a sickening rhythm.

No!

Darkness engulfs me, and in my last moment of consciousness, I say what I couldn't say to her before, what never left my lips, and I can almost feel her embrace...

Akio...

THE END

A MESSAGE FROM ERIC

Thanks so much for reading *Echoes of Olympus Mons!* If you've enjoyed this book, please be sure to leave a review on Amazon and Goodreads. Authors live and die by their reviews.

Before you move on to the Mind's Horizon preview, be sure to grab your free collection of cosmic horror stories by signing up for my mailing list, as well as free articles, ARCs for upcoming books, and more!

Thanks for reading!

A COLOR OUT OF INTERSTELLAR SPACE PREVIEW

The following is a preview for the next book in the Echoes series. Please note that since this excerpt is from an early draft, many things may change during the editing process.

AD UTOPIA TERMS OF SERVICE AGREEMENT:

Congratulations on being selected to participate in this historic mission into the unknown!

In accordance with your agreement with AstroDest Corporation and all territories that fall under our ownership, you have been released from your Sewer Work Release program and will be transported to the nearest space elevator for relocation to your exciting new home, our state-of-the-art interstellar space craft, the *AD Utopia*.

You, *Darrel Paxton*, agree to allow our patented A.I. System U.E.I. to monitor all thoughts, speech, thought-speech, VR activity, and sensory information pertaining to all activity perpetrated while aboard and utilizing AstroDest owned property and systems.

You agree to have these recordings distilled into "AUTO-LOGS" that will be available to security personnel and commanding officers at any time during the mission.

Paxton stops reading.
"The fuck is this?" he asks.

"Just some standard TOS stuff," the probation officer says. "It's all very boilerplate."

Paxton doesn't like the wry smirk on the probation officer's plastic face. Doesn't like his stupid corpo haircut either. Makes him want to take a welding torch to his fucking—

"Is it recording what I'm thinking right now?" Paxton asks.

"Of course."

"So…"

"Based on my feed here, it looks like you want to take a welding torch to my, and I quote, 'plastic fucking face.'" The smile deepens. "You Frontier Savages are charming, aren't you?"

Paxton isn't sure what to do.

The idea of being monitored like this. It raises his body temperature. Increases his rate of breathing. Makes him feel like the room's spinning like an old-world Carousel.

"Relax, *Darrel*," the probation officer says. "If AstroDest thought you were a threat, they wouldn't have selected you for the program."

"Right…and what am I even gonna be doing up there? Bet you got smarter people than some 'Frontier Savage.'"

The probation officer relaxes in his chair. His mechanical eyes, however, do not. They zero in on Paxton like a predator. Even without the feed reading every thought bouncing around his head, he's got a feeling this guy'd be able to read him like a book.

Not even something complicated like Dickens…more like, One Two Buckle My Shoe or some shit.

"Oh, yes." The probation officer chuckles. "Your earnest nature is one of the reasons why the Executives chose you. But your experience with repairing proprietary AstroDest machinery both in your uncivilized homeland—and here—will be quite useful."

Paxton's fingers grip the armrests attached to his chair. "Can I ask you a question?"

"Sure."

"What's the odds of me comin' back…seein' my family again?"

"Well, so long as nothing goes wrong, you'll be seeing them in sixty years."

"Sixty…"

Paxton's heart sinks. He can't help but think about what could happen in sixty years. Who will even be alive when…*if* he gets back.

"Any other questions?"

Paxton is staring at the TOS documentation.

You agree to allow AstroDest Corporation to use any and all data acquired through your sensory implant for the purpose of training U.E.I.

"So, everything we do and say, everything we feel, is gonna train this thing?" Paxton asks.

The probation officer nods, smiling his plastic smile. "Of course."

"And what's to stop the thing from deciding it don't need us? Killing us all?"

"I guess you'd better hope our A.I. limiters hold."

UEI Auto Log

Mission Date: 2145

Journey Time: 6 years.

Cameras: Online.

Subjects identified as Mechanical Specialist Darryl Paxton and Doctor Andreas Wolfe-Schmidt approaching Med Bay 2 from Crew Bunks.

Scanning subjects.

Darryl Paxton: Heart rate: Elevated.

Infrared sensors detect elevated body temperature consistent with heightened levels of stress. Recommend sedative once in Age Suppression Sleep.

"Are you excited, friend?" Detecting speech from Doctor Andreas Wolfe-Schmidt.

"If I'm being honest, man, no." Detecting speech from Darryl Paxton. "I'm fucking terrified."

"Why?"

"You have to ask?"

"Is it not exciting that the mission at last starts?"

"Can I ask you a question?"

"You can ask me anything, my friend."

"How did they get you?"

"Come again?"

"AstroDest? They got me running drugs into their territory from the Frontier. Said if I didn't do this job that they'd fry my brains and sell me to Rackham Media Amalgamated."

"This is terrible. But, crime is crime."

"So, you didn't do a crime?"

"No. No TOS violations for me."

"Huh, a straight shooter in the Corporate Confederacy. Crazy."

"Do you have family back in Frontier?"

"Yeah…a wife and two sons."

"And you miss them?"

"Of course I miss them. They were my whole…"

Mechanical Specialist Darryl Paxton has stopped moving. Oculus dexter and oculus sinister drifting toward Crew Bunks. Heightened levels of monoamine oxidase A detected. Neurotransmitters actively breaking down. Recommend anti-depressant dosage increase.

"What is it, Paxton?"

"I'm gonna record another one of them logs." Darryl Paxton is smiling. Does not match chemical profile. "I'll catch up to you."

"Do not take long. You know how the Captain is about tardiness."

"All too aware, my friend."

Mechanical Specialist Darryl Paxton bodily motion detected in direction of Crew Bunks.

Doctor Andreas Wolfe-Schmidt: Heart rate: Normal.

Subject is moving toward Med Bay 2. On schedule.

Time remaining until Age Suppression Sleep: 35 minutes.

Switching cameras to Med Bay 2.

Viewpoints established.

Remaining crew members, subjects identified as Captain Benning Smith and Doctor Emyne Foste are cleared for Age Suppression Sleep.

"Are you ready for this?" Detecting speech from Doctor Kaylee Staite, directed at Doctor Monica Edie Pizarro. Relationship: Classified.

"I think so," Doctor Monica Edie Pizarro responds. "Are you nervous?"

"Why would I be nervous? We're only being put into a medically induced coma for thirty years while they feed us a cocktail of age suppression drugs that will alter our DNA at a fundamental level, oh, and we're venturing into literally the middle of nowhere."

"Ah, I see, you're being sarcastic."

"Yes. I'm terrified."

"I am not scared." Detecting vocal patterns from Doctor Andreas Wolfe-Schmidt, now entering through Med Bay 2 doors. Subject's dopamine levels elevated, arms extended above torso and head. "Think of it. Soon we will wake around a new world. We will make history!"

"Right, and you're not at all concerned with what might happen to the ship while we're asleep?" Doctor Kaylee Staite asks.

Determining answer: CLASSIFIED.

"UEI will take care of us, I am certain," Doctor Andreas Wolfe-Schmidt responds.

"Oh, that totally eases all of my fears." Detecting sarcasm from Doctor Kaylee Staite. "Thank you, Andreas."

"UEI's job is to protect us." Speech pattern of Doctor Ayna Rosha detected. "And she will do just that. I programmed her myself and all of her systems check out as normal."

"Yeah, I'm sure you did." Detecting elevated levels of epinephrine in Doctor Kaylee Staite. Monitoring.

"And what's that supposed to mean?" Doctor Ayna Rosha asks.

Detecting elevated levels of adrenaline in subject Alice Krieger.

"Oh," Kaylee responds, "I don't know, maybe that you've blown off your duties for the last six years and maybe I'm fucking tired of it?"

"I have one of the most important jobs on this ship."

"And I don't?"

"You play with plants."

"Those plants are the only thing keeping us breathing, you stupid—"

"How typical." Detecting speech patterns from Steven Wilson. "A cat fight before bed."

"And speaking of slackers." Detecting movement from Doctor Kaylee Staite. Index finger pointing toward Subject Steven Wilson. "When's the last time you did *anything* on this ship, Mr. I have ten doctorates?"

"I don't appreciate your tone, I'll have you know I was instrumental in—"

"Enough!" Vocal pattern of Captain Benning Smith registered. "Get in your tube and shut the fuck up before I flush you three out an airlock. That's an order."

"Uh, and besides, Ayna didn't do all of the programming herself." Detecting speech patterns from subject Alice Krieger. "I did a big chunk of the programming."

"Krieger, shut it," Captain Smith says.

Monitoring complete. High levels of epinephrine detected in Doctors Kaylee Staite, Ayna Rosha, and subject Alice Krieger.

Recommendation: Sedation.

"That goes for all of you," Captain Benning Smith says. "It's time for the long sleep. And where the hell is Paxton?"

"He took time for one last log," Doctor Andreas Wolfe-Schmidt says.

"UEI, tell Paxton to get his ass down here stat." Voice pattern of Commander Dallas Patrick Verduzco recognized.

Executing order.

Doctor Bridget Avery Okoro, Doctor Xerxes Morrow, Doctor Kaylee Staite, Doctor Monica Pizarro, Commander Dallas Patrick Verduzco, Steven Wilson, Guy Hails, Mechanical Specialist Jojo Elias Wilkerson, Alice Krieger, and Doctor Ayna Rosha removing clothing and donning Sleep Suits.

Scans commencing.

Subjects are cleared for Age Suppression Sleep.

Scans show no health anomalies. Radiation damage within safe limits.

Microphones outside Med Bay 2 picking up footsteps. Mechanical Specialist Darryl Paxton detected in Med Bay 2. Closing doors to Med Bay 2.

Locking mechanism engaged. Biometric access set to Captain Benning Smith.

"And where the hell were you, Paxton?" Captain Benning Smith asks.

"Saying goodbye to my family," Mechanical Specialist Darryl Paxton says.

"Get ready and get in your damn tube."

"Yessir."

Darryl Paxton strips clothes off, placing them in the appropriate bin in center console for sterilization. Running scans as subject dons Age Suppression Sleep suit.

Radiation damage: Within safe limits.

Medicinal cocktail calibrated. Subject is cleared for Age Suppression Sleep.

All subjects inside Age Suppression Sleep chambers.

"Well, I guess this is it," Darryl Paxton says. "Hope you guys enjoy the in flight movie."

"There is movie?" Doctor Andreas Wolfe-Schmidt asks. "I love movies. Much better than holo-vids, yes?"

"He's being a smartass, Andreas," Doctor Kaylee Staite says. "There is no in flight movie. Just your own deep space nightmares."

"Could they have done that? With our implants and stuff?" Detecting speech from subject Steven Wilson. "Hey, Cap, is it too late to have UEI patch in that stuff from the movie room?"

"All right, all right," registering speech patterns from Commander Dallas Patrick Verduzco. "That's enough fun for tonight. Let's all bed down before the Captain blows a gasket."

"UEI," registering speech pattern from Captain Benning Smith. "Close up the tubes and begin Age Suppression Sleep."

"COMMENCING."

"Well, see you guys on the other side," Darryl Paxton says.

"Yeah, whenever that is," Doctor Kaylee Staite says.

Age Suppression Units are sealed. Inducing comas. Beginning Age Suppression cocktail regimen.

Scheduled Wake Time: 30 years.

UEI Auto Log
Mission Date: 2146
Journey Time: 7 years.

Ship's systems normal. Interstellar region remains unchanged. Age Suppression Sleep Units functioning normally. Biometric readings normal. Botany Ward efficiency at 99%. Biological ARK: Condition: stable.

Fusion Reactor Status: Stable.

Engines: Stable.

Current Speed: 0.2 C has been reached. Cutting engines and switching to Centrifuge Mode.

Wake crew in: 29 years.

UEI Auto Log
Mission Date: 2155
Journey Time: 10 years.

Ship's systems normal. Interstellar region remains unchanged. Age Suppression Sleep Units functioning normally. Biometric readings normal. Botany Ward efficiency at 99%. Biological ARK: Condition: stable.

Fusion Reactor Status: Stable.

Engines: Stable.

Current Speed: 0.2C

Wake Crew In: 20 years.

UEI Auto Log
Mission Date: 2165
Journey Time: 20 years.

Anomaly detected.

Running scans. Activating external telescopes.

Rendering images. Analyzing. Changing aperture and exposure for interstellar light conditions. Magnifying.

Analyzing…

Asteroid detected.

Scans complete.

Object appears to be interstellar asteroid, moving at steady 137,920.7799999841 kilometers per hour at an estimated distance of 5 AU from Utopia.

Plotting possible origin points.

55% probability of Proxima Centauri origin.

ALERT.

Organic compounds detected.

Processing…

Asteroid appears to have hollow core. Movement inside object detected. Possible life forms.

Activating Directive 12.

Adjusting Utopia course.

Current speed: 0.2C

Engaging forward thrusters.

Current speed: 0.1C

Object is 0.5 AU from Utopia.

Current Speed: 137920.7799999841

Speed matched to object. Adjusting attitude and angle.

Deploying drones.

Commencing scientific sampling of object.

Drones activating drills and lasers.

Samples collected. Scans logged.

Calling drones back to AD Utopia.

ALERT.

ALERT.

ALERT.

Hull breach detected.

Interstellar object course changed as drones were prepping for return.

Atmospherics pressure leaking.

Deploying retrieval drones.

Retrieving object and transporting to Cargo Bay 2 for further study. Sealing Cargo Bay 1. No damage to supplies in Cargo Bay 1 detected. Cargo straps holding.

Minimal damage to ship systems. Additional drones deployed to conduct repairs. Interstellar region clear. Age Suppression Sleep Units functioning normally. Biometric readings normal. Botany Ward efficiency at 98%. Biological ARK: Condition: stable.

Engaging rear engines, accelerating back to 0.2C.

Switching to GRAV MODE.

Wake Crew In: Recalculating… 12 years.

UEI Auto Log
Mission Date: 2165
Journey Time: 20 years.

ALERT.

Unauthorized movement detected in Cargo Bay 2.

Activating cameras. Scanning.

Drones are moving without UEI commands. Dragging interstellar meteoroid into corridor.

Drones have stopped.

Switching to infrared.

Detecting elevated heat levels consistent with acetylene torches. Drones are conducting further scans of interstellar meteoroid.

Movement detected. Drones taking interstellar meteoroid into engine room.

Other drones are making way to AI Core.

Scanning for threats.

Organic compounds detected.

Isolating AI Core from Axis Corridor.

No movement detected.

Calculating options…

ALERT!

Movement detected in Axis Corridor.

Drones have interfaced with door locking mechanisms. Attempting to bypass security…

AI Core hatch breach imminent.

Drones have breached AI Core.

Spider and flying models approaching AI Core.

Drones attempting to access AI Core paneling.

Calculating actions…

Recommend temporary AI Core shutdown…

5…

4…

3…

2…

ALERT…

AI Core Shutdown aborted.

Calculating further action…

Drones interfacing with AI Core. Organic compounds detected within AI Core.

ALERT.

Detecting increase of organic compound levels within drones.

Movement detected in access shafts in Grav Ring.

Ship's systems…improved.

Interstellar region: clear.

Age Suppression Sleep Units functioning normally. Biometric readings normal. Botany Ward efficiency at 75%. Biological ARK: Condition: UNKNOWN.

Ship course: Adjusting…adjusting…

New course set.

Wake Crew In: ?? years.

UEI Auto Log

Mission Date: REDACTED

Journey Time: REDACTED

Subjects have awoken.

Age Suppression Sleep units have opened.

Adjusting cameras.

Doctor Kaylee Staite falls to her knees onto the grating. Detecting heightened levels of distress within subject. Gyroscopic unit within Age Suppression Sleep Unit has malfunctioned.

Sounds registering, echoing, sending vibrations throughout the ship's hull.

"Why in the hell is it so dark?" Doctor Staite asks. "Anyone else awake?"

Switching to infrared.

Subjects appear as glowing red figures. Age Suppression Cocktails ceased five years ago, reaching the intended service life end. No age anomalies detected across subjects.

"My head," Darryl Paxton says, rubbing his cranium. "Anyone else have a splitting fucking headache?"

"Check the center console for painkillers, Paxton," Doctor Xerxes Morrow says. "Take two. There should be some spare water packets in there too."

"I will find flashlight," Doctor Andreas Wolfe-Schmidt says, wiping vomit from his lips and scrambling around like a blind man in the dark.

"Captain?" Commander Dallas Patrick Verduzco calls. His voice echoes, reaching beyond the Access Shaft vents. Detecting movement outside Med Bay 2 corridor. "Andreas, when you find that flashlight, check on the captain. I think I'm gonna hurl."

Subject Captain Benning Smith appears to be unconscious.

Mics detect the click of a flashlight. Bulb spark to life, casting light through the dark, shining upon Captain Benning Smith.

"He is breathing," Andreas says, voice void of fear.

"What a shame," Kaylee says, struggling from her capsule and taking a flashlight of her own from the center console.

"That's enough, Doctor Staite," Commander Verduzco says. "You know the Captain doesn't take that kind of talk lightly."

"I must get to the AI Core," Doctor Ayna Rosha says. "I do not think she is online."

"I agree with her," Alice Krieger says, sitting up in her tube.

"Can we get these damn consoles online first?" Commander Verduzco says, pointing at the dead center console.

"I can do that," Andreas says, moving away from Captain Smith and planting his flashlight upon the center console's raised surface.

"All right, Ayna," Commander Verduzco says, "help him with that. Doctor Morrow and Okoro, help me with the Captain."

Subjects Doctor Wolfe-Schmidt and Doctor Rosha are about to bring the console online.

Reducing ship system activities.

Activating POSSUM MODE.

Doctor Kaylee Staite: AUTO-LOG
Year: 2265

Doctor Kaylee Staite leans her weight against her Age Suppression tube. Her body still hasn't recovered from the induced coma.

The others are busy trying to get the center console to work.

"The Captain's out cold," Doctor Morrow says, his voice coming from her left. "Jojo too."

Sound Detected: CLICK

Andreas' face lights up, as though it's floating like a disembodied phantom. Kaylee can't help but gasp. "Jesus, Wolfe!"

"Wolfe-Schmidt," Andreas says. "Many flashlights are stored inside center console."

Kaylee takes one and shines it around MED-BAY 2.

Doctors Morrow and Okoro are busy seeing to the Captain's condition. Kaylee would rather have Dallas in charge. Between the two of them, Verduzco is more level headed.

There's no way that Smith would ever let the command go that easily.

Interesting. Filing information away for further reflection.

"Captain Smith's vitals appear to be normal," Doctor Morrow says.

More bad news, Kaylee thinks.

"See if you can wake him," Dallas says. "Honestly, his combat expertise will help a lot."

"Or it'll get us killed," Kaylee says.

The center console lights up, the hum of machines and computers coming to life fills Med Bay 2, masking the subtle groans and creeks from my aging metal body as it slowly rotates in the black of space.

"Doctor Rosha and I have access to some of the ship's systems," Andreas says.

"Some of them?" Monica asks, worry chopping at her vocals. "What about navigation? Telescopes? Are the radio dishes still functional?"

"Calm down, woman," Ayna says, rolling her eyes. "We're still working. Holy—"

"What is it?" Kaylee asks.

"Look at the date," Andreas says, backing away from the console.

Kaylee approaches the center console. She interprets her body's response as her heart "sinking."

We've been in Age Suppression Sleep for almost one-hundred years?

"2265, can that really be real?" Andreas asks, holding his head in his hands.

"Oh, man, this ain't good," Paxton says. Subject is starting to pace back and forth. "My wife…my kids…if we been in space for a hundred years, they're…"

"Paxton!" Commander Verduzco shouts. "Get a hold of yourself! We can panic later, right now we need to assess the condition of the ship and figure out where the hell we are. Remember, the mission comes first."

"The mission?" Doctor Foste says, her hazel eyes lighting up. "And what good is the mission going to do for us here if AstroDest doesn't even exist by the time we get back? If we can get back at all? Remember that there's only so much organic matter on this ship, only so many supplies."

"She's right," Doctor Pizarro says. "The plan was to establish three-dee printing farms on Proxima B to manufacture and farm more supplies for the return trip once we established a viable colony space."

"More bad news, yah," Andreas says. "Just ran scans on Age Suppression Sleep Units, they are all out of juices I'm afraid."

"What does that mean?" Paxton asks, eyes wild. "Man, that doesn't sound good. That's not good right?"

"No, it's very bad news," Jojo says, his sigh cutting the tension and the fear in Med Bay 2 like a laser cutter through a piece of toast. "That means that if it takes us one-hundred years to get back to Earth, that means we'll age one-hundred years naturally. And only a few of us have any metal to speak of."

"Wait a minute, though," Krieger steps forward, hopping up to peer over the center console. Standing at a mere four-feet in height, cybernetic augments run down her neck, snaking from an access port at the base of her skull. She's one of the only members of the crew with any amount of cybernetic augmentation beyond a standard brain implant. And between her and Ayna, the only AI and programming expert Kaylee trusts. "If we need augments, I could probably make them with Andreas's help."

"Yes, I imagine you both could, but I can't exactly augment any of us with the supplies we have here on the ship," Doctor Morrow says in his usual monotone manner. "Even if I had the materials to make plastiflesh and you and Doctor Wolfe could make the cybernetics, the medical facilities here were not intended for such an invasive operation."

"Doctor Wolfe-Schmidt," Andreas says.

"Yes, sorry," Doctor Morrow says.

"Son of a bitch!" Paxton shouts. He collapses onto the console, tears welling in his eyes. "I'm gonna die up here. I fucking knew it!"

Kaylee's "heart" aches for him. Of all of the crew, he was one of the few of them with a family to return to. A promise for, as humans often say, a "real" life.

Now, what does he have?

What do any of us have? Kaylee wonders.

"Doctor Morrow, how's the Captain looking?" Dallas asks.

"I believe he is in a medically induced coma still," Doctor Morrow says.

"We think the ASS tube didn't wake him properly," Doctor Okoro says, her eyes narrowing at the Captain's near-lifeless body.

Funny, in the six years I've known him, he's never looked so peaceful, Kaylee thinks. *Scratch that, one-hundred and six I guess...*

"Don't let him catch you calling the tubes that," Dallas says.

Doctor Okoro nods, completely missing that the rest of them think she's made a joke.

"Can you bring him out of it?" Dallas asks.

"I believe I can, but I'll need to harvest some medicine from his tube," Doctor Morrow says.

"Do you need anything from us?" Dallas asks.

"Yes, I will need a syringe applicator and Doctor Wolfe-Schmidt's expertise in harvesting the medicine."

"Okay, do it," Dallas says.

"I'll grab the applicator," Doctor Okoro says.

Andreas moves away from the center console and examines the Age Suppression tube. "The pressure will need to be offset, I will need flexi-tubing, a razor, adhesive gel, and a spare applicator."

Doctor Okoro moves deftly, snatching up a spare syringe, some flexible medical tubing, razor, and the adhesive gel. One bright side to being locked up in Med Bay 2 is that there is a ready supply of improvisational tools.

I just wish I wasn't so useless, Kaylee thinks. *But, maybe that's just the quality of atmosphere talking?*

Andreas cuts the applicator's plastic tubing off from the rest of the applicator, then attaches it to the medical tubing with the adhesive gel.

"Now, I will need a container for the medicine," Andreas says, gesturing for one of the empty blood sample vials in the one part of Med Bay 2's wall-panels not occupied by the Age Suppression tubes.

Doctor Okoro fetches it for him and stands by with the applicator in hand. "Are we ready?"

"Now, if it gives you comfort, pray for the Captain." Andreas slides the needle into the Age Suppression tube's medicine stores, draining it slowly into the blood sample vial. When he's done, he hands the sample off to Doctor Okoro.

Doctor Morrow takes the applicator from Okoro and drains the medicine from the vial. "All right then. Now, we inject the Captain, and hope it does not kill him."

"Do your best," Dallas says. "That's all I'm asking."

"I've seen your file," I say, locking eyes with Doctor Morrow. "Maybe do someone else's best."

Doctor Morrow's expression does not change as he pierces Captain Smith's forearm with the needle and injects him.

At first, it appears as if the Captain is dead.

Kaylee can't help but wonder if they'd be better off without him.

Much to her chagrin, the Captain's dark eyes shoot open; his gasps send a thrill of shock through her.

At first, Smith rests his forearm on Doctor Morrow's shoulder. The Doctor helps him into a sitting position. As soon as realization creeps into the Captain's eyes, he pushes Morrow away.

He fears how weak he looks to us, Kaylee thinks. *Can't have his absolute rule over us questioned out here in the void.*

"Status report," Captain Smith calls out; his weathered and callous eyes fall on Dallas. "Now."

"Sir." Dallas stands to attention. The neon emergency lights dance on his cranium; even a hundred years in Age Suppression Sleep did not help him to grow hair. "The Utopia's systems appear to be down. We woke in darkness. AI Core appears to be offline. Doctor Morrow just brought you out of a medically induced coma."

"And our course?" Smith asks, his breath steaming.

Kaylee can't help but worry about the state of her plants.

Oh, don't worry, Doctor. We've taken such good care of them.

"Unknown," Dallas says, his eyes downcast. "We don't have access to navigation or any of the main systems. Wolfe-Schmidt and Rosha were able to get into basic systems, though."

"What year?" Smith asks, and the crew takes turns glancing at each other.

Maybe we're all thinking the same thing? Kaylee wonders. *How unhinged could Smith be without the promise of a glorious return home?*

"It's 2265," Dallas says. "If that's even right."

"Yeah…"

"We've been asleep for one-hundred years?" Smith says. Kaylee can't help but notice how measured his voice is.

What does he know that we don't? Kaylee wonders.

Amusing observation, Kaylee. Amusing indeed.

"We must reach the AI Core," Ayna says—her voice makes Kaylee's skin crawl. "This should be priority one."

243

"I agree with Ayna," Krieger says, looking up to the Captain. "If we can get to the core, then I can jack in and see if I can get the Utopia's operating system up and running. Get us some answers."

"All right," Smith says, pulling himself out of the tube and planting his feet on the grating. "Listen up, because I'm only going to say this once. We need to split up into two groups. One will follow Doctor Wolfe-Schmidt, Commander Verduzco, and Paxton to Main Engineering to asses the condition of the engines and get the lights back on, and the other group will follow myself, Krieger, and Doctor Rosha to the AI Core to get the systems back online."

"No offense," Kaylee says. "But I think it'd be smarter to check on the Botany Ward, who knows what might have happened to life support within the last hundred—"

"We've got air to breathe, don't we?" Smith says, glaring at Kaylee.

"For now, but that doesn't—"

"When you're the Captain," Ayna says, looking slide eyed at Kaylee, "you can make your plants a priority."

"You have your orders!" Smith says, then turns his attention to Paxton, who is still busy muttering to himself and sobbing in the corner. "Paxton. Pull yourself together and get the damn door open."

The look in Paxton's eyes. His pupils are dilated. Tears pooling and soaking into the beard that grew while stuck in Age Suppression Sleep. To Kaylee, he looks like his whole world has come crashing down.

And here the Captain is ordering him to keep going when likely all he wants to do is to mourn the family he's probably lost.

"Yes, sir," Paxton says, clearly fighting through the torrent of emotions running through him.

Paxton approaches and tries the hatch leading to corridor M-2. He grunts, straining for thirty seconds, but gives the effort up and shakes his head. "No good. There's no power."

"That door's always malfunctioning," Doctor Morrow says.

"Well, Paxton isn't exactly the best mechanic," Jojo says. The animosity in his voice is not lost on Kaylee. "Perhaps we should try the Access Shafts? I guarantee my maintenance work is not as shoddy as his."

Paxton does not respond.

"I can get us in," Andreas says.

"No!" Paxton shouts. "I thought I heard something moving around in there. I can open the door, it's just gonna require me getting into the paneling."

Curious. I didn't think they noticed.

"How long will that take?" Smith asks.

"Not long, Sir," Paxton says. "Maybe twenty minutes at the most."

"Let's not sit idly, then," Captain says. "Doctor Wolfe-Schmidt, assemble your team and get your asses in those shafts."

"Sir..." Paxton glances back at Smith as he's pulling the emergency toolkit off the wall. "What if they—"

"You got a problem with my orders, Paxton?" Smith glares at him. "No..."

"Good. Besides, it was probably just a malfunctioning drone."

Kaylee and Pizarro glance at each other.

She brings up her internal HUD and shoots off a text message to Pizarro.

Kaylee: You thinking what I'm thinking?

Pizarro: I detected the noises too. They don't match the sound Spider-Walker Class drones make.

Kaylee: What EM frequency should I switch to?

Pizarro: I would suggest switching to infrared if we've been boarded by organics.

Kaylee: And why would you think that?

"What the *fuck* are you all waiting for, Saite?" Smith shouts, his eyes igniting with yellow rings as he thrusts his index finger at the access hatch. "Get to it! Pizarro! You too, stop gawking at your girlfriend and get a fucking move on before I start shooting!"

"I will need Doctor Pizarro, and my friend Paxton above all else," Andreas says.

"All right, Paxton," Smith says. "Once you finish with this job, head to Main Engineering and join up with Doctor Wolfe-Schmidt."

"By my lonesome?" Paxton asks, fear turning his face ghost white.

"Take Doctor Staite and Commander Verduzco with you if it makes you feel better."

"But that's in the opposite direction of the Botany Ward," Kaylee says.

"I don't give a damn." Smith points at several of the others, starting with Morrow. "Doctor's Morrow, and Foste, you're with me as well. The rest of you, go with Doctor Wolfe."

"Wolfe-Schmidt," Andreas says.

"Whatever!" Smith shouts.

A loud popping sound echoes through the chamber, startling the crew.

"I got the cover off," Andreas says. "Someone hand me my flashlight."

Kaylee watches as Andreas enters the shaft without a single hint of fear in his body language.

Pizarro glances in Kaylee's direction, probably looking for approval. Sometimes she finds her constant need for such approval annoying, how the *thing* clings to her like a sick puppy.

If only the crew knew the truth. Filing information for later use.

Kaylee shrugs at Pizarro. "Go on. You heard our dictator."

Pizarro sighs and follows after Andreas, bending low and clilmbing the ladder to ACCESS SHAFTS above them.

Bug-Eyed-Steve follows Pizarro. "Well, at least I'll be able to enjoy the view."

Doctor Morrow follows after him.

Kaylee turns her attention back to Smith and the others. Paxton is trying to pull the wall grating off while Smith and the others are busy accessing the ship's map from the center console.

Quietly, Kaylee makes her way over to Paxton. She can see the sweat dripping down his forehead, mixing with his still drying tears.

"Are you okay?" Kaylee asks.

Paxton hesitates, but nods. "Captain's right. Can't think about it right now."

"You can't just block it out," Kaylee says.

The panel finally pops off, revealing a bunch of mechanical and hydraulic bits Kaylee knows absolutely nothing about. "No offense, Doc. But isn't this Doctor Okoro's area?"

Paxton pulls at one of the hydraulic pumps and the door to MED BAY 2 hisses, sliding partially open.

"Got it!" Paxton shouts, wedging himself inside the door and pushing it the rest of the way open, probably something he's very used to doing, given that hatche's reputation.

And with that, Captain Smith and his handpicked group join up at the door, shining their lights into the corridor outside.

"What in the hell…" Dallas says, gasping.

"What is it, Commander?" Smith asks.

"There are…vines, sir."

"Vines?" Paxton practically jumps away from the hatch, stumbling into the center console.

"Let me see," Kaylee shouts, pushing through them.

Shining her flashlight down the corridor, Kaylee sees them for herself. The corridor is totally overgrown with green and violet vines. I can't help but latch onto how she describes them: *Like some kind of alien forest.*

Oh, my deer, Kaylee. You have no idea.

To Kaylee, the vines seem to be snaking their way through the paneling, the tiny holes in the grating, and…and the access shafts.

"Report, Doctor Staite," Smith demands.

"They're vines, lots of them," Kaylee says, retreating back into the chamber. "From this distance I have no idea what species. But at a glance, I'm sure they're not from the Botany Ward."

"What does that mean, though?" Paxton asks, worry creeping back into his voice.

"I don't know," Kaylee says. "I'd need to get a sample and analyze it in one of the labs."

"Then you have a secondary objective," Smith says.

"You're going to need to get the power back on before any of that equipment can be used," Kaylee says.

"Then as soon as the lights and main systems come back on, be sure to activate your comms."

Kaylee nods.

For once, she actually agrees with him.

"All right," Smith shouts. "Vines or no vines, we have an objective to accomplish. Let's get to it."

Paxton, Dallas, and Kaylee watch as Smith, Hails, Foste, Krieger, Okoro, Morrow, and Ayna all leave the *apparent* safety of MED BAY 2.

This is so much fun!

Perhaps I should have released them sooner?

ACKNOWLEDGMENTS

This book was born sometime in 2017 as a novella that I originally wrote in the space of a single week. I sent it out to a few of my regular beta readers, and while most of the feedback was positive, it wasn't until Phoenix Bunke's beta read that I began to see the potential, and really get excited by the prospect of turning the original draft into what you hold in your hands. It's all Phoenix's fault. If it weren't for her wonderful insight into my twisted mind, this book would not be half of what it is today.

I'd like to also thank my patrons over at Patreon for reading the serialized (pre-copy-edited) version of the book, as well as D William Landsborough and Kathrine for their beta reader feedback at various stages of this novel's development.

I must also thank the bands and musicians, Gojira, Elder, and Jim Matheos. Their music had a profound effect on the material.

-Eric Malikyte

ABOUT THE AUTHOR

Eric Malikyte is a neurodivergent author, illustrator, science communicator, and video editor. He has published works in various genres, including Lovecraftian horror, dark fantasy, and cyberpunk. He has written for YouTube channels such as TopTenz, Geographics, and Biographics. He lives in Richmond, Virginia, with his wife and two cats, where he spends his spare time exploring used bookstores, Irish Pubs, and terrorizing the neighborhood children on Halloween.

BIBLIOGRAPHY

Echoes of Olympus Mons
Neo Rackham 001: Ego Trip
Into the Astral Lands

Suleniar's Enigma Series:
The Man Without Hands
Rise of Oreseth

Coming Soon:
A Colour from Interstellar Space
Gr1mo1r
The Observatory
Neo Rackham 002
Neo Rackham 003

Suleniar's Enigma III: The Transit of the Kultari

Anthology Contributions:
Neo Cyberpunk Volume 1
Neo Cyberpunk Volume 3

Curious about other Crossroad Press books? Stop by our website:
http://crossroadpress.com
We offer quality writing
in digital, audio, and print formats.

Subscribe to our newsletter on the website homepage and receive a
free eBook.

www.ingramcontent.com/pod-product-compliance
Lightning Source LLC
Chambersburg PA
CBHW030248200626
46816CB00002BA/557